ROPE ON FIRE

A JOHN CRANE ADVENTURE

MARK PARRAGH

Waterhaven MEDIA LLC

Rope on Fire
by Mark Parragh

A Waterhaven Media Publication
First Print Edition – June 2019

Cover Design by Kerry Jesberger, Aero Gallerie
Edited by Courtney Umphress
Production Coordination by Nina Sullivan

———

CONTENTS

For Nina,
without whom the world would be
a very different place

.

CHAPTER 1

Adale, Somalia

The pilot's wife was an insufferable, nagging harpy, but she was right about one thing. One day, she often said to her husband, one day, all this smoking will be the end of you.

Just before 4:00 a.m., the pilot stood outside a Quonset hut at a deserted airstrip near the shore, waiting for his passenger to show up. At the far side of the cracked tarmac, a white Beechcraft Baron sat silhouetted against the pre-dawn sky. Beyond the plane, he could just make out whitecaps on the black water and hear the rolling of the surf. The pilot flicked his spent cigarette butt away and removed a crumpled pack from his dirty coveralls. They were Lebanese Cedars, cheap and not very good. But they were a quarter the price of Marlboros, and the pilot smoked incessantly. It added up.

His wife worried mainly about his health. Her best friend's brother had lost his larynx to smoking and had to talk through a little box that made him sound like a machine. The pilot wasn't worried. His grandfather had smoked even more than he did, and he'd lived into his 90s. The pilot was confident that he had cancer-proof genes.

What neither he or his wife had considered was how smoking had ruined his sense of smell.

The pilot didn't notice the stench of his coveralls, which hadn't been washed in months. He didn't notice his horrible body odor. He simply smelled nothing.

The figure that detached itself from the shadow of the hut was behind him, dressed in black, and moving in darkness. The figure advanced across the tarmac toward the pilot. He had been trained to move silently, and he made no sound. So there were good reasons why the pilot didn't see or hear the figure moving steadily toward him. But an odd medicinal odor might have warned him—if years of heavy smoking hadn't ravaged his sense of smell.

The pilot put another Cedar between his lips and dug for his lighter. Then some primal instinct alerted him. He turned and discovered a man standing barely ten feet behind him. The man was tall and lean, dressed entirely in black. A silenced pistol hung at his side, in his left hand. In his right he raised something that looked like a toy gun, with a plastic frame and a wide muzzle, and pointed it straight into the pilot's face.

The man smiled as the pilot's cigarette slipped from his lips and fell to the tarmac. Then he pulled the trigger. There was a soft *pop*, and a pale green ball smacked into the pilot's mouth and splattered like shaving gel.

The pilot stood in confusion for a moment. The green foam expanded and clung to his skin. Was it a joke? Then his hand crushed his pack of Cedars, and his eyes defocused. He went rigid for a moment, then completely limp, and collapsed in a heap on the tarmac. His crushed cigarette pack spilled loose tobacco which blew away in the cooling breeze from the sea.

———

John Crane prodded the pilot with the tip of his boot and got no reaction. He gave the Sandman a look of newfound respect, then put it away. The damn thing actually worked. For something that looked for all the world like a toy, he had to admit that was pretty impressive. The foam was called Trance-8, a very potent mixture of isoflurane, desflurane, and a couple other analogs. His handlers had made grandiose promises for the stuff. Crane hoped it would keep the pilot out long enough for him to complete his mission and get out. He could have simply shot the pilot, but why kill the man if he didn't need to? But mostly, Crane admitted to himself, he'd wanted to test the Sandman before he turned it on his target. He still had two doses of Trance-8 for al-Sarary.

Crane dragged the inert pilot inside the hut. There he stripped off the coveralls and pulled them on over his black mission uniform. He found a battered baseball cap on a shelf and put that on as well. The coveralls didn't fit well, and they stank like death. But it could be worse, Crane reminded himself. It could always be worse. He stepped outside into the pre-dawn breeze and waited.

John Crane was an agent for a US covert operations team known as the Hurricane Group because its budget and administrative personnel had been hidden away inside the National Oceanic and Atmospheric Administration. Crane was barely thirty years old and on only his second mission for the Hurricane Group. It was not going according to plan.

The mission brief had been simple enough. Grab Yemeni terrorist financier Musi al-Sarary at a point fifty miles north of here, where the highway ran close to the beach. Then load him into a zodiac and haul him out to the destroyer USS *Dunham* waiting in international water. He should have been back aboard the *Dunham* by nightfall. He should have enjoyed a hot meal and swapped stories with Chris Parikh, a fellow Hurricane agent on his own parallel mission. By now he should have been fast asleep in a comfortable bunk. But al-Sarary hadn't shown. Crane suspected they'd moved the location of his meetings with local terrorist leadership for security reasons. And so here Crane was, at four in the morning, at a remote airstrip in rural Somalia, wearing stolen coveralls that stank. Improvising. His handlers at the Hurricane Group weren't much for improvisation.

Nearly an hour passed before Crane heard a car engine in the distance, and saw headlights snaking toward him through the dunes. He pulled the cap over his short, dark hair and let the brim hide as much of his face as possible. Crane was clean shaven, with lean features and gray eyes. He looked nothing like the pilot: a short, doughy man with a three-day beard. But for security, al-Sarary took one plane in and a different plane out, so he hadn't met the pilot. Crane wasn't so sure about his escorts. If they didn't notice anything, he'd have al-Sarary to himself in the air. If they did, he'd have to fight them all here on the runway. Crane took a deep breath and strode toward the Beechcraft like he belonged there.

He was finishing his walk-around inspection when a battered Land Cruiser pulled up twenty yards away. Four men got out. Three were Somali, wiry, heavily armed. The fourth was clearly the important one. The others opened the door for him, carried his bag. The fourth man was of Middle Eastern extraction, shorter and heavier than his escorts. He looked like he'd kitted himself out from an L.L. Bean catalog. Musi al-Sarary looked just like his surveillance photos.

He walked toward the plane like he was eager to be out of Somalia. The others surrounded him, sweeping the perimeter with their Kalashnikovs.

"You're late," Crane snapped in French.

The nearest guard snorted. "Things take time here. You still get paid."

"Well, get him aboard," said Crane. "I need to finish checking the engine."

He walked around the plane and opened the port engine cover, letting it hide him from view. He pretended to tinker with the engine as the guards loaded al-Sarary's bags into the hold. Then he closed the cover and announced, "We're clear to fly," to no one in particular.

The guards had moved back a safe distance. Al-Sarary was already in the passenger cabin, in the right rear club seat. Perfect.

He stuck his head inside. "Are you ready to leave, sir?"

Al-Sarary waved a hand dismissively. "Go, go."

"Yes, sir," said Crane. "We'll be airborne in a couple minutes."

That much was true, Crane thought as he secured the door. Al-Sarary just wouldn't be going back to Nairobi. After a short visit with the US Navy, he would be headed for a black site somewhere, where he would provide invaluable intel about the financial underpinnings of Al-Shabaab and several other jihadist networks.

Crane climbed into the pilot's seat and ran through the checklist as quickly as he could manage. The last thing he needed was for someone to find the pilot. He started the engines and ran them up to speed. Then the nav and taxi lights. Just a few more seconds.

He set the autopilot and turned it off and then released the parking brake, and the plane edged forward.

Dawn light stained the sea red as Crane taxied down the airstrip. At the far end, he spun the plane around and went through the final checklist items: cowl flaps, props, mixture.

He was just ready to begin his run when he saw a wedge of light off to his left. The door of the Quonset opening. It was time to go.

Crane slammed the throttles forward, and the Beechcraft obediently shot down the runway, gaining speed.

As soon as he could, he pulled back and felt the nose wheel rise off the tarmac. Figures were running now in the darkness. But it was too late. The Beechcraft leaped into the air. Below, Crane saw muzzle flashes, but the plane was moving fast now, climbing sharply. He couldn't hear the gunfire over the roar of the engines, and no bullets hit the plane. Al-Sarary didn't seem to notice.

Then Crane turned and took the plane away, out over the Indian Ocean and into the breaking dawn.

He climbed to ten thousand feet and put the plane on autopilot. Now came the interesting part. He slowly slid the Sandman from a pocket of the coveralls and unfastened his seatbelt. Movement would be tricky in the tight cabin. At least the plane's owners had helped a bit by removing the two rear-facing club seats right behind the cockpit.

Behind him, al-Sarary was jotting on a legal pad in his lap.

"Everything okay back there, sir?" Crane asked. "I'm getting a warning light on the cabin door." He folded down the co-pilot's seat.

"It's closed. Of course it's closed. Look at it."

"I'm going to put us on autopilot for a second and check it out, okay? Don't worry."

Crane started to climb around his seat when al-Sarary suddenly whipped a pistol from beneath the legal pad.

Crane froze. "Sir! Be careful!" The Sandman was in his other hand, still hidden behind the seat. He flipped off the safety.

"Who are you?" al-Sarary asked in English. "American? CIA?"

Crane dropped his French. "Actually, we're part of the National Oceanic and Atmospheric Administration." Al-Sarary looked skeptical. "No, seriously."

Al-Sarary held the gun steady. He'd be weighing his options, realizing they were few and none of them good. Slowly, painfully slowly, Crane began to move the Sandman around his body.

"You know how to fly this thing?" Crane asked dubiously. "How to navigate over open ocean? You don't have much of a future if you shoot me."

"What future in your black sites?"

Crane could see him summoning his courage. Christ, he was going to do it!

"Better to die here. Without torture, without betraying my friends ..."

His grip tightened on the pistol. Desperately Crane thrust his leg back against the rudder pedals. The plane veered hard to starboard, and al-Sarary was thrown hard against the opposite side of the cabin. The pistol went off with a thunderous roar, but the shot punched through a side window.

Crane was pressed against the edge of the pilot's seat. His legs hit the yoke, and the plane went into a steep climb. Al-Sarary was pressed back against the rear seats, and Crane slid back into the passenger cabin and landed on his side on the floor.

Then the plane leveled out as the autopilot started to bring it back under control. Al-Sarary fell across Crane's legs, and his head slammed into the bulkhead. He pushed off Crane's body, scrambling for purchase on the seats.

As al-Sarary raised the gun for another shot, Crane sat up and fired the Sandman directly into his face. The green anesthetic foam expanded across his face. Al-Sarary had perhaps three seconds of consciousness, and he spent those trying to figure out what was happening to him.

Then he was out. Crane carefully pried the pistol from his inert fingers.

Breathing hard, Crane crawled back into the cockpit. The autopilot had brought the Beechcraft back on course. Crane confirmed that the plane wasn't damaged—there was only the hissing of wind across the bullet hole—and then got to work.

He pulled a waterproof plastic bag from his chest pocket and collected al-Sarary's papers and his smartphone. Then he dragged the unconscious man forward. With some difficulty, he managed to belt him into the copilot's seat and secure his wrists with a zip tie. He'd be out longer than Crane needed, but he didn't want al-Sarary's arms flailing around in the cockpit.

When he was done, he climbed back into the pilot's seat and rechecked the instruments. He took the plane down to five hundred feet and then reached into his collar and thumbed the switch on the mic he wore there.

"Control, this is Ocelot. I have the package and am inbound your location. ETA thirty minutes."

A few moments later, a tired voice came back on the secure channel. "Roger that, Ocelot. You're late."

Crane sighed. Yes, obviously. Things happened in the field.

"Control, be aware I am flying a civilian aircraft," and he gave them the plane's tail number. "Be prepared to receive."

"That's not protocol, Ocelot."

Crane placed his face in his palm in a moment of exasperation. Then he shook his head and thumbed the mic again. "Wow, I can't argue with that, Control. When you're right, you're right. That is not protocol."

There was a long, static-filled pause. Finally, "Understood, Ocelot. Proceed. We are standing by to receive you."

Crane confirmed and switched off the mic. At least they probably wouldn't blow him out of the sky now.

The sun was above the horizon by the time Crane reached the USS *Dunham*, and the destroyer cast a long morning shadow across the calm surface. Crane saw the dark shapes of small boats in the water alongside her. They were ready for him.

He brought the plane down to just a few yards above the water and came in slow. The destroyer's bow was pointed toward him into the wind, so he flew slowly past on her starboard side and turned around, bleeding off speed. He adjusted the flaps and turned into the wind. He remembered his instructor telling him that eighty-eight percent of controlled ditches resulted in "few" injuries to the pilot and passengers. He supposed that was reassuring.

Then he just did what they'd told him to do. He pulled the circuit breaker for the landing gear. He was going very slowly now, the plane nearly at stall speed. He edged it down, down, and then he switched off the engines and feathered the props.

At the last moment, he opened the cockpit door so the airframe wouldn't bend on impact and seal it shut.

He felt the tail hit, and then the bottom slapped the water hard and the plane bounced. Crane went into crash position. Then they hit the water again, and he was thrown hard against the straps.

Water poured in through the open cockpit door. The plane had stopped, but it was canted to one side, morning sun glaring off seawater right outside the canopy. He popped his harness and leaned over to struggle with al-Sarary's. He got him loose, but the plane was going down fast. He hooked one arm through al-Sarary's bound arms and grabbed the lip of the doorway with the other. Seawater was pounding his face. Crane took a deep breath, and then arms were grabbing him. The black fabric of wetsuits. The rescue divers hauled him out of the cockpit, his target dragging behind him.

———

Crane stood on the deck of the *Dunham*, looking out across the sea where the ditched Beechcraft had sunk without a trace. Behind him, the medics had strapped al-Sarary onto a stretcher and were making sure the anesthesia hadn't harmed him. He doubted he'd see the man again. That was fine. He had no particular desire to. He'd done his job and that was that.

A door opened, and Chris Parikh stepped out. His fellow agent looked rested and relaxed. He looked like someone who'd gotten his man back to the ship according to plan and enjoyed a good meal and a night's sleep.

Parikh grinned. "Damn it, Crane. You just can't help grandstanding, can you?"

"Once I realized I wasn't going to beat you back, all that was left was to go for style points."

Parikh said nothing for a long moment. They watched the sun on the ocean and the distant towers of clouds over the African coast. The medics carried the stretcher off to a secure sickbay. Package delivered as ordered.

"I'm going to miss this," Parikh said with a nod toward the horizon. "Beats Peshawar, doesn't it?" He was referring to Crane's first mission. Parikh had been on that mission as well. It had also not gone according to plan.

Crane laughed. "Five days in a safe house with nothing to pass the time but a DVD of *The Princess Bride*? Yeah, I'll take this."

"It was a good movie, though."

"Not blaming the film at all," said Crane. "Or the company."

"Agent Crane."

A navy lieutenant approached and handed Crane an envelope. "New orders, sir. There's a helicopter en route to pick you up."

"What?" That didn't make any sense. "We've still got Stage Two!"

"I don't know, sir," said the lieutenant. "I just know we've got orders to get you back to D.C. by fastest available means."

He saluted and then turned and walked off the way he'd come. Crane realized he was still holding the envelope out as if it was radioactive.

"What the hell is this?"

Parikh unzipped his flight suit and produced his own envelope from an inside pocket. "Well," he said, "if it's anything like mine, you're fired."

CHAPTER 2

Key West, Florida – Five Months Later

Crane nursed his beer and looked out across the beach. The Southernmost Beach Café was supposedly, true to its name, the southernmost bar in the United States. It was part of a hotel called the Southernmost Beach Resort. Across the street was Southernmost House, an old mansion that had been converted into a bed and breakfast. And next to that was the old concrete buoy the town had painted up for tourists to take photos with, called the Southernmost Point.

Key West took its southernmost-ness very seriously.

But it was a good place to get away, and Crane wanted to get very far away from his old life. Well, not his old life itself so much as the sudden way it had ended.

They'd rushed him and Parikh from the middle of the Indian Ocean back to the United States, and Crane had reported to the Hurricane Group's offices in the basement of a nondescript building that, like the Hurricane Group itself, was technically part of the National Oceanic and Atmospheric Administration. In the cube farm, everyone was packing family photos and plants into cardboard boxes. Someone was crying in the kitchen. The entire operation was folding up. Everyone was out of work.

He didn't know the stern-faced HR drone who met him in a small conference room, gave him the standard exit briefing, and had him sign and initial page after page of security regulations. Crane managed to slip a couple questions of his own in, but the answers were vague at best. Apparently Hurricane's funding had been pulled, but he couldn't get a reason.

"Idiots," he'd overheard a voice from another little meeting room say, more loudly than was polite. "Think all they need to do is read everyone's e-mail and send up a drone once in a while." And that made as much sense as any other reason Crane could think of. Perhaps he'd chosen a career as a field agent just as that career was ceasing to exist. Maybe there was just no place for field agents anymore.

The waitress brought him his cheeseburger and another beer. Outside, kids played in the sand and tourists slathered themselves in sunblock before lying out on plastic chaise lounges. Crane noted the fingertips of his left hand drumming the tabletop in annoyance. He'd been unceremoniously tossed over the side.

He couldn't even take satisfaction in blaming the anonymous accountants for the free fall his life had become. Agents like Crane knew enough to rate golden parachutes, or silver ones at least. The HR drone had explained that a friendly beltway bandit contracting firm had agreed to take them on as mid-level consultants doing what the HR drone called "Enterprise Operations Management." Crane had no idea what that meant, but he doubted there would be much real work to do, anyway. It was basically free money in exchange for staying hidden away, out of sight someplace where the government could keep an eye on them. The HR drone hadn't been pleased when Crane turned down the job.

At some point he would need to find work. And at that point, he realized, he might start to regret the little flush of pleasure that came from rejecting the one they offered him. His résumé was mostly classified. But he had an unusual combination of skills. He could probably find something here if he decided to stay. He could fly the seaplanes that ferried tourists out to Fort Jefferson. He was dive-rated, so he could work the excursion boats. He could translate Russian intelligence briefings in case there was a market for that here. He'd find something. In the meantime, he was having a fine time feeling sorry for himself, and Key West was a great place to do it.

After lunch, Crane walked back up Duval Street to his little B&B and stretched out with a book in the shadow of some palm fronds beside the fountain. The fountain's soft gurgling took the edge off the bass beat from the gay bar down the block. Crane would spend his afternoon reading. Later he would take a run around the southwestern tip of the island, past the Naval Air Station and old Fort Zachary Taylor, and end up at Mallory Square to watch the sunset with everyone else. Then it would be back to Garbo's for tacos. And tomorrow would be more of the same. He realized he was falling into a predictable routine. Already his tradecraft was going to hell.

"Mr. Crane?"

Crane looked up to see a man of about fifty wearing a dark gray suit that was very out of place in Key West, and probably just as uncomfortable.

Crane sat up. "Good afternoon. Yes, I'm John Crane."

"Oh, good," said the man. "Good. They said at the desk I'd find you back here."

Crane noticed the man's cuff links were gold, and his watch looked like a Rolex. He stood there sweating into his expensive suit and didn't seem to know where to begin.

"My name's Gough," he said at last. "I'm CEO of a company

in Miami called Spencer-Tate Capital Strategies. We mainly do financial planning for high-net-worth clients."

"Okay." Crane gestured to another lounge chair. "Won't you have a seat?"

Gough perched on the edge of the cushion and studied Crane intently. Crane looked back, and they examined each other for a long moment. Crane wasn't sure which of them was more confused as to why their paths had crossed.

"What can I do for you, Mr. Gough?" he prompted at last.

Gough swallowed. "Well, apparently I'm here to offer you a job."

What was it with people offering him jobs he was obviously unqualified for? "I'm flattered," he said, "but I don't know the first thing about financial planning."

"No ... not with Spencer-Tate. We're part of a multinational conglomerate called the Myria Group. Are you familiar with it?"

Crane shook his head. "It doesn't ring any bells."

"It's owned by Joshua Sulenski?" Gough looked expectantly at him.

"Sorry."

"Well, Mr. Sulenski has certainly heard of you. I'm here because apparently, out of Myria's many global holdings, Spencer-Tate is the one closest to Key West. We started getting urgent calls and e-mails very early this morning, followed by a call from Mr. Sulenski himself. That never happens. He was very specific. Client meetings didn't matter. Quarterly filing deadlines didn't matter. Nothing mattered except that I get down here as soon as possible and locate you. There are a lot of little hotels and inns in Key West, Mr. Crane. My staff has been calling them all morning while I drove down."

"Because this Sulenski wants to offer me a job. Okay, what kind of job?"

"He didn't specify. He wants to talk to you himself. Since you don't know who he is, let me emphasize this. That. Never. Happens. Not ever. To my knowledge, he's literally never taken a direct role in company operations."

"What does he expect me to do, then?"

"He's on his yacht, the *Normandy*, somewhere in the Gulf of Mexico. He told me he expects to arrive in Key West tonight. He'd like to invite you to lunch tomorrow. He'll have a boat waiting for you at twelve thirty, at the ferry docks near the cruise ship pier, wherever that is."

"I know it."

"You don't have any idea what this is about, do you?"

"Not a clue," said Crane.

Gough shook his head. "Will you meet with him?"

Crane considered it. The only thing that made him interesting was his previous job. He gathered Gough didn't know what that was, but Sulenski must know about his work for Hurricane. And wanted him for something.

Why did this Sulenski need a former spy?

"I don't know," Crane answered. "I guess he'll have to wait and see if I show up at the pier tomorrow."

"Well, that," said Gough as he stood up, "is not my responsibility. My job was to find you and deliver the invitation."

"And nobody can say you haven't done that."

"No, they cannot," said Gough, already walking toward the B&B's back porch. "I wish you well, Mr. Crane."

"Have a safe trip back," he said to the back of Gough's suit. "Watch your speed around Big Pine. They'll pull you over in a heartbeat."

The porch door slammed as Gough vanished back into the building.

Crane sat watching wispy clouds pass by overhead for several minutes, thinking. Then he wandered inside. Mary, who ran the B&B's front desk in the afternoons, agreed to let Crane use her PC. He fired up a browser and searched for Joshua Sulenski. He wasn't hard to find, though Crane entered a few different search terms before he believed what he was seeing.

Joshua Sulenski was twenty-five years old. In the most recent picture Crane could find, he looked like a college freshman who'd accidentally wandered onstage at an insurance convention and was trying to bluff his way through a speech. He wore wire-rimmed glasses and had sandy blond hair that he wore long and floppy so it fell over his eyes. In videos, he was endlessly brushing it out of his face.

And he was very, very rich. Sulenski was in the upper half of the *Forbes* Billionaire list, and tied as the youngest person on it. He'd started Myria Group within the last two years. Its business, as far as Crane could tell, consisted of simply owning whatever Sulenski wanted to own.

Crane assumed he must be a trust-fund baby, heir to some huge corporate empire, but he discovered he was mistaken. Sulenski had become insanely rich, seemingly overnight, in his junior year in the math program at Stanford. Crane didn't understand exactly what he'd created. Some kind of mathematical formula or computer algorithm. But it apparently made it possible to predict the movements of the stock market almost fifteen seconds in advance, with an accuracy of about sixty percent. The articles he read went to some lengths to warn Crane he shouldn't quit his day job and expect to get rich investing. To take advantage of Sulenski's technique, he'd need to start with several billion dollars to spread across the market and hedge all his bad bets.

So Sulenski's invention created nothing new. It just helped billionaires become somewhat wealthier billionaires. But apparently that was all it took. Wall Street hedge fund managers poured money into the company Sulenski formed, and he'd invested that in a series of Internet startups. He was very good at picking those, too. Several had already sold for more billions. Sulenski was now a couple years out of Stanford and richer than several third-world countries. He wasn't a celebrity like so many young Internet prodigies. He kept a low profile and went about his business.

So why did he want to meet with a recently unemployed covert government agent? Why did he need a spy?

There was one way to find out, Crane decided. And it came with a boat ride and what he suspected would be an excellent lunch.

CHAPTER 3

The next day, Crane wandered the promenade that led to the pier. A Disney cruise ship was docked at the far side of the little square harbor, and tourists were swarming the line of shops. The ferry to Sunset Key pulled away and made its way around the enormous cruise ship's bow. A few other small boats rode along the docks. And at the top of one of the ramps stood a man holding an iPad displaying "John Crane" in large black letters. Crane wasn't sure he'd expected him to actually be there.

The man recognized Crane as he approached, and put down the iPad. "Mr. Crane," he said. "Good day, sir. I'll run you out to the *Normandy*."

He led Crane to the only boat on this particular pier, a small tender, all teak and brass fittings. It looked appropriately expensive. They climbed aboard, and Crane settled in the back. The pilot brought the engines roaring to life, a dock tender cast off their line, and they pulled away. He was committing himself to ... whatever he was getting himself into, he realized. But he didn't think he'd passed any point of no return just yet. And this was certainly more interesting than wasting away in a bar somewhere.

"It'll be about fifteen minutes, sir," the pilot called back. Crane nodded, and then he relaxed and watched the scenery slide past. They moved slowly out of the harbor area, rounded the bow of the Disney ship, and then accelerated out into open water, leaving Key West behind.

After the promised fifteen minutes, they approached a large yacht. There was no mistaking the *Normandy*. Crane estimated she was about 350 feet long, sleek and dark. The top decks were white, but the lower hull was black. Toward the stern was a wide red band bearing the legend "Normandy SR1" in huge, squarish white letters.

As they drew close, a port opened in the hull. The pilot cut his engines and carefully steered directly into the ship. They came to rest in a chamber inside the hull. A crewman closed the door behind them from a control panel, and a web of black straps cradled the boat as the water was pumped from the chamber.

As the pilot was helping Crane up onto the deck, a door opened and a figure burst in.

"John Crane. Welcome aboard! Josh Sulenski. Great to meet you! What do you think?" His voice was loud and enthusiastic. "This is sweet, huh? I put a boat in my boat! So I can boat! While I boat!"

He seemed to think that was very funny for some reason. Sulenski looked like he did in the photos Crane had found online. He was about five eight, with the same floppy hair and glasses. He wore cargo shorts and a T-shirt with a female cartoon character Crane didn't recognize saying, "Let's Mess with Texas!"

They shook hands, and Sulenski led him up a stairway. "Sorry about sending Gough after you," said Sulenski. "Sounded like he had a huge stick up his ass. But he was the quickest way to find you. When I found out you were in Key West and we were only a couple days' sail away, I knew I couldn't miss the chance."

"First question," said Crane. "How did you know I was in Key West?"

"I had people looking for you, and they came back with Key West. Credit card probably. You buy anything recently?"

"Second question. Why were you looking for me?"

"Hope you're hungry!" said Sulenski. "We've got some killer wagyu rib eyes on the grill!"

"Okay, fair enough. I know why in the larger sense; there's only one thing interesting about me."

"Oh, I doubt that," Sulenski said. At the top of the stairs, he waved his hand at a pair of frosted glass doors, and they slid open to reveal a partially shaded rear deck with a café table and a serving station. Two of the crew waited at attention. A third was operating a grill burning carefully cut wooden planks. Folding screens separated them from the rest of the stern deck.

"But maybe you shouldn't mention that thing to my other guest," said Sulenski. "Someone I want you to meet. I think she can help explain things."

"Mr. Sulenski, I'd really—"

"Josh. Please."

Crane took a breath. "Josh, I'd really like to discuss why you want to talk to a spy before we—"

"Too late for that!" Josh said, leading Crane past the screens. "We're here. Melissa! Come here! Someone I want you to meet."

On the port side of the deck was a dining table and chairs. On the starboard side, a woman in a pale orange bikini lay on a chaise lounge. She stood up. She was tall and lean with a rich tan and medium-length blonde hair. She took off her sunglasses and lay them down on a table beside her chair. She was stunning, Crane realized.

"John Crane, Dr. Melissa Simon," said Josh. "Melissa, John.

John, Melissa, Josh, Melissa. John, Josh. There. I think that covers everybody."

"Pleased to meet you," said Crane. They shook hands.

"The same," said Melissa. "I want to thank you for coming. I really hope you can help."

Crane was about to ask what she meant when Josh interjected. "I haven't filled John in on the details yet. I thought you could do that better than I could." He tapped the screen of his smart watch, and a waiter appeared and served three margaritas from a silver tray.

The drinks were perfect, of course. They enjoyed them and made small talk for a few minutes while admiring the view from the yacht's stern. Crane took another look at Dr. Simon and reminded himself to keep things professional.

"Melissa is a microbiologist," said Josh after a few minutes, signaling the shift to the matter at hand. "She runs a biodiversity project that I fund in Puerto Rico."

"We're doing a species census in the rainforest at El Yunque," she explained. "My own specialty is microorganisms living in mud along stream beds or benthic zones at the bottom of lagoons. But we're sequencing all kinds of things. Bacteria, diatoms, dozens of small invertebrate species, along with the usual plants, birds, frogs, and insects. We've published sequences for more than a dozen undiscovered species this year alone."

"Which we can talk about over steaks," Josh said. He seemed to be enjoying the role of magnanimous host immensely, thought Crane. As if he was playing dress-up on his toy boat.

They seated themselves around the table, and the rich smell of grilled steaks preceded the waiters.

"Melissa calls her project a census," Josh said as the waiters served lunch. "As I see it, it's a gene bank. That area's threatened by development, by climate change, and we have no idea what lives there. Melissa's identifying species and preserving them before they're lost forever."

"At least we were," she said, "but we've run into a snag. That's why I've come to Mr. Sulenski—"

"Josh. Come on."

"That's why I turned to Josh for help."

"What's the problem?" Crane asked.

"Someone's tampering with our equipment," said Melissa. "We set up all kinds of equipment out in the field. Insect traps, timed water sample collectors, pH recorders. We never had a problem until a couple months ago. Then things started disappearing."

"Stolen?"

Melissa nodded. "If it was just once in a while, I'd think the wind, or maybe an animal got something. But it was a dozen instruments in a night. It was very deliberate."

"Is this equipment valuable?" Crane asked. "Could someone resell it?"

"Not really. I mean, they cost money, of course, a lot of it. But there's nobody around there who would pay for them. They're really only useful to us. After the first couple times, a thief would have figured that out. But we looked anyway. We checked local flea markets. I even sent a couple people to canvass pawn shops in San Juan. But we never found anything. Then it escalated."

"Escalated how?" Crane said over the clicking of Josh's silverware against his plate.

"They started destroying things. Just trampling everything and leaving the wreckage behind. We lost a fifteen-thousand-dollar gas analyzer once. They had to break a padlock to get into it. Then they even smashed the data cards."

"That's not greed, then," said Crane. "That's malice. Someone objects to what you're doing."

"Who has a problem with a gene bank?" said Josh. "It doesn't make sense."

"Nobody's ever complained to us," said Melissa. "The land isn't contested. It was set aside by the king of Spain! It's been forest preserve for more than a century. We reached out to local environmental groups. They were as upset as we are. They all think we're doing important work that will help Puerto Rico."

"And the police?"

Melissa shook her head and sighed. "They haven't been much help. They just think it's bored kids. And they're not going to put officers out in the rainforest all night to watch over some insect traps."

"Tell him about the cameras," said Josh.

"Right. We tried putting out game cameras to catch them in the act. That didn't work. They stole the cameras."

"How many cameras?" Crane asked.

"Two the first time. Four the second. They got all of them."

"All of them?" Crane's instincts were flaring. That didn't fit. "You never got a single camera through the night?"

"Not a one. This is putting the whole project at risk," Melissa said. "We've got a backlog of samples we're still processing. But we haven't collected any new material for more than a month. We're dead in the water. Josh is our primary backer, so I turned to him."

"And here we are," said Josh. "I explained to Melissa that you have a strong background providing security for government installations."

"And I'd appreciate any insights you can offer," said Melissa. Crane could hear the diplomatic "but" in her voice. He wasn't what she wanted from Josh.

"I want to send John back with you," Josh said quickly, nipping whatever objection she planned to raise in the bud. "I want to know what he thinks once he's seen the situation on the ground. John, I'd like to put you on retainer to Myria Group to help Melissa out any way you can. This project's important to me."

Crane hesitated. He quickly added up the pros and cons. Josh clearly liked his toys, and Crane had no interest in becoming one of them. On the other hand, Josh had money to burn, and Crane would run out of cash in another few months. He'd rejected the golden parachute and let himself fall. Well, here was someone throwing him a rope. He'd already rejected one. How many more could he expect the world to toss him?

Also, there was the beautiful woman in distress angle. He wasn't doing anything at the moment except letting his skills degrade. He wanted to feel like he was doing something helpful. And he'd never been to Puerto Rico.

Crane gave Josh and Melissa a smile. "I'll be happy to see what I can do."

———

After lunch, they left Melissa sunning on the rear deck and went forward to work out the details of his employment. Then Josh walked Crane back down to the tender. It would take him back to Key West where he'd pack his bag, check out of the B&B, and meet Josh's Gulfstream at Key West's airport in a few hours. Josh had promised he'd have them both back to San Juan in time for dinner.

"She doesn't really want me there," said Crane as they descended the steps to the tender's launch bay.

"I know," said Josh. "She wants to hire locals to guard the site. She thinks that will protect her equipment and make her local friends as well. But I've got reasons for sending you instead."

"You mean the cameras?" said Crane.

Josh stopped at the bottom of the stairs. "What about the cameras?"

"They got all of them. Those cameras are built for conceal-ment. They're meant to be tucked out of the way where they won't be noticed. But they found every one of them. In the dark. That's not bored teenagers with flashlights and hammers. And it's not someone who resents all that money being spent studying bugs while they're broke. Whoever you're up against went looking for cameras, and they brought specialized gear to find them."

"Huh." Josh exhaled. "I'm going to like you. I can tell." Then he glanced back up the stairway to the closed door. "But that's not it. There's something else I haven't told Melissa because I don't want to freak her out, but there's more to it than vandalism in the forest." He led Crane slowly toward the door to the dry dock. "A few months ago, we had a fake reporter sniffing around my foundation asking about this project. She pestered us for interviews, but her background didn't check out. Then she tried to social engineer her way around my gatekeepers. After that, someone tried to hack into the project's cloud servers. We traced that as far as Eastern Europe before the trail went cold."

So the interest wasn't just local. "Is there anything you want to tell me about this project before I head out there? Is it a front for something?"

"No!" said Josh. "That's what's so weird. It's just what it looks like. And they put all their data on the net under a creative commons license. Trying to hack it doesn't make any sense. It's all right there, for free."

Josh opened the door and gestured Crane through. Two crewmen were already prepping the boat.

"I need to know who's messing with this project and why," he said as Crane boarded the tender, and the bay doors slid open to the sea. "But be careful. So far nobody's gotten hurt. I'd like to keep it that way."

"I will," said Crane.

But he was troubled as the tender left the *Normandy* and sped back toward Key West. The reasons for the attacks might not make sense to Melissa, but they made sense to whoever was behind them. And that meant they knew something about her project that she didn't. If he was going to help her, Crane needed to find out what that was.

CHAPTER 4

Brno, Czech Republic

Anton Kucera swept into the lobby with his two best men, Vladan and Lubor, at either side. The building was some government heap from the old days. Kucera was too young to remember the communists, or their stitched-together state of Czechoslovakia, but there was no mistaking the flat ugliness of their buildings, despite the attempts to pretty it up with lights and wood panels.

Kucera took off his sunglasses and slipped them into his jacket. It was a brown leather recreation of a World War II flyer's jacket, complete with a sheepskin lining and a pinup girl straddling a bomb on the back. He strode through the metal detector, and it went off like a car alarm. Kucera locked eyes with the nearest of the guards. He waited until the man looked down at his shoes, and then gestured Vladan and Lubor through. The metal detector bleated its warning two more times. The guards stood like statues.

There was a pretty girl at the main counter. She looked up from her PC and smiled.

"I'm here to see the old man," said Kucera, leaning against the counter and checking out her cleavage.

"Yes, sir," she said, her voice steady. "Mr. Skala is expecting you." She gestured to the elevators. "You can go up."

He winked at her and led his entourage away. She was afraid, of course, but she played it cool, kept her composure. Kucera respected that. He'd probably keep her on. Unlike the guards. Useless. They'd have to go.

This was a historic day, he thought as the elevator hummed upward. Branislav Skala ran everything in Brno: hookers, gambling, liquor and cigarettes, stolen cars. Everything. It had been that way since the communist days. He was always going on about it. How tough it was back then. How he got started smuggling out old family gravestones for rich Jews in the West. It was all StB agents and SNB national police and government snitches, and none of it meant a damn thing to Kucera. Nobody had seen a communist since before he was born.

Skala got rich purchasing state assets when the new government privatized them. A bribe here, a broken leg there, and Skala bought up half a dozen factories, a brewery, a hotel, this hideous office building, and more, all for a song. So now he was rich. But that was ancient history and so was Skala. Being rich made him soft. Both of his sons were in America. They said one of them was a veterinarian in Minnesota. A fucking veterinarian!

Kucera had clawed his way out of the gutters. From street wars with other gangs, he'd moved up to challenging Skala himself, and he'd won. He'd demanded this meeting, and Skala had accepted. Maybe the old man could see it was time to surrender and leave the field. If he was that smart, then Kucera would be happy to let him retire to his country estate and grow his stupid grapes. If not, then he could die right here today.

The elevator opened to a well-furnished foyer. There were

no soldiers here. Just a pair of glass doors with Skala's name. Kucera strode in like a general ready to receive his vanquished enemy's sword.

———

Skala's spacious office was furnished in steel and leather. The old man sat behind a broad, angular desk. Behind him was a sweep of glass with a panoramic view of an empty apartment tower slowly crumbling away in the weather.

"Come in," he said. "It's good to see you, Anton."

Kucera sat in one of the old man's fancy chairs, and Vladan and Lubor stood behind him on either side. Their jackets were open to show off their shoulder holsters. The old man tried to make small talk, like they were old friends catching up. But Kucera got right to the point. He told the old man that his operations were in tatters. He'd already taken over some of his operations, and Skala's men had failed to push him out. He could take what he wanted.

"You're old and soft," Kucera said. "Maybe you were something back in your precious communist days, but that was a long time ago."

Skala acknowledged this with a shrug.

"It's time for a new boss," said Kucera. "One who knows the streets. Who has the guts to fight."

"And that's you?"

Kucera laughed and Vladan and Lubor laughed with him. "You see anybody else sitting here in your nice office telling you how it is?"

"No," said Skala. "No one else would dare. And you're right, Anton, about a lot of things. But there's one thing you're wrong about. I took your meeting because I think you might be smart enough to see that."

"I know you have a shit view from your office," said Kucera, waving at the empty tower across the way with its empty windows and crumbling, naked balconies. "I'm smart enough to know if you put it on the other side of the building, you'd have a nice view of the river."

"Yes, you're clever," said Skala. "And tough. I watch the street gangs. You let nothing stop you. You're ruthless when it's called for. This is good. You're like I was before I got old and soft, as you say. I wanted a better life for my sons, and I gave it to them. But doing that, I lost them. They're in America now, and they aren't coming back. It's been three years since I saw my grand-children. Eh." He shrugged again. "Everything comes at a price."

Kucera paused for a moment. He'd expected more bluster. He came here to win a fight, but it looked like all the fight was gone from the old man.

"You did very well to get here," said Skala. "But you made mistakes, too. You killed Miloslav Babic. He was a good man. Loyal. We went way back."

Kucera shrugged. "I killed a bunch of your guys."

"Yes, but I'd already agreed to meet you when you shot poor Miloslav. You killed him for nothing. We have to settle that before we finish our business."

Kucera tensed his shoulders slightly. Behind him, Vladan and Lubor would pick that up. They'd be ready to gun the old man down if he decided it was necessary.

"So you brought your two favorite soldiers with you," said Skala. "I'll leave it to you. Which one can you do without? Maybe you like one more?"

Kucera laughed, and Vladan and Lubor echoed him a beat behind.

"Shit, I don't know. They're both stone-cold killers." He turned, grinning. "Which one of you is the better shot?"

"That's him, boss," said Lubor, and he cocked his head toward Vladan. "But I'm better looking."

They all laughed again. Skala sat patiently behind his desk and said nothing.

"He is better looking," said Kucera. "The girls like him. But he sucks his teeth. Drives me crazy."

"Very well," said Skala. "The one on the left, then." Kucera's ears perked at the faint chink of breaking glass. What was—he saw the tiny hole in the window. Then Lubor fell over backward and hit the floor. A neat hole in his forehead was edged with blood.

Shit! Kucera dove to the floor. Out of the corner of his eye, he saw Vladan whip out his pistol. "Boss!" Vladan shouted.

"Get down!" Kucera yelled.

Kucera sprang to the edge of the desk and popped up just enough to level his own gun at Skala's impassive face. A moment later, Vladan slid into place beside him.

"You bastard! I'll kill you right here!"

"You see now," said Skala, "the reason I have my office on this side instead of over there with the nice view of the river is because I own that building behind us."

Kucera's eyes swept the building, looking for the shooter but finding only dark window frames.

"And indeed, you could surely kill me," said Skala, "but then you'd never leave this office alive. Wouldn't you rather be the king of Brno's underworld?"

Kucera slowed his breathing, tried to calm the tide of adrenaline. But he kept his pistol trained on the old man's forehead.

"One of my sons told me about something he learned in college in America," said Skala. "It's called game theory." Skala's tongue worked its way hesitantly through the unfamiliar words. "There's a clever strategy they call 'tit for tat.' They proved it works with computers, but I learned it long ago the hard way. If a man hits you, you knock him down. Then you help him up and offer to buy him a drink. If he takes it, fine. If he hits you again, you knock him down. Then you offer him a drink. You keep doing this until he gets the idea, and then you can be friends."

"You want to be my friend?" Kucera said, stalling for time while he looked for a way out.

"I think we can help each other. Put that away and have a seat."

There was no way out, he realized. Skala's sniper could hit anything in the office. He glanced at the door. Too far. He'd never make it. He was screwed. He nodded to Vladan. Then, slowly, carefully, he put away his gun and edged back into his chair. Unsure what else to do, Vladan resumed his post, glancing down at Lubor's corpse.

"It's very important that you understand, Anton. You're not taking my throne from me. I'm giving it to you. I'm making you my heir because you have what it takes to run things. So you'll take over. I'll pass the word down the line, to everyone. They'll accept you."

"And what do you want?"

"I want to move up to the next level. You think this is the top of the heap, don't you? I used to. But there's another game out there. It's bigger than cops, politicians, judges. There's more money and power than you can dream of. That's where I'm going. But I'll need someone with your talents and with an eye on the street."

Skala opened a desk drawer and Vladan flinched, but Kucera waved him back. Skala produced a bottle of whiskey and two glasses.

"So you'll be the new king of the hill in Brno," he said as he poured one shot and then another. "And I'll be your mentor. I'll smooth things out for you with my connections. And sometimes

I'll need you to do some work for me—for which you'll be very well paid. So what do you think, Anton? Can I buy you a drink?"

Kucera took a deep breath. Did it really matter who had "won" this meeting if he got what he wanted? Especially given the alternative.

"I don't need to get hit twice to see how things work," he said as he leaned forward and accepted the glass.

"Very good," said Skala. "You see? Now we can be good friends."

Kucera wasn't sure of that. But he clinked his glass against Skala's and drank. He could wait to see how things shook out. For now.

CHAPTER 5

San Juan, Puerto Rico

The Gulfstream's wheels screamed for a moment as it touched down, and then they were in San Juan. Crane checked his watch. Sulenski had been true to his word. It was dinner time.

Dr. Simon sat opposite Crane, reading something on a tablet. The bikini had been replaced by khaki slacks and a blue linen shirt, but no matter how she dressed, she was a very beautiful woman. It was too bad she didn't like him, Crane thought.

"Here we are," he said, realizing how stupid he sounded.

She folded the cover over her tablet and slipped it into her shoulder bag.

"Here we are."

The Gulfstream taxied to a ground handling terminal outside the main traffic flow, and the engines wound down.

"I guess we may as well make the most of it," said Crane.

She smiled politely. "I guess so. There's no point in going out to Benitez tonight. It'll be dark and the lab will be closed by the time we get there. I've got a place I stay in town. Can you get a room?"

Josh had provided Crane with a company credit card and told him not to worry about expenses. Coming from Josh, Crane figured that meant something.

"Won't be a problem."

"Great," she said as the copilot opened the door. "I know a good place for dinner!"

The ground crew unloaded their baggage. There wasn't much. Melissa had just brought an overnight bag for a short trip and Crane traveled light by habit. He slung his battered duffel over his shoulder, took Melissa's bag, and they walked through the terminal to the taxi stand.

Melissa guided the taxi to a guest house in the Ocean Park district, near the beach. She quickly dropped off her bag, and they were off again.

"Condado Vanderbilt," Crane told the driver.

Melissa raised an eyebrow but said nothing. They'd passed through the Condado district on the way, and Crane had noted the Vanderbilt. It was the most expensive-looking of the row of hotels along the beach. That suggested it was more likely to have a room available for someone without a reservation. And, he thought, he might as well put Josh's credit card to the test.

Twenty minutes later, Crane had a luxury suite on the hotel's ocean side. The card was approved without a second thought. He looked briefly out from his balcony, over the beach into the setting sun. Apparently working for Josh had its advantages. Then he dropped his duffel bag onto the bed and went down to rejoin Melissa.

The next stop was Columbus Square at the edge of Old San Juan. Melissa explained they'd walk from there, both to enjoy the sights and because it was probably faster than taking the cab. Old San Juan was a maze of narrow streets designed when the city had been crowded into high stone walls, part of a Spanish fort complex. They passed restaurants and shops, and

Crane reacquainted himself with the rhythms of spoken Spanish. Thanks to the Defense Language Institute, he was rated ILR 4+ in Spanish, as well as a half dozen other languages, but he hadn't used it in a while.

Melissa led the way to a little restaurant called Rosa de Triana on a narrow, tree-lined side street across from the Hotel El Convento. They sat in a small courtyard out back with high cement walls and lights strung in the trees overhead.

"How did you end up running a gene bank in the rainforest?" Crane asked over sliced manchego and a bottle of Rioja.

She shrugged. "I grew up in the country. I liked science. I was always off on my own in the woods, digging around in stream beds. One thing led to another, I guess. I got my bachelor's in biology and specialized in grad school. From there your course is pretty much set."

"But why this specific project?"

"Because there's so much left to find out there! Rainforests really are almost unexplored. The medical applications of undiscovered plant species alone are ridiculous. And we're losing the biome. We're losing all of it before we even know what's there. I wanted to do something about that."

"How'd Josh get involved?"

"He has a grant foundation. He's not the only one on the board. There are half a dozen other big donors, plus some foundations with a hand in. But Josh was the most interested. I submitted a grant proposal and he actually called me. I think he had to talk the rest of the board into funding us."

The waitress came by, and Melissa ordered a set of small plates. "Trust me," she said with a grin.

"Absolutely."

She took the last slice of the manchego and finished her wine.

"My background's pretty standard for a scientist. I get it."

Crane emptied the rest of the bottle into her glass and nodded to the waitress for another.

"But you, I don't get," Melissa went on. "Who are you? What exactly do you do? And how does it help me with my problem?"

Crane laughed. "Okay, that's fair enough."

Then he stopped and covered the silence by finishing his glass of wine. What was he going to tell her? The truth was out of the question. If nothing else, he'd be violating several national security regulations. He'd known since before he joined the Hurricane Group that this part of his life would become complicated. But nobody had actually asked him about it before.

"I just always wanted to make the world better," he said at last. "But I didn't know what that meant, really. By the time I got to college, I had no idea what to do with my life. So I majored in philosophy."

Melissa's laugh mid-swallow almost choked her.

"Honestly?"

"Eh, it seemed like a good idea at the time. Big questions, no answers, you know."

"And did it work?"

"Not really. When I graduated, I still didn't know what I wanted to do with my life, except now I had student loans to pay off and no obvious career skills. I ended up joining the Coast Guard. I figured they helped people. And that turned out okay. I rescued people from sinking ships and stopped drug traffickers. From there, I just sort of drifted into security work."

And that, Crane thought, was where he had to stop telling the truth. In fact, Hurricane had recruited him out of the Coast Guard. They were looking for people with elite level physical skills, but they were reluctant to recruit from the usual branches of the military. They wanted agents, not soldiers. Crane had the athleticism and the initiative, but he was more effective operating solo than as part of a unit. Apparently his performance ratings and his scores on a battery of psychological tests had rung some bells somewhere, and before long, he was detached from the Coast Guard and in field-agent training. Crane had taken to it, and he thought he'd found his path, until it all fell apart.

Melissa was looking at him thoughtfully. The waitress brought another bottle of the Rioja.

"Things like setting access policies, determining what went wrong after a breach," he added. "I really do know what I'm doing."

She gave him a conciliatory smile. "I'm sure you do. I'm not questioning that. I'm just not sure this is the right approach."

"No, I get it," Crane said. "Josh said you want to hire some locals. You want to build bridges. It's not a bad idea."

"Of course it's not!" she said, warming to her subject. "Hiring locals will buy us double the impact! We can put people in the woods to keep an eye on the machinery. And these are poor people! There's not a lot of jobs out in the back country where we are. If we inject some money into the local economy, we'll buy a lot of goodwill. That might solve our problem right there."

"If it really is just area kids causing trouble, it could help. But there could be more to it than that." In fact, Crane was convinced there was more to it than that, even before Josh had mentioned the hackers probing the project from Eastern Europe. But there was little to be gained by explaining all that to Melissa.

"Look, I'll make a deal with you," Crane said. "Take me to your facility. Show me where you've been losing equipment. Answer my questions. Let me do my job. After that, if I think your plan makes sense, then I'll talk to Josh."

"You'll back me up?"

"I'll do what I think is best for your project. If I agree that's the right way to handle this, I'll tell him so."

"Okay," she said. "I guess that's fair."

Crane lifted his glass. Melissa followed suit, and they clinked them together.

"I'll take you out in the morning and show you around," she said. "Dress for a hike in the rainforest."

CHAPTER 6

Branislav Skala left the office early. He'd accomplished enough for one day. And besides, the building staff needed to replace the carpet in his office.

Out front, he got into the back of his armored Mercedes.

"The estate," he told his driver.

As the car made its way out of the city and sped through the Czech countryside, Skala smiled. The boy he'd been, the boy who had made his money rolling drunks and running errands for old Domenek, couldn't have even imagined the life he led now.

Deep in the countryside, the car turned off the highway onto an unmarked side road, and now Skala rode through land that he owned. That in itself would have been impossible when he was a boy; the estate had been the personal retreat of some high party official. Even after the communists fell, there was no way he could have bought something so grand. He'd started at the very bottom of the ladder and had been clawing his way up all his life.

Now he was the ruler of Brno—still in charge when it

mattered, as young Kucera would learn soon enough. And he had his own personal kingdom here, a palatial chateau and four hundred hectares of the finest vineyards in the southern wine country. A fine meal was waiting for him, prepared by a Cordon Bleu–trained chef, along with a couple bottles of Cabernet Moravia from his own vineyards.

The chateau rose up from among the vineyards as the Mercedes sped up the private drive. It was a three-story expanse of seamless white in the Louis XVI style with steep black roofs and high chimneys. Two expansive wings swept out on either side of the main house. It was a palace, originally built by some nobleman from the old Austro-Hungarian Empire. When he bought the place, he imagined he had reached the summit, that there was no higher goal to aspire to. But there was more. There was still so much more. And if there was more ladder left to climb, Skala meant to climb it.

The Mercedes pulled up on the crushed gravel driveway, and a servant opened the door for him. Skala strode through the front doors into a large entry hall with fluted columns set into the wall, supporting a domed ceiling painted with clouds and angels. His butler appeared to greet him and take his briefcase. Skala walked on, through a large sitting room full of antique furniture. Old paintings lined the walls, hanging three deep from railings near the ceiling. The place smelled of wood polish, and he heard classical music piped softly from hidden speakers. He knew this one ... Beethoven. Yes, this was the *Moonlight Sonata*. The culture lessons were paying off. Soon he would join the rulers of the world, and no one would know he was just a Brno gutter rat.

For much of his life, there had been powerful men above him, and Skala had succeeded by knowing who to attach himself to, how to get their attention, how to make himself indispensable to them.

When he was young, the powerful man had been old Domenek, and his problem had been a police lieutenant who didn't know enough to take his money and go. Skala had solved Domenek's problem very suddenly one night on a moonlit path along the banks of the Svratka. And that bold move had lifted him out of the gutter and set him on a new trajectory.

The particulars of the present situation were different, but the idea was the same. A consortium of investors stood to make billions when their biotech concern patented a new drug. Or a "line of therapies," whatever that was. Skala wasn't a doctor. He just knew they were keeping their work secret until it was time to claim the patents. But now there was a scientist in Puerto Rico who threatened to put their secret drugs on the Internet for nothing and make their investment worthless.

He knew how to make that problem go away, just as quickly and as finally as that old policeman.

Skala's private suite was a departure from the rest of the chateau. He lived in a bedroom with its own bathroom and walk-in closet, and an office. He'd closed off hallways so his suite was accessible only by one well-secured door. The rest of the palace looked like a museum, but here the furniture was chosen for comfort. There was a big flat screen TV on one wall. Clothes were tossed in the corners. Skala only allowed the maids back here once a week. Here, he felt at ease.

He took off his shoes and tossed them onto the closet floor. Then he settled back into a plush armchair with a loud, groaning sigh and tapped the button on a nearby table.

"Sir?" his butler said through the speaker.

"A glass of wine, Tomas. I have a little more to do. Tell chef, dinner in half an hour."

"Yes, sir."

He waited until the wine had come and Tomas had left again before he opened a panel in the console beneath the television and took out his laptop. It was still mid-afternoon in Puerto Rico. His man there would be standing by. He powered up the laptop and put his fingertip on the reader, waiting for it to boot. The laptop was perhaps the most precious thing he owned. Skala had discovered a world of wealth and power beyond his dreams. But it was a complicated place, full of secrets: concealed identities, secret alliances, rivalries, and fierce vendettas. If he wanted to navigate that world, Skala needed to understand it. So he gathered intelligence wherever he could and kept careful notes on his laptop. Skala didn't really like computers. They were too new for an old dog like him. But computers were like guns now. If you couldn't use one, you'd run into someone who could, and that would be it.

So Skala had his technical people set it up for him and teach him how to use it. When the machine was done powering up, it read his fingerprint. Then a screen appeared with pictures of all the people Skala had watching, following, reporting back to him.

He tapped the photo of Emil Zajic, and a chat window popped up. Half a world away in Puerto Rico, Zajic's own laptop would be sounding a tone and he would be scrambling to respond. As always, Zajic was prompt.

Here, said the chat window.

What is your progress? He typed in return.

More stuff smashed two nights ago. Nothing put out since then.

That was promising. He had read about these projects. They were always run on a shoestring. If he kept destroying their expensive equipment, they would quickly run out of funding to replace it.

The woman, Dr. Simon, left to ask rich backer for help. They say he's sending a man.

Skala hissed through his teeth. That could be bad.

WHO? WHO DID SHE GO TO?

He'd researched the people funding the project. The money came through a foundation with several wealthy donors on its board. A few of those people were tied to other groups, and those were tied to other groups. They were careful to hide the strings they pulled. A good lesson, one Skala had taken to heart.

DON'T KNOW. SOMEONE WHO GIVES THEM MONEY.

Damn it, he knew that much. It might be nothing, but if the woman had gone to the right donor and he'd called in a favor from the right people ...

IS IT TEAM KILO?

No, Zajic wouldn't know that.

He backspaced that out and typed, HAS ANYONE MENTIONED TEAM KILO?

DON'T KNOW. WHAT IS TEAM KILO? JUST KNOW BACKER IS SENDING SOMEONE. SHOULD GET HERE TONIGHT.

Damn it. Just when he had everything under control.

FIND OUT WHO IT IS. BUT STAY IN BACKGROUND. IF THIS MAN IS FROM TEAM KILO, INFORM ME IMMEDIATELY AND THEN BREAK ALL CONTACT WITH LOCALS AND COME BACK.

A few moments, and then Zajic typed back, HOW DO I KNOW? WHAT IS TEAM KILO?

Skala knocked back the last of his wine and slapped the glass down on the table harder than he'd meant to.

JUST FIND OUT ALL YOU CAN ABOUT NEW PLAYER. AND SHUT PROJECT DOWN FOR GOOD. NO MORE SCREWING AROUND.

UNDERSTOOD.

Skala closed the window. Coming up through the under-world, at least he'd always known the score. He knew who was on whose side, what they wanted, what drove them. Now he just knew there were shadowy forces moving around him, groups he didn't know about, with motives he could only guess at. The man coming to Puerto Rico was probably nothing, but the not knowing unsettled him.

He folded the laptop closed and went out to his waiting dinner. Of course the meal was excellent, but Skala couldn't truly enjoy it.

CHAPTER 7

After dinner, Crane and Melissa strolled back through Old San Juan. The mood was lighter than it had been walking these same streets in the other direction, Crane realized. Thanks to his promise, she was warming to him. He doubted he would agree with her plan to hire locals to guard the project's equipment. There were forces at work that she didn't know about. But he'd meant what he said. If what he found tomorrow was less serious than Josh feared, if it really was just a local matter of bored vandals, then he would support her plan to Josh.

In the meantime, he was enjoying her company, and she seemed to be enjoying his.

"This came up pretty suddenly," he said as they approached a taxi line on the Calle Tetuan. "If we're going into the rainforest tomorrow, I'm going to need some gear. Do you know a good outdoor store?"

She looked at him, and Crane could see her gauging his intent. Was he looking for an excuse for them to stay together? As it happened, he did need some things before they went out to Benitez in the morning. Her company, that was a good thing too.

"Yeah," she said at last. "I know a place in Hato Rey. Come on."

They caught a cab, and Melissa told the driver where to go. It took them across town to a large store designed to look like a ski lodge, with wooden trestles and canoes hanging from the ceiling. It was a little cheesy, but it did have a large selection of clothes and other gear.

Crane started with a pair of black Fjallraven hiking pants. They were made of a microfiber fabric that was light enough to be comfortable while still providing UV protection. They also had plenty of pockets for the other things he was planning to buy. He modeled the pants for Melissa, who had him spin around for her before she gave him two thumbs up. He added a pair of Scarpa Kinesis boots and a couple T-shirts to the pile, and then they headed to the equipment section. There Crane bought a GPS receiver, a point-and-shoot camera, a compact multi-tool, a rucksack, and a few other things he thought he might need. Again, Josh's credit card absorbed it all without a peep.

They were loaded down with shopping bags when they left.

"I totally would have bought you those boots, you know," Crane said in a playful tone. "The leopard print ones. I saw you eying them."

She laughed and punched his bicep. "Oh God, can you see me wearing those things around my team? They'd lose all respect for me. It would be anarchy."

"So what? You want them. You know you want them." He started to turn around. "It's not too late! We can go get them. It's the least Josh can do."

"If you're feeling generous with Josh's money, you can get me another gene sequencer," she said with a grin.

"Mom always said the way to a girl's heart is through her lab equipment."

"You know it."

She flagged down a cab and told the driver to take them back to Condado.

On the ride back, Crane felt an energy between them. He knew he'd been attracted to her from the moment he saw her on Josh's yacht. He thought she had dropped her initial wariness. If, when they got back to the Vanderbilt, he asked her up to his suite, he thought she'd come.

But no, he decided. It was too soon. More than that, he had work to do.

The cab pulled up outside the Vanderbilt, and Melissa helped him unload his bags and carry them to the doors, where a bellman put them on a cart and took them upstairs for him.

"What time do you want me to pick you up?" she asked as they stood beneath the overhang in front of the lobby doors.

"Let me get some breakfast first," said Crane. "Nine-thirty? When will that get us there?"

"By eleven or so. Is that okay?"

"That works," he said. "Thank you for showing me around. Dinner was excellent."

"Any time," she said softly. It felt like an invitation, and Crane was again tempted. But not now. Not yet. Part of him argued that he was working for Josh, not Melissa, but he knew better than that. He had no business getting involved with her while he was investigating the threat to her project.

"Have a good night," he said, and watched her walk back to the waiting taxi.

Afterwards might be a different matter.

CHAPTER 8

A little after midnight, Police Sergeant Javier Acevedo sat in his cruiser in the parking lot of a dark strip mall outside San Juan and waited for the Little Russian.

The Little Russian was, of course, far from little. The man was six and a half feet tall and built like a tank. He must have weighed three hundred pounds. And Acevedo knew he wasn't really Russian, either. He was from one of those old eastern bloc countries; Acevedo didn't bother to remember which one because he didn't really care. Russia was close enough. His name was Zajic, or something like it. Again, Acevedo didn't care. He only put up with him at all because he was paid well to do so.

Acevedo turned his radio down until the dispatch chatter was barely audible through the whine of traffic on the highway in front of him. The pale dash lights cast his angular face in sharp relief.

Acevedo took a long drag on his cigarette and wished he was home in bed with his wife.

He was a simple man, an officer in the Puerto Rico Police, the state level police force. It wasn't a bad job, but the pay wasn't great, especially with the government going broke. There was a pay freeze for public employees, and the taxes kept getting higher all the time. All Acevedo wanted was enough money to buy a little plot of land at the western end of the island, somewhere outside Mayaguez maybe. A place with a nice house he could retire to. That and a boat for fishing. It wasn't so much to ask.

He'd assembled a group of officers with similar inclinations. They were assigned to the Carolina district, which meant their patrol area included Luis Muñoz International Airport. They had a simple enough system going. Drugs came in from partners in Colombia or Mexico. Acevedo and his men collected them and repartitioned the shipments into smaller packages. Those went to the airport and then out on direct flights to Spain or Germany, and eventually on to other partners in Southern and Eastern Europe. They were just middlemen. They passed the drugs up the chain and took their cut. It was simple.

Then this bullshit.

Acevedo had no idea what the Little Russian's boss had against some science project in the middle of nowhere in El Yunque. He just knew he was sick of tramping around the forest in the dead of night, tripping over roots and getting soaked, all to tear up cardboard moth traps and smash test tubes. Yes, they were getting paid for it, but it was still bullshit. And he didn't like the way Zajic's boss assumed he and his men were there just to run whatever errands he came up with. He didn't like that part at all.

Headlights swept around the edge of the building and then the Little Russian's black BMW appeared. Acevedo tossed his cigarette out the window, and it fell to the pavement like a tiny red comet.

The BMW gave off thumping bass from some kind of fast, Slavic rap. Thankfully it cut out suddenly, in mid-beat. The Little Russian killed his headlights next. He turned in a wide arc across the parking lot's orderly yellow stripes and pulled up opposite the cruiser so the driver's side windows were only a couple feet apart.

"Anything new?" the Little Russian said. His voice was deep and guttural, and his Spanish was horrible. It was like talking to a three-hundred-pound toddler who broke kneecaps if he didn't get his treats on time.

Acevedo shook his head. "We checked the forest again last night. They didn't put anything out for us."

"The boss doesn't like the woman went away for help. He lost his shit. Not good. The man they sent back. What do you know about him?"

Acevedo shook his head. He'd put a tap on the center's phone lines, but it was another waste of time. They just didn't use the phone very much. The call from Florida was the only useful thing they'd gotten. "Just what I told you. She called yesterday. Said they're sending someone back with her."

"They're not here yet?"

Acevedo shrugged. "Nobody's seen them."

"The boss says no more fucking around. He wants them shut down for good."

Well, who the hell didn't want that? Acevedo had enough on his plate without running around the rainforest doing favors for his clients. He didn't even know what the hell Zajic's boss had against these people. They were harmless. Acevedo needed this to be finished. They had a delivery on its way, the biggest one of the year. And he was pretty sure the Special Investigations Bureau had sniffed something in the air. If they kept this up, it would bring attention to him and his men.

"How does he want to handle it?" he asked.

"Shut them down for good," the Little Russian repeated. "Go in tomorrow. In the daytime. Shoot the place up. Kill everybody. It's easy. It's done."

Jesus Christ. The last thing he needed was to turn this into a high-profile mass murder. "We're not killing anybody," Acevedo snapped. "That's not what we agreed to."

The Little Russian snorted in disgust. "Bunch of pussies."

That couldn't go unchallenged or the bastard would be pissing on him forever. "Hey, fuck you, jackoff! We need to keep it on the down low, you follow? We've got real business to think of. Business which this shit is not!"

They locked eyes for a tense moment. Acevedo knew the Little Russian had a gun and a short temper. He let his fingertips quietly unsnap his holster, slowly edged his pistol free.

Then the Little Russian laughed. It was not a happy sound.

"I don't get it either," he said. "The boss is worked up, but he doesn't tell me shit. Just 'is it done? Is it done?' He showed his right hand by scratching his head for a moment. "So get it done, yes? Whatever you have to do. Just get it done, and then we can get back to business. Business we understand, right?"

Acevedo let out a breath he hadn't quite realized he'd been holding. "Yeah, we'll get it done. But we're not killing people. Believe me, your boss doesn't want that kind of heat."

"Okay, okay," said the Little Russian. "Tomorrow. Tell me it's done. Here."

He tossed a heavy envelope through Acevedo's window. Then the BMW slid away into the night, erupting with bass once again and a voice snapping off clipped Russian phrases.

Acevedo hefted the envelope of cash and then tucked it into a gym bag in the passenger seat. Christ, he'd be happy to see the last of that asshole.

CHAPTER 9

The next morning, Crane waited in front of the Vanderbilt, practicing his Spanish with the doorman. Just before nine thirty, Melissa rolled up in a battered Jeep Wrangler. She had taken a somewhat different approach to preparing for the rainforest, he realized as she jumped down out of the Jeep. Her boots were like his, though obviously well used. She wore tight shorts in green twill and a T-shirt with an open plaid shirt over it. The overall effect was ... effective.

"Damn," Crane murmured.

The doorman nodded in agreement.

"Morning!" Melissa said cheerfully as she looked Crane over. "A little touristy, but you'll do."

"We'll have to get me scuffed up a bit," Crane said. He tossed the rucksack into the back.

"Yeah, that won't be a problem where we're going. Climb in."

Crane grabbed the Jeep's roll cage and swung himself into the passenger seat.

Melissa coaxed the engine back to life, and they were off. They took the main Highway 26 past the airport and then south out of San Juan until it turned into Highway 66 and led east toward El Yunque. The air was comfortable. A few high clouds scudded across the sky.

"What kind of weather are we expecting?" Crane shouted over the wind rushing through the open Jeep.

"It'll be fine!" Melissa answered. "It warms up during the day. Might see some showers by late afternoon, but we should be done before then."

When they reached Canovanas, Melissa turned off the highway onto a much smaller road and headed south, away from the town.

"Benitez is a few miles ahead," said Melissa. "Then we get into the real back country!"

Crane could tell this was not a prosperous area. The houses thinned out as they got farther from the highway, and those that were here were in poor repair, set well back from the road amid thick groves of trees. They passed a number of bars and little barbecue stands and then a large sign informing them they were entering the Caribbean National Forest. A few minutes later, they passed through a small village that Crane supposed must be Benitez. On its far edge, Melissa slowed and took a sharp left onto a narrow gravel road.

Within a few hundred yards, they were surrounded by tropical greenery. There were palms with enormous trunks, lush ferns, a dozen types of trees Crane had never seen before. He could hear bird calls and another chorus of voices that Melissa identified as tree frog cries. "Coquis," she said. "Thirteen different species of them. Only here. That's why we need to catalog this place while it's still here."

They rattled across almost two miles of the poorly maintained road, climbed a ridge, and descended the far side. Crane counted only three houses along the way.

"We're near the river," Melissa said. "The Rio Cubuy. Runs south from the mountains. Then it turns west here and curves all the way around to the north until it hits the Canovanas. Fantastic place to collect samples. Used to be, anyway. We're here!"

They rounded a bend and passed through an open steel gate. A faded sign read "Kaplan Foundation–Caribbean Biodiversity Project. Benitez Research Facility."

Crane's first impression was that someone had taken poured concrete slabs and dumped them here in a pile. The place was all tilted cement walls, ramps, and walkways. Crane could see the seams where the cement had been poured in pieces and irregular green stains of moss were taking hold. The rainforest had grown up among the walkways and ramps and threatened to absorb the building in its entirety.

"This was supposed to be another visitors' center for the park," said Melissa. "Like the one up at El Portal. But they dropped that idea halfway through and never finished it. The foundation bought the place a few years ago. Cleaned it up. Put in new glass, power and data lines. It's perfect for us. You get used to the architecture after a while."

She parked the Jeep next to a handful of other cars, and they got out.

"Come on. I'll introduce you to the team."

They went up a ramp to a cement walkway that crossed a shallow ravine. At the bottom, a stream threaded its way between tall trees that shot up past them. On the other side of the ravine, the walkway dumped them near a pair of large glass doors, set in a sweeping wall of glass panels. Melissa opened one and led Crane inside.

"Welcome to my domain," said Melissa. Then she let out a loud whistle and shouted, "Anybody home? We've got company!"

"In here!" a woman shouted from somewhere. Her voice echoed off the cement until Crane had no idea where she was calling from. Melissa led the way down a dim corridor with bare cement walls. It appeared to run the length of the building to a glaring bright rectangle of light at the back. Crane imagined the original designers had meant for the place to be more brightly lit and decorated with displays about the local flora and fauna. All that was here was rust stains where rain had leaked through the roof and dripped down the cement.

Eventually the corridor opened up into a two-story circular atrium with a skylight. Melissa led him down a flight of stairs to the atrium's floor level, a large open space with rooms around the outer edge. Crane spotted power and data cables running along the walls, bundled up with zip ties so the researchers wouldn't trip over them. The doorways looked indistinguishable to Crane, but Melissa led him through one.

"This is our sequencing lab," said Melissa. The room was cluttered with metal tables loaded down with instruments the purpose of which Crane could only guess. Stainless steel refrigerators lined one wall. Their humming competed with a boom box putting out old school R&B.

Four young people stood in a ragged line, shuffling nervously as if they were about to be inspected.

Melissa quickly introduced him. "Dorothea, our botanist. Lupe—insects mostly. Thom, our IT support. And our biochemist Sabelio. He handles the sequencing and DNA analysis."

Crane shook hands all around and left his own role vague. It was probably best if they remained uncertain about what he was really here to do. They shook his hand, smiled nervously, and seemed happy to get back to what they were doing. Crane guessed they thought he was a wealthy donor, or at least someone with power over their funding.

Then Melissa showed him around the rest of the complex. It was a huge space for a half-dozen people, with long, empty corridors and large rooms devoted to classifying, preserving, and analyzing everything from insects and lizards to diatoms and microorganisms.

"This is my part, right here," said Melissa as she showed Crane into a chamber scattered with plastic boxes full of river mud. Some had irrigation systems with hoses that leaked water onto the cement floor. "I mean, I cover what needs to be covered, but my specialty is actinomycetes."

"Which are?"

"Soil and freshwater bacteria. DNA slanted toward guanine and cytosine. Most of our antibiotics come from them. And they do a lot of good work decomposing compost and fixing nitrogen in the soil so crops can grow. "

She was entirely in her element here. Crane found her enthusiasm charming.

"There's a lot of debate about how to classify them," she was saying, "which I hope to make even worse with the paper I'm working on. There's something odd about the chemical profile of the soil here. If it's what I think it is, then I'll discover whole new species of the little guys and change science forever in my own small way."

"I'm sure you will," said Crane.

"If we can keep the project from falling apart," she muttered, half to herself.

"That's what I'm here to help with, remember?" said Crane. "Maybe you should show me the sampling sites."

Melissa nodded. "Let's go."

———

While Sosa cut the telephone line, Acevedo sat on the edge of the van's deck, in the side doorway, and let the others gather around. There were five officers besides himself: Gavilan, Sosa up on the pole, Old Rodriguez, Acosta, and Fat Rodriguez. Like him, they all wore black tactical gear and boots. Surplus stuff, not actual police gear. Black ski masks bulged in their pants pockets. They were armed with seized Kalashnikov knockoffs from Vietnam or someplace. They were shit guns, but they looked scary and they made a loud noise.

This road was the only way in or out of the facility, and Sosa was cutting its only phone connection. There were a couple houses between here and the center and their phones would be dead too, but Acevedo doubted they'd even notice. These hicks kept to themselves.

"Okay," he said. "They're cut off. They'll probably notice right away when their Internet goes down. But it's too late to do anything. Besides, it's down half the time. They don't know we're coming. We're going to move fast. Roll in, take control. The van stops inside the gates and blocks the road."

"Rodriguez." He gestured to Fat Rodriguez so they'd know which one he meant. "You stay with the van."

"Ah, man, come on!"

"Someone has to hold the gates. Nobody in or out. You hold the gate until we're ready to go. It's important."

"All right, Chief," Fat Rodriguez said, somewhat mollified.

"The rest of you, we'll move in through the front doors and fan out. Destroy anything that looks useful."

There was a metallic snap, and the thick phone and data cable crashed down into the undergrowth.

"Got it, boss!" Sosa shouted.

"All right, get down here. Everybody mount up."

They loaded back into the van. Acevedo rode shotgun while Fat Rodriguez drove.

"Floor it," he said. "Let's move."

Rodriguez jammed down the pedal, and the van shimmied

fast across the washboard surface, throwing back gravel on the curves.

"Once more," Acevedo shouted over the noise. "Nobody gets hurt. We don't need these folks dead, and we don't want heat. So let them run away. Some idiot tries to fight back, beat him up a little, but don't shoot them. They're not our enemies. They're just in the way, so we're moving them along. Everybody clear on that?"

One by one they sounded off that they were indeed clear on that. Acevedo figured they probably got it. They weren't killers. They were just some guys who wanted to retire someday. They'd get the job done and get out clean, and then they could get back to doing things that made sense.

"All right. Now give me a radio check."

They inserted their earpieces and checked in, one by one. "Good. Stay in touch!" said Acevedo. "You see something, sound off. And listen to me. I'll be keeping the time."

The van slewed around a curve, and Acevedo saw the facility's open gates, a line of dusty old cars parked off to one side.

"We're in there no more than five minutes, and then back to the van! In the meantime, anything looks expensive, shoot it up. Anything looks important, shoot it up. Computers, file cabinets, whatever. We don't want to have to come back here!"

Then Fat Rodriguez sped through the gates and slid the van to a stop. Acevedo pulled on his mask.

"Okay, it's on!" he shouted, and bailed out. He heard the van's side door slide open behind him.

Some skinny white guy was standing in the parking lot, halfway between the building and the cars. He just stood there and looked at them, slack-jawed with confusion. Acevedo fired two quick bursts over his head, and the guy turned and bolted back across the walkway.

It was definitely on.

CHAPTER 10

Crane knelt in the marshy ground and examined shattered fragments of plastic from an instrument case. Some were clear, others a dull gray. And they were thick; it had taken hard work with a heavy tool to do this. Crane powered up the Canon point and shoot he'd bought the night before and took a few pictures.

Melissa stood a few yards away, looking around in disgust.

Crane listened to the rustle of the Rio Cubuy, not much more than a stream here. Over that, the calls of birds and tree frogs. In every direction was green. Huge fronds and clinging vines shot through with the dark vertical slashes of tree trunks climbing through the lower levels of the forest in search of sunlight.

"I assume your people have been here since it happened," said Crane.

"Yeah, Luis, our intern. He found this and brought me and Thom out to see it."

So most of the boot prints Crane was seeing were probably theirs. But whoever did this had to get in and out somehow. He and Melissa had come down a narrow, packed dirt trail from the edge of the facility grounds. It gradually descended the ridge and followed the river upstream for almost a mile. Here they were deep in the rainforest, in a relatively narrow part of the valley. Directly across the river, the land angled sharply up to the far ridge. On this side there was a bit more flood plain, but still the only way out besides the trail itself was over one ridge or the other, through thick forest.

"Did you cross the river after it happened?"

"No, no gear over there. Why?"

Crane rose and made his way down to the water's edge.

"I'm trying to figure out how they got here. Best way would be just like we did it. Drive in and then hike down this same trail. Is anyone in the lab at night?"

"Sometimes," said Melissa. "Maybe. After this started up, we began locking the gates at night."

So they couldn't be sure someone wouldn't see them if they crossed the grounds. Maybe they were careful. Maybe they just didn't care.

He studied the thick mud of the riverbank. It would be easy enough to ford, but they would have left tracks here. Deep ones. He considered following the river to look for signs of a crossing.

"Why would someone do this?" Melissa said in frustration. "We're not hurting anybody!"

Crane snapped a few more photos of the riverbank, the unbroken stretches of thick, sandy mud scattered with stones.

"Have to disagree," he said. "To do this, they'd have to hump it through three or four miles of forest. In the dark. Carrying heavy tools. That's dedication. They've got a reason for this. We just don't know what it is."

Crane checked the map screen on his GPS, looking for fire roads or some other means of access. But the map showed only the thin blue trace of the river and some contour lines. If there were any trails through here, they weren't mapped.

"All right," Crane said finally. "I've seen enough. Let's head back."

Melissa was quiet as they walked back up the trail. They were nearly to the edge of the clearing before she spoke. "So what are you going to tell Josh?"

"I'm not ready to tell him anything just yet," said Crane. "I want to try a couple things first. Looks like you've got plenty of room to spare. Can I set up a cot in one?"

"We can do that." Her voice was controlled. Crane could sense her irritation. "I'll talk to Luis."

Then she started as a chattering sound echoed through the rainforest. Birds shrieked and the forest itself seemed to shudder. "What was that?"

Crane knew exactly what it was. A Kalashnikov. A short burst, followed quickly by another. He grabbed Melissa's hand and led her a few yards off the trail. "Get down and stay here! Right here! I'll come back for you."

She looked stunned for a moment, and then she met his eyes and nodded.

Crane patted down his pockets. The closest thing he had to a weapon was a folding utility knife.

More gunfire echoed through the forest. Bursts over bursts. More than one gun.

He gave one last look back at Melissa and ran down the trail toward the labs. He stopped at the edge of the clearing to survey the building. From here, everything looked calm. But he could hear more gunfire. Four of Melissa's people were there. They were civilians, untrained, unarmed. He had to get inside.

Crane sprinted across the thirty yards of open ground to the rear wall. To his left was a window. To his right he would eventually reach an outside walk leading around the far side of the building. That would get him to the front doors.

He was considering which route to take when the window

exploded in a burst of bullets. Shattered glass sprayed out, glittering in the sun as it fell into the grass. Crane ran to the window and edged up against the hole, ready to jump the shooter if he stuck his head outside.

But nothing happened. After perhaps twenty seconds, Crane risked a quick glance around the edge of the steel window frame. The room was empty, as if the shooter had paused in the doorway just long enough to spray the room with fire before moving on.

At least it made his decision easier.

————

The kid had found a mop somewhere and jammed it into the door handles. Acevedo could see it through the glass doors. What an idiot. Frightened people did stupid things. Acevedo leveled his gun and unloaded a long, sweeping burst that shattered the doors and the glass panels on either side of it.

Then he stepped through with the others at his back. The place was still for an instant. The scientists had retreated deeper into the building. Probably hiding someplace. That was fine. If they stayed out of the way, they'd be all right.

He waved his men off in groups, and they jogged down the hallways, checking doors as they went. Acevedo himself went straight ahead. He'd seen the blueprints of the building, but it was a mess—a rats' maze of hallways and ramps dotted with stairwells and large chambers with skylights.

He took the first door on the right and found himself in a conference room. Windows on the opposite side, a long table with leather chairs, a ceiling-mounted projector, and a screen on the wall at the end.

He caught a glimpse of motion beyond the table and leveled the gun. A terrified woman crouched there, clutching a phone.

She was desperately flashing the hook, trying and failing to get a dial tone. She looked up at him, her eyes wide, trembling.

Acevedo raised the gun and fired into the projector. It exploded into a rain of plastic and sparks that fell across the table. The woman screamed and cowered.

"What the hell's wrong with you?" he shouted. "Run away!"

She hesitated for an instant and then dashed around the table, the long way so she wouldn't have to pass him. She disappeared out the door like a rabbit with a hungry dog on its tail.

His earpiece beeped. "This is Acosta, lower level, east wing. I've got equipment here."

"So wreck it."

He heard gunfire over the channel for a moment before it cut out, and then echoes off the cement walls and floor. He took a deep breath. This was going to be easy.

———————

Crane stepped through the shattered window and into the empty room beyond. The air conditioning made it feel like stepping into a refrigerator. He heard gunshots, short bursts. People screaming. Hoarse voices shouting in Spanish.

He moved quickly across the room and pressed his back against the wall by the doorway. It was hard to locate sounds in this warren of bare concrete, but he thought the gunshots were coming from farther away. He popped his head around the doorway for an instant, and then back, and then· out again looking the other way. Nothing.

He stepped out into a long corridor lined with identical doorways. He tried to call up a mental map of the place from his tour, but the design was too sprawling and complicated. So Crane did the next best thing. He followed the noise.

When he reached the atrium, he knew he was close. The

shots echoed much louder here. Then a figure in black appeared on the level below him. Crane registered a dark ski mask, the instantly recognizable shape of a Kalashnikov. Crane dropped behind the safety railing at the edge of the mezzanine. It was made of enameled metal panels between posts, and it gave him gaps to look through. He watched the gunman step into a doorway, raising the rifle to firing position. Then he disappeared into the room and Crane heard him empty the clip, hosing down the room.

A few moments later, one of the scientists—the biochemist Sabelio—ran out and sprinted for the stairs. From the room he'd left, Crane heard the shooter slam another clip into his weapon and resume firing. He heard the ragged clatter of shell casings ejecting, the impact of bullets on fragile machinery. He'd let the person in the room escape unharmed, but he was still shooting up the equipment. That wasn't accidental. He could have easily killed Sabelio, but he hadn't. So they weren't here to kill the staff. That was something, at least.

The biochemist reached the second level and took off into the nearest hallway, away from Crane. Crane stood and hissed "Over here!" as loudly as he dared. But Sabelio wasn't listening. He was running on adrenaline and pure terror, and he was likely to blunder into another shooter the way he was going.

Crane shook his head and then took off after him. He entered the hallway he'd seen Sabelio go down just in time to see him duck into a doorway. Crane followed and found himself in what looked like an improvised break room with folding lounge chairs, a cooler, and a plastic trash can overflowing with empty bottles. He saw Sabelio leap out the shattered window and hit the ground running in the direction of the rainforest. That would do, Crane thought. He was moving off the battlefield. That left three unaccounted for.

He stepped back out into the hallway—and nearly collided with another armed man.

For both of them, there was an instant of shock. Their eyes met through the shooter's black ski mask, and Crane picked up his surprise. Crane was an unexpected factor. He wasn't supposed to be here.

In the next moment, they both reacted on instinct. The shooter raised his gun, and Crane grabbed the barrel and the receiver. Crane forced the muzzle up toward the ceiling, and the shooter was pulled off balance. He fell against the wall even as he tried to yank the gun out of Crane's grasp. Crane pushed him back hard, and the man's elbow slammed against the cement wall behind him. He cried out in pain and released the grip. Crane punched him hard in the face and bounced his head off the cement. The man staggered, still trying to regain control of the weapon. Crane finished him off with a flurry of strikes. Even though he was fading, the man grasped at the trigger again, and Crane twisted the gun hard, heard the arm snap. The man slid to the floor and didn't move.

Crane quickly swept the AK across the hallway and then spun and checked the other end. No one was there. He didn't know how long it would take the others to realize one of their men was down. He had more pressing concerns.

He checked the magazine. It was nearly empty, but the unconscious man had three more. Crane took them and loaded one into the gun. The Kalashnikov didn't seem to have been very well cared for. It was certainly not up to Hurricane Group standards. But it obviously worked. And least he was now armed.

———

Melissa crouched at the edge of the woods, her torso pressed hard against the rough back of a Tabonuco tree as she listened to the gunfire. She wasn't sure how long Crane had been gone. It felt like a long time, but some part of her kept popping up through her fear to observe that adrenaline could be tampering with her sense of time passing. As if she gave a damn about that.

Those were her friends in there.

She'd recruited most of them herself. She'd gotten funding for them and talked them into coming out here and living on what she could scrape up. She'd brought them all here, and someone was ... no, she wouldn't think they were killing them.

Another burst of fire startled her. She looked around, but nothing moved. Erase the sound of sporadic gunshots, and the day looked calm, lazy. A good day to leave the electrophoresis units to run while they hung out on the roof with some cold beers.

But they'd probably never do that again. There was no coming back from this. It was hard enough scraping up the funding the first time around. There were plenty of other projects for the big donors to back. Projects that didn't have armed terrorists hanging over their heads.

She'd worked so hard. She must have given that damn presentation a hundred times—to foundations, corporate citizenship boards, even garden clubs. Anybody with some money and an interest in plants.

She breathed out hard. She had gone begging to garden clubs full of little old rich ladies for this! And now someone was destroying it all, and she didn't even know why.

To hell with that.

Melissa had broken out of the undergrowth before she quite realized it. She picked up her pace and ran toward her building. Around the corner to her right was an access door into the basement. The keys were in her pocket. Just inside that door was a room they'd used to store construction supplies during the renovation work. She remembered a pile of metal pipes there.

The part of her brain that had been commenting on her perception of time was sounding alarms and reminding her that the men inside had machine guns, but she was done listening to it.

She unlocked the door and slipped inside. The gunshots were louder, of course, but she didn't see anyone, living or dead. She turned quickly into the first doorway and found the supplies, just as she'd remembered. She grabbed a milk crate and used it to block open the back door. If any of her people were alive, she'd get them out this way and take them back to the safety of the woods. Then she went back and grabbed a pipe. It was perfect. About the size and weight of a baseball bat. All she needed now was someone to hit.

CHAPTER 11

Acevedo knocked several computers off the table where they were lined up, and then fired a burst into each of them. He swept the room and didn't see any other likely targets.

He checked his watch.

"Three minutes," he said into his mic. "Check."

The responses came back quickly. "Okay." "All good." Four of them in quick succession.

There should have been five.

"Gavilan?"

Nothing. He repeated the call.

"I saw him headed for the back west quadrant," said Sosa.

"Find him."

Acevedo didn't like this. It should have been clockwork.

"He's down!" Sosa shouted over the open channel, and Acevedo could hear the sudden fear in his voice.

There was a burst of frightened chatter from the others, and Acevedo barked at them to shut up.

"He's alive," Sosa reported, "but somebody beat him up. He's out. I can't find his gun!"

What the hell was going on? There was no way any of the

scientists could have done that, even if they got the drop on him somehow.

But the woman had gone to the mainland for help. Supposedly a man was coming back with her. One man. Probably unarmed—he hadn't shot Gavilan; he'd taken him down and then claimed his gun. It didn't make any sense. Gavilan was a beast. If this man had dropped him like that ...

No. The others needed him to stay in control, tell them what to do. He had to pull this together.

"Sosa, get him out!" he snapped. "Take him to the van. The rest of you sweep the building again. There's someone else here. Find out what we're up against. And the gloves are off. You see someone with a gun, kill him!"

————

Crane worked his way through the downstairs rooms, searching for the rest of Melissa's team. He found only piles of dusty junk left over from the construction. He did notice a sliver of sunlight at the end of a dark hall and found a door blocked open by a milk crate. Perhaps the others had escaped this way. At any rate, they weren't down here.

Crane headed back up toward the rooms Melissa had shown him earlier. Everything had been shot to pieces. Computers and microscopes, even a ventilation hood had been peppered with bullets. He smelled chemicals. As he moved through what looked like a storage room, he caught movement and spun, the gun ready.

"Don't shoot!" a terrified woman cried. Crane lowered the muzzle.

Three figures stepped out from behind a bullet-scarred metal cabinet. The rest of Melissa's team, alive. Crane felt a flood of relief.

"Is anyone hurt?"

"We're okay," said the woman; Lupe, he remembered. "What about Melissa? She was with you."

"She's in the woods. I'll take you there."

He led them back downstairs, to the open door.

"We got separated from Sabelio," one of them said.

"I saw him get out. Melissa's probably found him by now."

At the rear door, Crane looked outside, saw nothing. "Okay, stick close to me and keep moving."

"Did Melissa give you her keys?" It was Lupe again. Crane could see in her expression that something wasn't right.

"No. Why?"

"How did you get this door open?"

"I found it this way." Crane had a sudden bad feeling. He examined the door. This was no fire exit. The lock was a deadbolt, separate from the knob. There was no manual latch anywhere. Even from the inside, the only way to unlock it was with the key.

Which Melissa had. She must have sneaked in to try and get her team out. Damn it.

"All right, go," said Crane. "Move. Get to the woods. I'll find her."

He sent them out, watched them run for the cover of the trees. Then he turned and headed back down the hall.

The moment he stepped into the atrium, he heard a shout from above. He jumped back, and a burst of gunfire splattered off the cement floor in front of him. That was no warning shot fired over his head. They must have found the man he'd taken out and realized someone was fighting back.

He heard the shooter's footsteps coming down the stairs and dropped to a crouch, ready to fire when the enemy came around the curve of the stairway. Then a second man appeared across the atrium, running toward him. Crane had no cover. He moved back into the darkened hallway and ducked through a doorway.

He stepped into an empty room, lit only by a faint column of sunlight from the ceiling. It looked like the opening for stairs that had never been built. But someone had left a metal ladder behind. Crane climbed up into another empty room, this one with windows that looked out on the rainforest. Crane pulled the ladder up behind himself.

Where would Melissa go?

The best place to look for her was the atrium. He'd have visibility down the long hallways. He made his way back there. It was empty. He checked the hallways in all directions and saw nobody. Then he knelt by the railing and looked down between the panels to the lower floor. One of them emerged from a storage room, speaking into a mic on his collar. Then he crossed the atrium toward one of the hallways.

Crane was considering whether to shoot him when Melissa popped out of the same doorway. She was carrying a length of pipe like a club. She didn't see Crane.

"Melissa!" he called quietly, hoping not to draw the attention of the man she was following. But she didn't hear him.

Crane swore under his breath. He might catch up with them if he headed downstairs, or he might not. The man with the gun had to come back upstairs, though. Crane was getting enough of an idea of the layout that he thought he knew where to intercept him. He set off at a trot, hoping he could get to them before Melissa got herself killed.

———

"I found him!" a voice shouted into Acevedo's earpiece. "I've got him!"

"Who is that?" he demanded. "Acosta? Where are you?"

"Yeah, I've got him cornered. Bottom floor of the atrium. Tall guy, anglo, dark hair, black pants, and a T-shirt. He's got Gavilan's gun."

"All right," Acevedo answered, already moving fast. "Keep him pinned down. I'm coming to you."

A few moments later, "Shit. I lost him. There's a hole in the ceiling in here. He's on the first floor somewhere."

Acevedo swore. Whoever the interloper was, he was slippery. They needed better coordination. There were four of them now, against one guy. They needed to work together, herd the bastard into a corner and overwhelm him. No matter who the son of a bitch was, he was still just one guy.

"Keep after him," he snapped into his mic. "He's probably heading toward the front doors. Push him that way and I'll move to head him off. The rest of you, start moving back in toward the center. We want to corral the son of a whore. If you get a shot, take him down. This guy's trouble."

He checked his watch. Just over four minutes since they'd come in. If things had gone to plan, they'd be finished now, falling back to the van, and this whole business would be over. But things weren't going to plan. It was a bullshit job from the start, and it just kept getting worse and worse.

A man shouldn't have to put up with all this shit for a fishing boat, Acevedo told himself as he swapped a full magazine into his gun and headed for the center of the building to meet up with Acosta.

———

Melissa looked with dismay at the sample storage room. Crates had been knocked over, trampled, shot to pieces. Coolant pooled on the floor. Nothing here could be salvaged. At least she hadn't found any bodies.

Then she heard a man's voice outside. "Roger that," it said. "Coming to you."

She ducked behind the wreckage of a storage refrigerator as a masked figure appeared in the doorway. He looked around, sweeping the room with his gun, and then disappeared again. Melissa hurried to the door, peered around the frame, and saw the man moving off down a corridor. She followed.

He turned and found the stairs to the main level. Moving quietly, she followed him up. She knew this building better than anyone. The stairs would take him to a side passage that opened into one of the main central corridors.

Melissa took a deep breath as she reached the top of the stairs, and hefted the pipe. Then she sprinted forward. She was already into her swing when she realized he knew she was there—had known all along. He wheeled to face her, raising the gun and parrying her swing with it. The pipe hit the gun's metal frame and skated down the barrel. The impact jarred her arms, and she felt herself overextending. The pipe slammed against the wall, and there was a terrible scrape as the end gouged a scar into the concrete. She was off balance, stumbling forward.

A moment later, a blast of agony swept through her as he jammed the rifle butt into her ribcage. She gasped out a loud, ragged breath and couldn't breathe in. She fell and lost her grip on the pipe. It clanged away down the hallway as she hit the floor hard. The man kicked her in the stomach, rolling her over onto her back with another gasp.

He leveled the rifle at her. His eyes glared through his ski mask.

"No," she tried to say. "Please, don't." But the words didn't make it past her throat.

Then the left side of his head erupted in a spray of blood and bone, and he pitched forward. She felt the blood spatter her face, saw him toppling forward toward her, and this time she did scream as he fell on top of her.

A dark shape approached from down the hall. It resolved into John Crane.

He stalked toward her, gun leveled, dark eyes peering down the barrel, and she suddenly realized that this was who he was. For all his looks and charm, he was a killer and this was his world, not hers, that she'd gone charging into with her stupid pipe.

"Are you all right? Can you walk?"

He didn't look down at her. He turned, keeping his eyes on the spot where his gun was aimed. She could hear the calm anger in his voice. For the first time, she was afraid of him.

"Can you move?" he repeated. Then he suddenly let one leg go limp and fell into a roll. Melissa heard the shots, heard the bullets spatter off the cement where he'd been.

Crane rolled over one shoulder and came back up into a crouch. He sprayed a long, uncontrolled burst down the side passage, filling it with bullets, and she caught just a glimpse of a figure retreating around a corner.

"Jesus Christ," she breathed.

He rose and now looked down at her. His eyes were fierce.

"Come on," he snapped.

And now she got to her feet and ran back toward the stairs and out the basement door as Crane moved, quick and calm behind her, covering her as she fled.

———

Acevedo moved carefully. The stranger was nearby. He could feel it.

"Fourth junction, still nothing," said his earpiece. That was Sosa. He'd met up with Old Rodriguez and they were sweeping forward. The target was in front of them. He had to be.

"Keep moving," Acevedo said, his voice steady. His control had slipped a little when the stranger took out Gavilan. That wasn't good. But he had things under control now. His men were working together as a team, the way they'd been trained.

"Acosta, where are you?" he asked. If they could hook up, they could trap their quarry between themselves in front and Sosa and Rodriguez behind him.

"Coming upstairs," said Acosta.

"Pick it up. I don't want him slipping through."

"I'm coming, I'm—" Then Acosta shouted. Acevedo heard metal hitting metal and then something metallic ringing hard against the cement. He realized he could hear it, not just on the radio. The next junction, and then right.

He was almost there when he heard the single shot. Acevedo froze. Why just one shot? Why now?

Acevedo looked around the corner and saw Acosta on the floor. His head was a bloody wreck; a pool of blood was spreading against the pale gray cement.

The woman lay near him—near his body—but she hadn't killed him. At the far end of the hallway stood the stranger, his body leaning over the rock-steady barrel of Gavilan's AK. He had killed Acosta.

Killed Acosta.

He'd lost a man. His friend was dead. Acevedo had a vague sense of everything coming apart around him, a moment of terror. He fought it down. For Acosta. He stepped into the inter-section and fired a burst, aiming for center mass just the way they'd done it in the academy.

And yet, somehow, he missed. The figure seemed to collapse, and for an instant Acevedo thought he'd hit him. But then he came up to one knee and a long burst sprayed the hallway.

Acevedo sprang back, hearing bullets drill through the air nearby and ricochet off the walls.

Who the fuck was this guy?

His watch started to beep. Their time was up.

Now the wall of his reserve gave in earnest. Panic washed over Acevedo. He had a dead officer to explain and a man out there he couldn't seem to just kill. He needed to get out of there, get the others out, before this all went more to shit. Get out and figure out what to do next.

"Fall back!" he shouted. "To the van, get to the van! Rodriguez, get ready to move. Everyone get to the van, now!"

Then he turned and ran down the corridor toward the front doors.

They were outside when Crane heard the engine and ran to the parking lot in time to see a white van disappearing around the bend in the road. They were gone. It was over. At least the shooting part. The rest was just beginning.

His first priority was Melissa and her team. He'd gotten them out of the building and left them in the safety of the forest before he went back inside. They were still there, in a tight huddle at the tree line. He put the gun down and brought them back across the rear lawn. They were silent, docile. The adrenaline was fading.

Once he got them inside, Melissa took charge again, leading as they moved in a group from room to room, taking inventory and surveying the damage. Few words were spoken. Just an occasional awed, "Oh, no," as they discovered the ruins of expensive gear in each new room. Lupe was crying, and the IT guy was trying to comfort her without much success.

"We should call the police," Sabelio said dully.

"I tried," said the botanist. "Lines are dead."

That seemed to break the dam of silence, and Crane was bombarded with questions.

"Who were they?"

"Why are they doing this to us?"

"Why didn't they kill us?"

Melissa took her team to the conference room where they got the chairs back in place and sat down. Then she spoke softly to Crane. "We should take care of ..."

He nodded. "Stay here. I've got it."

But she followed, and he didn't stop her. She stood back as he turned the body over. She winced at the sound his clothing made as it pulled free of the drying blood on the floor. But she stayed.

Crane pulled up the ski mask to reveal his face. He'd been a good-looking man. In his late thirties, Crane guessed. Removing the gloves revealed a tattoo on the inside of one wrist, and a wedding ring. This man had a family waiting for him. But he wasn't coming home, because he died trashing a research facility for no damn reason that Crane could see.

He checked the rest of the body. He had a pistol—a Glock 18, a much better weapon than the cheap AK knockoff he'd been using. Crane took it, along with a pair of spare magazines in a pouch on his belt. His wallet had a few dollars and a driver's license that gave him a name: Hector Acosta.

"The hell did you think you were doing, Hector?" Crane murmured.

"Who was he?" Melissa asked.

Crane had a bad feeling about that. He checked the chest pockets in Acosta's shirt and felt a squarish shape.

He pulled out a leatherette case and flipped it open to show her Acosta's badge with the seal of the Puerto Rico police.

"He was a cop."

CHAPTER 12

Melissa blanched. "A cop? That doesn't make sense."

"They were all cops. This is a police-issue radio." Crane listened to the earpiece, but the channel had gone dead. He doubted it would come back.

Then he turned to Melissa. "Is there any reason why the police would take an interest in your operation?" he asked, his voice stern. "Anything you kept from Josh? Is anything going on behind the scenes?"

"No!" she protested. "This project's too important to me! And I'd know if my people were up to something."

Crane heard the indignation in her voice. He believed her. The other explanation made more sense, anyway.

"I had to ask," he said. "That means they're working for somebody. We need to find out who and what it's about."

"How do we do that? What do we do now?"

"Well, we don't call the police yet. We don't know who'll show up, what they know, or what side they'll be on. We need to contain this. Send your people home. Tell them not to talk to anyone, forget this ever happened. If they want to take some vacation, this would be a good time."

She nodded, still lost in the implications.

"Nobody was here today. Do you understand? Monday morning, you'll come in to open up and you'll find the place trashed. That's the story."

He took her arm and gently turned her away from Acosta's corpse. He walked her back toward the conference room.

"How do we explain the body?" she asked.

"There won't be a body. I'm going to need the keys to your Jeep."

Lupe offered Melissa a ride back to her place in San Juan. Once they had all left, Crane wrapped the body in a paint-stained tarp he found in a storage room downstairs and carried it outside. He loaded the body into the back of the Jeep and drove out.

Once he hit the paved road, he drove steadily north as development grew denser and the traffic became heavier. He was surrounded by people going about their lives with no idea that the battered Wrangler had a dead cop in the back.

Crane glanced over his shoulder at the tarp rattling in the wind. Acosta's death was bothering him, and he tried to unpack it, figure out why. It wasn't that he was a cop. That was happenstance, even though it complicated things going forward. He didn't regret killing him. Acosta had put himself in that situation, as had the other men Crane had killed.

Of course, when he'd killed before, he'd always had the full force and authority of the United States government behind him. Now he was just some random civilian. If he were caught, his future would be bleak. There was no way he'd get a self-defense verdict for killing a cop. He'd be lucky if he ever made it into a courtroom.

But that wasn't really it, either. He'd only been on two missions for the Hurricane Group before they'd shut it down, but on both, he'd spent long days risking capture and death.

He'd been well trained, and he knew what to do to avoid that outcome. He wasn't afraid of being caught.

He picked at the emotion as he drove through Canovanas and on northward toward Carolina. He wasn't ready to dispose of the body until he'd sorted this out.

Yes, he'd shot people before, abstract bad people who threatened him or other innocents. And to be sure, Acosta had done that. But this one had a name. He was Hector Acosta. He was a police officer, if a corrupt one. He had a wife somewhere who didn't know she was a widow. Maybe children without a father.

That was it, Crane decided as he drove through the outskirts of Carolina. Acosta had somehow gone from an anonymous enemy to a real person with a life, one that had collided with Crane's and stopped. That's why he was driving into a populated area with a dead body in the back of his open Jeep instead of burying it in a shallow grave in the rainforest. Because that family at least deserved a chance to bury their loved one and mourn.

He needed someplace where the body would be found but where he could get in and out without being noticed. A few miles farther along, he saw blue signage with a white "H" pointing off the highway. A hospital. That would do.

The hospital was a sprawling three-story complex surrounded by parking lots and landscaped grounds. Crane pulled in and followed the signs that directed him toward visitor parking. At the end nearest the building, he found another lot announcing it was for doctors' parking only. Crane pulled into that lot and let the Jeep roll slowly past the spaces, ranking the cars by vulnerability. Deep in the lot was an older Cadillac. Perfect.

Crane stopped behind it, hopped out, and went through the toolbox in the back of the Jeep. He found a long, thin metal rod for cranking the jack, and an oil-stained wooden wedge that

Melissa probably stuck behind a tire to keep the Jeep stable on steep hillsides.

He forced the wedge into the rubber window molding on the driver's side door and slowly forced the glass away from the Cadillac's doorframe until he could get the rod inside. Then he simply slid the rod in and turned it to hit the lock button. The doors unlocked with a satisfying *thunk*.

Crane tossed his tools back into the Jeep and took another look around to make sure no one had noticed. Then he carried Acosta's body to the car and wrestled it into the driver's seat. The body fell over, but Crane pulled it back up to a sitting position so it would be visible.

"I'm sorry, Hector," Crane murmured as he dug under the dash for the car's alarm wiring. "I don't know what you thought you were doing back there, but it was a useless death."

The Cadillac's alarm went off like a banshee's wail, which Crane figured was about all the funeral he owed the man. He slammed the door, jumped back into the Jeep, and was out of the lot and gone before anyone came to see what was happening.

————

It was dark by the time Crane returned Melissa's Jeep and caught a cab back to the Vanderbilt. It had been a long day and not a good one. He poured a drink from the minibar and turned on the TV. Officer Acosta's death lead the news. It was the typical "police are searching for the killer of one of their own" story. It explained how Officer Hector Acosta, shown smiling in an undated photograph, had been shot during a routine traffic stop somewhere east of Carolina, a good thirty miles from Melissa's lab. There was a plea for witnesses who had seen something along that stretch of highway to call police.

They'd covered it up well enough, but Crane knew they'd be looking for him behind the scenes. The question was how high up it went. That was something he'd have to discover for himself.

Now came the other unpleasant and risky thing he had to do. Crane took out his phone and dialed the private number Josh Sulenski had given him.

There was a thin background hiss when Josh answered. Crane guessed he was on an airplane, speaking into something that was trying to cancel out the engine noise.

"John, how are you? Do you have any news?"

"Are you somewhere you can talk?"

A note of concern entered Josh's voice. "I'm on my jet. What's going on, John?"

Quickly and concisely, Crane recounted what had happened, from his arrival at the facility to disposing of Acosta's body. To his credit, Josh remained quiet and let Crane detail what little he knew about who and why.

There was a long beat of silence when Crane stopped speaking. Finally Josh let out a breath. "Are Melissa and her people safe?" he asked. "I can get them out of Puerto Rico tonight."

"If they wanted to kill her team, they had plenty of opportunity. They just wanted the project dead. I think as long as it stays that way, they're okay. Just tell them to lay low; they can't start up until this is settled."

"Melissa won't like that."

Crane chuckled. "No, she won't. She damn near got herself killed taking one of them on with a steel pipe."

"She doesn't back down from much. That's why I decided to fund her."

"Well, talk her down. I'll need her help, but I can't do this if she keeps going off half cocked."

Josh paused. "Are you?" he said at last. "Doing this, I mean?

A dead cop … I mean, this is a lot more than you signed on for, John. Say the word, and I can get you out of there tonight too."

Crane stood up and walked over to the window. Outside the wind blew strong and steady off the sea, and whitecaps glowed in the moonlight as they rolled up the beach.

"No," he said after a moment. "I'm all in if you want me. But that means you're all in too. No questioning my tactics or complaining about my expenses. And there's no backing out after this call. I'm not planning to stop until I know why this happened and who's responsible. And they're going to have a problem with me. I just told you I killed a police officer, Josh. It's gut-check time."

There was another long silence, no doubt while Josh considered the implications of becoming an accessory after the fact.

"Do what you need to do," he said at last. "You'll have all the backup I can give you. So we're up against the Puerto Rican state police. What do they have against Melissa's project? Did she get too close to something? Are they up to something out there in the rainforest?"

"No, there's nothing out there. I've been all over that place, and I can't see any reason why they'd give a damn. Best guess is that they're working for somebody else who does care about it."

"How do we find them?"

"We follow the chain back to whoever's pulling on it. You don't advertise on Craigslist for cops to do your dirty work. These guys were already bent. They're into something else, and that led to this. So I'm going to find them and get into their business. I'm going to shake things up until something falls out."

"What do you need from me?" Josh asked.

"I'll need some things I can't just pick up at the mall. I'll send you a shopping list. You should be aware not everything on it will be entirely legal for civilian use."

"I've got a guy who can source whatever you need," said Josh. "Might even surprise you. I'll send you a care package."

"Thank you."

"Don't mention it. This means a lot to me, John. I want to be clear about that. If you weren't there, today still would have happened, and it would be just as bad, or maybe worse. We just wouldn't have any way to fight back."

"Take care," Crane said. "I'll call when I've got something to tell you."

"Okay. I'll keep an eye out for your shopping list."

Then Josh hung up and Crane stood there for a long time, looking out over the sea. He opened the sliding glass door and let the breeze sweep over him as the tide rolled in, and dance music drifted up the beach from the clubs in Condado.

He wasn't a government agent anymore. He was out here without the US military and intelligence machine as his lifeline. All he had backing him up now was a rich kid who wanted to do the right thing.

He hoped that would be enough.

CHAPTER 13

Acevedo sat in his cruiser with a flask of rum and waited. It was a bad end to a bad day. Acosta's body had turned up in a hospital parking lot of all places. He'd had to fix things with the local cops who got the call. Thankfully, cops tended not to think straight when another officer died. They bought his story about Acosta working undercover to catch drug thieves working the hospital. They'd helped him sell the official story—that he'd been shot during a traffic stop and left to die on the side of Highway 3.

He'd just come from telling Acosta's wife that version, hearing her shrieks, swearing he'd track down whoever killed her husband. Then there was the rest of his crew, all thinking it could have been them. Thinking he'd led them into this mess and gotten one of them killed.

He took another pull on the flask, felt the liquor burn its way down his throat. He'd lost a good friend today, and he didn't even have a chance to mourn. He was too busy trying to contain the damage before everything blew up in his face.

The Little Russian's BMW appeared, and Acevedo slipped the flask under his seat. Then he got out of the car, walked around it, and leaned against the front fender. Some instinct told him he didn't want to be shut inside the car for this.

The Little Russian pulled up alongside and eyed him for a moment before he cut his music.

"Is it done?"

"Yeah, it's done," he said, a little too quickly. "They're out of business."

"Something's wrong. What?"

"Someone was there, that's what. Someone who killed Acosta."

He recounted the story of the attack. All the details. Zajic grew more agitated as he went on. "This man," he said afterward. "Who was this man?"

"The hell if I know! She went for help. She came back with one man. We figured he was an insurance man or something."

"We need to find him. He's a threat."

"What the hell do you want now? Track this guy down for you? How do we do that?"

Zajic swore in his native tongue. Acevedo didn't understand the words, but the intent was clear.

"You're the fucking cops! Don't they teach you how to find somebody? Jesus. You need a clue? Okay? The woman. She brought this guy, right? Put some guys on her! Follow her until she leads you to him!"

"No. This is not our problem. This is your shit that you dragged us into. We're done. You want the guy, you go find him."

"Not how it works, little police man. You fucked up. You need to make it right. And fast."

Acevedo's temper surged. "Make it right?" He slapped the hood of the cruiser. "Fuck you, make it right. This shit is not our job, you hear me? We pick up the drugs, we get them to the airport, we get them on planes. That's what we do! Shooting up somebody's fucking lab in the jungle is on your side of the fence, you understand?"

The Little Russian opened his door and stepped out. Jesus, he was huge. Acevedo couldn't figure out how he moved around on that stupid boat he lived on with its tight quarters.

Zajic moved right into his space, inches from Acevedo's face, cold eyes looking down into his. It occurred to him that it was a very dangerous thing he'd done. But it wasn't the most dangerous thing he'd done today. Acevedo held his ground.

There was a long, tense moment. The only sound was the odd truck rolling by on the road, the sound of engines peaking and then fading away into the night. Finally, Zajic stepped back with a shrug.

"Okay, if that's how you want it, okay," he said. He took a phone out of his jacket pocket. The screen gave off a greenish glow. He held out the phone, and Acevedo took it because he didn't know what else to do. "You can talk to the boss yourself."

Acevedo looked at the phone in confusion. There was an active call in progress. What the hell was going on? How did he ...

He put the phone to his ear but heard only static.

"Hello? Is somebody there?" he said.

Zajic sighed and reached around to whack him on the back of the head.

"Not Spanish. Come on. Think. Use English. And talk slow."

"Hello, this is Sergeant Javier Acevedo, Puerto Rico Police," he said in English.

There was a long beat of silence, just the soft hiss of network noise on the phone. Then a heavily accented voice said, "Do you know who you are speaking to, Sergeant?"

"I think so."

"Good, good. I'm glad Emil has told you something about me. He's told me a great deal about you. You're part of the chain that moves my product. So I learn all I can about you. Do you understand?"

The silence dragged until Acevedo decided it hadn't been a rhetorical question. "I understand," he said.

"Yours is a small piece of the operation," the voice went on. "I have to watch all of it, beginning to end. That means I must keep my eye on more than you must to do your part. And so when I asked you to shut down the research project in the jungle, I understand this makes no sense to you. I ask you to trust me because I have my eye on the big picture."

Acevedo glanced at Zajic. He stood in a wide, ready stance. His expression was unreadable.

"So I ask you to do this strange thing for me, knowing you will think I'm a crazy old man who wastes your time. But you did it, and I thank you. But there are complications, yes?"

"There was a new man there," he said. "A stranger. He was no scientist. He killed one of my men."

"I share your grief. I too command soldiers," the man said, and now Acevedo could hear truth in his voice. "When one of my men is killed, at least it's simple. We bury him, we grieve, we take care of his family. But no one questions it. In our world, there is violence and men die. For you, I know it's not the same. When a policeman dies, there are many questions."

"Yes. I put out a cover story. But there will be investigations, scrutiny. I told your man here, this endangers our operation—"

"I know that," the voice interrupted. "Which is why I understand your reluctance. But this man ... appearing here now, it puts us all in danger, Sergeant. In much more danger than you understand.

"A man in my business makes many enemies. I succeed because I know what my enemies are doing. This isn't easy. Say someone attacks one of my gambling rings and kills my men. I have many questions. Who did it? Who were they working for?

Why hit me exactly there and now? The answers aren't always clear. Maybe two enemies have joined forces against me. Maybe a newcomer wants to muscle in. It can be very complicated. Many times I can only guess, and that is what I am doing now. There is a group that has a reputation in my field. A very bad reputation. I have been worried they will interfere with me, and now someone has done just that."

Acevedo didn't know how much of this he was supposed to know. But he knew more than they thought he did. He'd heard Zajic talking about something they called Team Kilo. Acevedo had no idea who this Team Kilo was, but he knew Zajic and his boss were scared to death of them. Scared enough to break protocol this way. Scared enough that Acevedo began to be afraid himself.

"If they've taken an interest in our operation there, then I need to know that. So though I know you don't understand why and though I know you have a problem with your dead cop, I'm telling you this is more important. I need you to find this man. I need to know exactly what he's told his people. And then I need him dead."

"It is difficult for me to act unobserved—"

"My own safety is, of course, my first priority," the voice interrupted, suddenly ruthless and cold. "If I have to, I will act myself to cut the cords leading back to me. It's not as though this man would spare your life, Sergeant. Or that of your lovely wife, Emilia. Or Ruben or little Belinda."

He let the threat hang there. Acevedo struggled to control his fear and anger.

"They know nothing about this," he finally choked out.

"Of course not. But they can be used to squeeze you, and that means they aren't safe. Do you understand me now?"

Acevedo felt himself trembling involuntarily. He clenched his muscles, trying to hide it from Zajic.

"I understand," he said.

"Good. I know you will do all you can. Now I need to talk to Emil. Good hunting, Sergeant Acevedo."

Acevedo thrust the phone at Zajic like something radioactive. Zajic took it and listened for perhaps five seconds. Then he said a couple words in his native tongue and hung up.

"So now you know what we're up against," he said. "We live or die based on whether we find this man. I suggest we find him before the Colombians get here."

CHAPTER 14

The sky was gray, and mist hung in the morning air as Crane and Melissa drove back to the lab. Neither spoke until they pulled through the gates into the empty parking lot. The building sat there, surrounded by dripping greenery, its front glass wall now a gaping dark hole. It looked like some lost ancient tomb, Crane thought.

He'd gone shopping again, for cleaning supplies this time. They unloaded them from the back of the Jeep and silently headed inside. Their footsteps echoed off the bare cement.

They found the dark stain of dried blood in the hallway. Crane glanced over at Melissa and saw her reliving that moment again.

"Is it just here?" she said.

"Nobody else got hurt," said Crane. "But I carried him out. We should double-check my route from here to the doors."

"I'll have a look around," said Melissa.

While she was gone, Crane carefully scrubbed away Acosta's blood with a wire brush and a wet sponge. He soaked the area down with detergent and cleaned it again. Then he washed the area with bleach, and another wash with water to clear the bleach.

When he was satisfied that he'd done all he could, he sprinkled the area with luminol powder and went over it inch by inch with a portable UV flashlight. It would do. Even if they went over the scene in depth, which Crane doubted, there was nothing left to prove what happened here. He cleaned up the luminol and took the supplies back to the Jeep.

Melissa still hadn't returned when he got back. He went looking and eventually found her in one of the lab spaces off the atrium. She was surrounded by the remains of esoteric lab equipment, and Crane could see she'd been crying. He put a hand gently on her shoulder.

"That's a high seek ten," she said softly, pointing to a large metal box that had been shredded by bullets. Crane spotted a label that read HiSeqX. "Do you have any idea how hard it was to get our hands on that? They cost a million dollars, but you can't buy just one. You have to buy ten. We found a biotech startup in Boston that wanted five, so we scraped around until we found four other projects looking for one and we went in together on them. When it showed up, we all just sat and looked at it for like an hour because we couldn't believe we had one of our own. A high seek. Out here in the middle of nowhere. We'll never replace that."

She walked around the wreckage of the machine, turned over something with her foot. Crane smelled chemical reagents from smashed plastic bottles.

"All gone," she said. "All that work. We'll have to start from scratch. I'll have to get an inventory to Josh."

"About that," said Crane. "I talked to Josh last night. He wanted to extract you and your team."

She turned to face him. "We're not going anywhere!"

"I talked him out of that. But I advised him not to restart your project yet."

She reacted with rising anger, but then it seemed to simply pop like a balloon and she shook her head. The energy simply wasn't there.

"Of course you did," she said with resignation. "I forgot, in the heat of it all. I thought you were on my side for a minute."

"I am on your side," said Crane. "But look around. Whoever has it in for your project isn't kidding. And we still don't know who they are, or why."

"The dead cop ..."

"They had no reason to come after you. I doubt they even knew about this place. They were working for someone else, someone who gains something by shutting you down. Right now, they've got what they wanted. You and your people are safe. But if you start trucking in loads of new gear and looking like a working project, they'll send those men back again. Or worse."

He could see her thinking it through, realizing he was right.

"I'm going to get to the bottom of this. And then Josh will be here with his checkbook in hand. But right now we're going to go through the motions, and then you're going to play dead."

"All right," she said. "You win."

He smiled at her. "Well, don't be too morose. I need you angry for a few more hours."

"What do you mean?"

"We have to call the police."

"The police?"

"That's what you'd do if it really happened the way we want them to think it happened. Nobody here when this happened. You came in this morning, found the place shot up. Nobody was hurt. And you're not scared. You're angry. You want the cops to catch whoever did it."

"They're not going to—"

"No, but you don't know that. This wasn't a police operation. Just a handful of dirty cops. They already covered up their dead man. The story is he got shot making a traffic stop. The safest thing we can do is hold up our end of that."

She was quiet for a long moment, working out the implications. "Why wasn't anybody here when it happened?" she asked at last.

"You went to the mainland to get some face time with your donors. Got to keep them happy so the money keeps flowing. That's part of your job, and the trip checks out. Without you, nobody else had much to do, so they took a couple days off."

She let out a breath. "Okay, I can do that."

They drove back out to the main road and stopped at a convenience store with a payphone outside. Crane walked her through the call and asked a few different questions he thought the responding officer might ask. Once or twice he advised her to change an answer slightly.

"Okay, you're ready," he said eventually. "Can you handle this? I can't be here when they show up."

"I've got it," she said, some of her old confidence starting to return.

"Good. Call me later and tell me everything."

"Okay. Wait ... how are you going to get back?"

Crane smiled. "I spotted a roadside grill shack a couple miles up the road. I'm going to hike up there, have myself a beer and some pinchos, make some new friends. Sooner or later I'll find someone going my way."

"Seriously?"

He grinned as reassuringly as he could. "I'll be fine. So will you. Call me later."

Then he turned and strolled away up the road as Melissa picked up the phone and pushed a quarter into the slot.

———

By late afternoon, Crane was in a camera store in San Juan's Hato Rey neighborhood, putting Josh's credit card through its paces once again.

"The Canon 70D body," he said to the very attentive clerk, who had laid out a selection of cameras and lenses on the counter. Crane considered them, pointed to a long black metal model. "The 200-millimeter f 2.8 telephoto and the AstroScope low light module."

"That's a big lens. With the AstroScope, the camera will be very unwieldy," the clerk said, stating the obvious. "You will want a tripod for stability, I think?"

"No, I'll make do," said Crane. "And give me two 8-gig SD cards, 10X speed."

"Very good, sir. And perhaps one of the 50 millimeters?" said the clerk hopefully. "For daylight shooting at closer range? And if you can get closer to your subject, you will find it much easier to use with the AstroScope."

Crane nodded at one. "The f 1.4, obviously."

"Of course, sir," said the clerk, sounding exactly like a sommelier approving of Crane's choice of wine.

Crane's phone rang. He checked the screen and recognized Melissa's number. He handed the credit card to the clerk. "If you'll ring those up, I'll be right with you."

Crane walked to the far end of the display case and answered.

"Is everything okay? How did it go?"

"I'm home," she said. "I did it. It was … easy, actually."

"What happened?"

"I waited almost an hour outside that stupid store for somebody to show up."

"Uniformed officer?"

"Yes. He followed me back to the lab, and I showed him around. I took a good half hour going through everything that was destroyed, and that wasn't much fun, by the way."

"What did he say?"

"Very little. He just took everything down. He didn't question anything. Then he filled out a police report and left me his card. He took my number and said a detective would follow up. That was it. He left, and I came home."

"You're at the guest house? Stay there. A courier's going to bring you a new phone. From now on, if you need me, call me on that phone. Don't use it for anything else."

She made a confused sound that shifted into concern. "Wait, are you saying they're going to tap my phone?"

"It's not impossible," said Crane, "but it would take some time to set up. More likely they'll pull your call records. They'll be looking for me, and you're the only lead they've got."

"But if they do that, they'll see this call, won't they?" Crane could hear the rising alarm in her voice.

"It won't tell them much. I'll be switching phones too. I'll text you the number. After this, you won't see much of me for a while. That's to protect you."

The clerk returned with Crane's credit card and a large shopping bag.

"I need to go," he said. "Don't worry. You're safe."

"Okay," she said doubtfully.

Crane disconnected. He put his phone into airplane mode before putting it away. He collected his bag and his card from the beaming clerk. "If you need anything else while you're in Puerto Rico, sir, we are here to help."

"Thank you," said Crane. "There is something, actually. Can you tell me where I can get a phone around here?"

CHAPTER 15

Hector Acosta's funeral was held at midday, at a cemetery in his hometown of Campanilla, several miles west of San Juan. John Crane made sure to arrive early. He found a position among old, moldering family crypts, far enough from the gravesite to go unnoticed but within range of his telephoto lens. He made sure he could cover the approach road that looped lazily around the grounds. Then he waited.

Eventually a hearse appeared, a line of cars creeping along behind it. The procession moved slowly among the headstones and pulled in to park in neat order along the edge of the road. Mourners made their way in twos and threes to the gravesite. Many were police officers in dress uniform. There was a grieving widow in black and a priest with his cassock rippling in the warm breeze. Crane noted faces, who spoke to whom. The ritual seemed almost mechanical viewed from the outside.

More cars drifted in after the main procession. Crane spotted an officer in dress uniform getting out of the passenger side of a silver Mustang with his arm in a sling. He snapped a photo as the man walked around the car and joined the woman who had driven. They walked together to the grave. The man with the broken arm spoke briefly to the widow and then joined another group of officers in dress uniform off to one side. There were five of them in a small cluster beneath an oak.

Crane watched how they interacted with each other and with the other mourners. That was them, he decided. There were five of them, which was right, and the broken arm was strongly suggestive, but it was more than that. As he watched them, he sensed there was something invisible that fenced them off from the others, especially the police. It was as if there was some subconscious agreement that those five were different. Their presence at the funeral was accepted, but they were somehow not of the same kind.

As the priest began to speak, Crane realized there were fewer people than he expected. For a police officer killed in the line of duty, it would be reasonable to see a flood of officers there to support the force even if they didn't know the dead man at all. There might even be a politician with his entourage and some reporters. A respectable group had turned out to see Acosta off, but nothing on that scale. Perhaps it was because of the remote location. Or perhaps Acosta hadn't been very popular with his fellow officers. Maybe they sensed an air of deception about him, found something dubious about the official manner of his death, and their protective instincts were keeping them at a safe distance.

Crane swept the rest of the mourners with his camera. The family sat in a row of folding chairs beside the grave, all dressed in black. The priest stood beside the flower-laden casket. He was too far away for Crane to make out his words. His voice was a stale, emotionless drone.

That was death. Prettied up and dusted off from the death Crane was used to, of course. There was no violence here, no screaming, no blood. It was all very orderly, but it was still death. There was the widow, surrounded by relatives trying in vain to comfort her. There were the dead man's children, now without a father. Acosta had brought it on himself, but Crane was the instrument.

Crane had never actually seen this part of it before. He'd killed to survive, and he'd done it without remorse. But then he'd moved on, eyes fixed on the mission. He was always long gone by now, when other people had to come along behind him, clean up the mess, and live with the consequences that Crane never saw. Well, this was what they looked like.

After the service was finished, the mourners drifted away a few at a time. There was a line waiting to pay respects to the family. Crane watched his little group of rogue cops move through it. The tall, slender one with the close-cropped dark hair was clearly the leader. The others all looked to him as they talked, and he was the first of the group in the line. Crane zoomed in and snapped more pictures.

Eventually they had all embraced the widow and shaken the hand of the son, who was perhaps twelve years old, trying to act like the man in charge now. They moved off and walked back toward their cars in a tight group. Crane snapped the cars as they got into them, made sure he could identify make and model and plate number.

One by one they pulled out and drove slowly out of the cemetery. Someone led the family back to a black town car behind the hearse. It was over. Workmen collected the chairs and rolled up the artificial turf that covered the bare earth at the edge of the grave.

Crane sat back and waited, his back against the rough, lichen-coated cement of a crypt. The mid-afternoon sun bore down on him, and the humidity made him sweat. Occasional drops of perspiration ran tingling down the back of his neck, feeling strangely like some instinct warning him of danger..

When the grave was filled and the workmen had left, the

cemetery was still once more. Crane walked to Acosta's grave and looked down at the headstone with the name and the dates that contained his life. "Beloved Husband and Father."

Crane knew he would eventually have to kill again if he maintained the course he was on. He might well have to kill one or more of those men he'd come here to see. He needed to remember this, the cost of his choices for people who had nothing to do with him. Before he killed another enemy, he needed to be certain that was the only way to avoid something even worse. Because when he did kill someone, it would be like this again.

But of course, it always had been.

―――――

Crane spent the rest of the day at the beach, watching the surf roll in and couples walking hand in hand along the waterline. The funeral had put him in a dark mood, and he needed to get out of it. He considered calling Melissa on his burner phone, asking her to meet him here. They could sit on the sand together, stroll along the water themselves. Then they could go for drinks and pionono from a food stall up the beach, and what might come after. But after what she'd seen him do, Crane sensed a wall had crashed down, cutting off whatever attraction might have been there.

So he waited alone. Eventually the sun began to set and the wind shifted. Clouds rolled in from the west, stained deep red by the sun. Crane got up and drove back to San Juan.

A large package was waiting for him when he arrived back at the Vanderbilt.

Crane signed the slip, and a porter rolled out a rather large box on a luggage cart. He took it up to Crane's room and placed it on the foot of the bed.

"Care package from home," Crane said as he tipped the porter and showed him out.

Then he locked the door and sliced through the packing tape with his pocket knife. Inside the box was a black suitcase covered in rip-stop fabric. Crane slid the zippers open and flipped up the lid. Then he let out a low whistle of appreciation. Josh's source had come through.

The suitcase was packed with tools and electronics. Crane organized the contents into piles by function. There were GPS tracers, radios and concealable microphones, and fisheye cameras with built-in burst transmitters. That all went into one pile.

The next pile was smaller but made up for it by being not just suspicious but flat out illegal. At least Crane assumed Puerto Rico had the usual laws against possession of burglary tools. There were lock picks, plus a snap gun for quickly opening tumbler locks. There was a small, specialized computer with firmware for decrypting signals and a software-defined radio for sending its own signals back out. It would let Crane infiltrate and decipher a home or business alarm system and take control of it from a block away.

Then there were a few other special-purpose items that went by themselves. A pair of compact night vision goggles. A silencer for the Glock he'd taken from Acosta's body. A pair of USB flash drives with a note from Josh promising that they would load a back door into any computer they connected to and start sending data back to Josh's servers. The prize was a mil-spec ruggedized tablet with a battlefield intelligence system. Crane had included that on his shopping list to see how far Josh was willing and able to go. He hadn't expected him to actually come up with one. Josh's resources continued to impress. He supposed that was what it meant to be richer than several countries.

He reminded himself that he was no longer official. If he was found with these things, it wouldn't all go away with a couple phone calls behind the scenes. For the whole suitcase, Crane guessed he was looking at about twenty to twenty-five years in prison. But that couldn't be helped. He'd just have to avoid getting caught.

He loaded everything back into the suitcase, put some clothes on top, and put it away in the closet. Then he fired up his laptop and went through the pictures he'd taken at the funeral. He studied the faces until he knew he would recognize any of the men on the street, in or out of uniform. He memorized their cars: the plate numbers, the identifying scrape on the front fender of a Dodge Charger, the third-party light kit on the grille of the leader's F-150.

He was considering a drink at the hotel bar when his burner phone rang. It was Melissa.

"Is everything okay?" he said when he picked up.

"I don't know," she said. "They want me to come to the police station tomorrow morning. A detective wants to talk to me about my case."

"That's routine," he said, trying to sound reassuring. It very likely was routine, but he'd told her to call him if she had any contact with the police at all. "He'll want details from you that the responding officer didn't ask for."

"What do I do?"

"You go in and answer his questions. Just like you told the first cop. The story's simple. There's not a lot you can tell him. He'll have you go through it again, but he won't get much."

"If I get arrested, so help me," she said, adding a laugh that sounded more forced than she probably intended.

"You'll be fine," he said. "Call me afterward and let me know how it went."

"All right. I'm just nervous. All right, yeah. I'll call you when I'm done."

They hung up, and Crane had a scotch from the minibar and went out on the balcony. He watched the moonlit white caps rolling up the beach in the dark for a while. Then he went to bed early. Tomorrow was going to be a long day. Crane lay in the dark for a moment, listening to the sound of the waves dimly creeping through the glass balcony doors, and thinking for the last time of the man he'd killed. Then he put those thoughts away and was fast asleep within minutes.

CHAPTER 16

Melissa found a parking space down the street and walked toward the police headquarters building off the Avenue Franklin Delano Roosevelt. She took a couple deep breaths and looked up at the building. It was a tall, squarish tower of white cement studded with high, narrow windows that made it look like a fortress.

She gathered her wits and strode into the front lobby, trying to look like a crime victim slightly peeved that she had to come in and deal with more bureaucratic annoyances.

A female officer at the front counter looked up her name in a computer and had someone escort her to an interview room on the first floor. They promised her an Agent Arias would be in to speak with her momentarily. She took a seat and waited.

The room looked comfortable enough. It had none of the features years of TV cop dramas had taught her to expect in an interrogation room. There was no one-way mirror on the wall. No way to fasten a suspect to the table. It looked like a small government office with aged carpet and a table covered in cheap plastic veneers meant to look like wood. Perhaps she really wasn't a suspect.

She was startled by the door opening, and then a man entered. He was tall and slender, perhaps forty, with serious eyes and a crooked smile. He wore a tan suit. She looked for a gun but didn't see one. He had a manila folder in one hand.

He smiled and they shook hands. "Good morning," he said. "I'm Agent Roberto Arias, Special Investigation Bureau." He offered her a business card from his inside suit pocket. "You're Dr. Melissa Simon?"

"That's right," she said as she released his hand and sat back down again. "Have you found the men who attacked my lab yet?" She hoped that was what someone would say in a case like this. Then she noticed Arias look back up at her.

"Did you say there were more than one?" he asked suddenly, his hand pausing in the act of placing the folder on the table.

She took a second to recover her composure. "Well, they did a great deal of damage. I suppose it could have been one man. But it would have been a lot of work."

Arias nodded. "Of course. To answer your question, I don't believe there has been anything to report regarding your case. I should make clear that I'm not the investigating officer. My role is to oversee the investigation, to make certain that it is handled appropriately."

Melissa wasn't sure what that meant. She smiled and waited for him to continue.

"You told the responding officer that this attack came after several previous incidents where valuable equipment was damaged outside the building. In the forest."

She nodded. "That's right."

He paged through the documents in his folder. "You've contacted the police about these incidents on two occasions," he said. "Most recently on March nineteenth of this year."

"I don't remember the exact date," she said. "That sounds right."

"It would help me to understand the nature of your project," he said. "What kind of scientific research are you doing?"

She explained the project to him—the layman's version of the elevator speech. That part was certainly easy. She'd delivered it hundreds of times. Arias nodded, took notes, asked the occasional question.

"And your team usually works in the lab on the weekends," he said when she'd finished. "Is that correct?"

"That's right. Nobody was there when it happened because I had to leave Puerto Rico to talk with my backers about the damage to our sampling equipment."

"It's expensive to replace," he offered.

"That's right. I had to make the case for more funding. So I gave the team the weekend off while I was gone. Thank God I did!" she added, feeling pleased with her improvisation. "If we'd been there when they came ..."

He looked at his papers again. "But you returned to Puerto Rico on Friday evening."

She felt a sudden rush of panic and fought it down. The cop who'd come out to the lab hadn't cared where she'd been. Why was this one poking at her story? Christ, he did suspect something. Crane had been wrong. An answer. She had to answer him.

"I didn't know when I'd be back when I left," she said. "Plus we haven't been able to collect much in the way of samples lately anyway, with the lost gear."

"So there isn't much work to do," he said, nodding and noting something down on his memo pad.

"Right. And honestly, this has been really hard on me. I just needed some time away from it. I stayed at home for the weekend and tried not to think about things."

"This is the address in Ocean Park?" he asked.

"That's right."

"Do you own a firearm, Dr. Simon?" Arias asked suddenly.

"What? No!" Again that trill of panic. She felt the adrenaline rush, felt her flesh tighten, the hairs on her arms standing up. She hoped it wasn't obvious to Agent Arias, but she was afraid it was. She tried to turn it back on him.

"Why would that matter? Are you suggesting I shot up my own lab?"

"Not at all," he said softly. "It's quite all right, Dr. Simon. Please calm down. I ask because we haven't been able to identify the weapon or weapons used in the attack. I was wondering if it was possible they used a weapon belonging to you that they found on the premises."

"Well ... no, none of my team has a gun. Certainly not at the lab, at least. I'd know about that." This time she couldn't tamp down her fear. She was convinced he knew something more than what she'd told the uniformed cop. Somehow he knew she was lying. She was convinced of it.

"I have one more question," he was saying. He pulled a sheaf of photos from his binder. "Can you tell me if you recognize any of the men I'm about to show you."

"Of course." She leaned forward as he lay down an eight by ten headshot on the table. It was a man in perhaps his middle thirties, dark hair and eyes, a military bearing.

"No, I've never seen him before. Are these the men who sabotaged my project?"

Arias didn't answer. He laid down another photo, not unlike the first. Then a third. Both times Melissa shook her head no.

Then, the fourth photo. It was a face she could never forget. She could still see Crane pulling the blood-soaked ski mask away, the horrible quiet sound as bits of skull came away with it, and that face, still in death. She involuntarily drew in a breath and looked up to see if Arias had noticed. His serious brown eyes met hers, and she knew that he had seen her react. He knew she recognized him.

"This one you have seen?" he said.

Melissa thought furiously. "I don't know where," she said. Then the answer came to her and she knew what to say.

"That's the policeman who was killed," she said as if just realizing it. "He was on the news."

"Hmm," Arias said, and she detected disappointment in the sound. "That he was ..."

"Are they all policemen?" she said. "I don't understand."

"It's not important," said Arias. "Thank you, Dr. Simon." He collected his papers and closed the folder—without bothering to show her the one photograph remaining in the stack. "I don't have any more questions at this time. On behalf of the Puerto Rico police, let me thank you for your cooperation."

"Are we done, then?" she asked.

"That's all I have at this time," he repeated. "We'll continue to investigate what happened at your lab, and someone will be in touch if we find a suspect."

He guided her around the table and out the door. "In the meantime, if you think of anything or have any questions, you can always reach me at the number on my card."

"Thank you very much," she said. Then he ushered her out into the main lobby and she was walking toward the front doors. She tried very hard to keep her pace comfortable and slow, but all she wanted to do was run out of there into the warmth and the sunlight.

She made the door, half afraid Arias would call her back. Then she was outside, crossing the parking lot to her Jeep. She fumbled with the key and realized she was shaking. She took several deep breaths, started the Jeep, and pulled out onto the street. She lurched out on the Avenue Franklin Delano Roosevelt and cut off a taxicab. The driver honked and shouted something at her, but Melissa didn't care. She just wanted to get as far away from here as she could and call John Crane. She hoped he would know what to do.

CHAPTER 17

In a post office parking lot, John Crane sat in a rented Hyundai and watched the police headquarters building across the street. Melissa was in there, giving her statement to a detective. He'd coached her on what to say, and the story was simple enough. It was more believable than the truth, in his opinion. Crane didn't expect there to be any trouble. He was here because of what he expected to happen when she left.

Crane knew there would be pushback from the adversary, whoever that was. They didn't know anything about him, but they obviously knew a lot about Melissa and her project. So they would use her to try to get to him. In turn, he would use that to get to them.

He waited another few minutes until Melissa emerged from the building and hurried across the parking lot to her Jeep. She looked flushed through his telephoto lens, and she was moving a little faster than normal. Something must have spooked her.

She started the Jeep and pulled out onto the side street. And a few moments later, a black Charger pulled out after her. It was the same one he'd seen at the funeral. Crane smiled to himself and started up the Hyundai. Game on.

At the intersection with Avenue FDR, Melissa pulled out at the wrong moment and cut off a taxi amid honking horns. The Charger waited for the taxi to clear the intersection and then the cars that had backed up behind it. Then it turned and followed Melissa's Jeep north. Crane pulled out and kept an eye on it. He stayed well back. He doubted he would lose the car; plus, he had the advantage of knowing where Melissa was going.

She led the entourage back across town to Ocean Park, where she parked up the street from the guest house where she stayed. She was walking back up the sidewalk as the Charger slid past, and then Crane's Hyundai. She didn't see him, but she had her phone out, nervously punching at the screen. A moment later his burner phone rang. Crane put it on speaker.

"Are you okay?" he asked. "How did it go?"

"They know something!" she said, and he could hear the nervous energy in her voice. "It wasn't like you said at all!"

"Calm down and tell me what happened," said Crane. For a moment, he considered turning around and going back to her. But he didn't want to lose the Charger. It turned around the block and headed back out of the neighborhood to the south. Crane gave it a few moments to pick up some distance, and then followed it.

"The detective knew more than he was telling me," Melissa said. "He had a picture of the man you ... and some others too. He asked if I owned a gun!"

"How many others?"

"Three," she said. "Does that matter? Wait, there was another one that he didn't show me."

"It's interesting," said Crane. It could mean a couple things, he thought. Some more helpful to him than others.

"What am I supposed to do now?" she said. "I've lied to the police!"

"It's going to be fine," he told her. "Nobody's after you. If they're trying to rattle you, it's to get you to lead them to me. That's why I'm keeping my distance. It's why we've got these phones."

Ahead of him, the Charger took an on-ramp to the expressway, heading east. Crane slipped through a yellow light to follow.

"You just keep a low profile," he told Melissa. "Stay close to home. Don't go back to the lab or talk to anybody else from your team."

She sighed. "I've got some reading I can catch up on."

"That's a good idea."

"If I end up in prison, I swear to God ..."

"I'll smuggle you a file," he said.

She laughed at last, and they finished the call.

The Charger led Crane east, into the Carolinas district. It dropped off the expressway and followed a twisting course through side streets, eventually pulling into a bar off the Avenue Monserrate. It parked next to the silver Mustang from the funeral. There were a couple of marked Ford Taurus police cruisers in the lot as well.

Crane parked on the street half a block up and watched in the side mirror as the driver walked into the bar. Crane got out and walked back up the sidewalk, looking around for any curious onlookers and concluding that no one was paying attention to him. In his pocket he had a collection of the tiny GPS tracers Josh had sent him. He walked through the parking lot, between the rows of parked cars, and slipped a tracer into the Charger's wheel well. The magnets leaped from his fingertips and thumped into place. He dropped another one on the Mustang and then crossed the lot and tagged the two police cruisers as well. He continued through the lot to the next street and walked around the block to return to his car.

Back in the Hyundai, he switched on his tablet and there

were the traces, a tight group of four red dots pulsing away on the street map, right up the street from Crane's blue dot. He assigned them labels. PV for the personal vehicles, CR for the police cruisers. The Charger was PV-2, the Mustang PV-3. He was saving number one for the leader of the group. Crane hoped he was in the bar and would claim one of the cruisers when they came out.

While he waited, he pulled up a page on his phone about the PR Police. The colloquial term for them was *La Uniformada*—the uniformed. They were a layer above the municipal police, the equivalent of a state police force on the mainland. They were organized into thirteen geographic regions covering the island. At the moment, Crane and his band of rogue cops were in the middle of the Carolina region, so Crane assumed that was where they were assigned. Canovanas and Benitez, and Melissa's lab, were also in the Carolina region.

Eventually the group left the bar together and split up in the lot. Crane recognized the leader, in duty uniform now. He crossed to one of the cruisers and pulled out. Crane tagged it CR-1 on his tablet. The other one became CR-4.

In theory, Crane didn't need to follow any of the cars now. He could sit right here and track all four of them around the island. But he wanted to keep an eye on the leader, to see if he would lead him someplace interesting. So he gave the cars a couple minutes to disperse and then pulled back out into traffic and followed the red dot marked CR-1.

He followed him around San Juan for the rest of the afternoon. He kept far enough away to remain unseen, but close enough to figure out what the officer was up to. Nothing of interest as far as Crane could tell. He patrolled stretches of the expressway, answered the occasional call. It looked like a routine day on the job. Crane didn't expect the man to immediately lead him where he wanted to go, but this part of the job had always been his least favorite.

He was following the Taurus up the expressway when a Boeing triple seven suddenly dropped out of the sky alongside him, on its approach run into Luis Muñoz International. Crane followed the cruiser into the airport but had to veer off when the cop flashed an ID card at a guarded gate and pulled into a secure area. There was a lot for people waiting for arrivals, so Crane pulled in. He swept the area beyond the chain link fence with his telephoto, but couldn't tell what the cop was doing. But it looked as though Muñoz was in Carolina's jurisdiction, not in San Juan proper. He looked it up on his phone and confirmed it. Now that was interesting. Crane could think of quite a few things a ring of corrupt cops could do with secure access to the island's international airport.

When CR-1 left the airport, Crane followed it back out again. It headed west now, across the border into the city of San Juan. Perhaps he lived there and was going off shift.

Crane followed, again keeping well behind the trace so the cop wouldn't notice him. The Hyundai was inconspicuous, but there was no need to take chances on his powers of observation. The cop drove across town to an area Crane's map called Monacilla Urbano. When the trace stopped moving, Crane drove slowly past the spot. The leader lived in a working-class neighborhood of smallish houses with driveways and small front lawns of well-kept grass. Many of the yards were walled off and the driveways gated. The cop's place wasn't walled. Crane could see the Taurus in the driveway and the F-150 pickup from the cemetery parked beside it on a paved pullout.

Crane drove past and left the neighborhood behind for the time being. He pulled over a few blocks away and ran a search on the address. The property belonged to one Javier Acevedo. That name belonged to a sergeant in the PR Police, assigned to the Carolina district. Crane found a photo of him and confirmed it. That was his man.

"Nice to meet you, Sergeant Acevedo," he muttered. Then he started up the car again and drove off. He found a place to fill up the Hyundai, grabbed a light snack, and waited for nightfall. When it was dark, he drove back and tagged Acevedo's F-150 as PV-1. Then he knelt in the darkness between the two cars and took out something that looked like a smartphone but wasn't. He called up an app and flipped through two long menus until he found "Ford" and "Taurus." When he pressed the red button, the device's radio fired off the appropriate codes until the cruiser's doors unlocked with a quiet *thunk*. Crane opened the passenger door and slipped an audio bug under the seat. Then he closed the door, relocked the car, and was gone.

It had been a productive day, Crane thought as he made his way back to his car. His tablet was now tracking three personal cars and two police cruisers, and he had a voice-activated recorder in the ringleader's cruiser. All he had to do was wait, then get within range of the bug again, and it would download everything it had picked up in a burst transmission to his laptop. It had been a very good day, but a long one. He'd been meaning to find a place that made good mofongo. Now seemed as good a time as any.

CHAPTER 18

Javier Acevedo drove his cruiser down the expressway. The day was bright and warm. The city gleamed in the sunlight, and palm trees waved in the breeze. Acevedo rejected all of it. His thoughts were gloomy. His talk with the Little Russian's boss had left a nagging fear deep in his bones. The man had threatened his family. The situation was spinning out of control around him. He had to do something, but he didn't know where to start. He'd caught a glimpse of the man who killed Hector, but he wasn't even sure he'd recognize him if they met on the street. He was just one more tall anglo with dark hair. The island was full of them.

But this morning an idea had come to him. He'd realized he did know something else about the stranger. He knew that the woman, Dr. Simon, had brought him back with her from the mainland. So he knew they'd come through Muñoz, and he knew roughly when. Maybe that would be enough.

He drove through the security entrance with a wave at the airport officers manning the gates. Nobody gave him a second look. He headed for the cargo-handling section and parked outside the satellite security office. The place was an ant's nest of activity with trucks, cargo lifts, and baggage trains going in all directions. To his right, a catering truck pulled out of a loading dock and headed for the main gate area. To his left, a scissor truck lifted a Unit Load Device up to the rear hatch of a FedEx jet. So much cargo moving so quickly from place to place. It had been so simple to slip a few packages of their own into the stream and make sure they made it out to the mainland or to Europe. It had seemed so simple when it started; easy money. How the hell had it turned into this?

He walked into the security office and found Eric Montalvo right where he expected to find him—sipping coffee from their battered machine while he tried to talk up one of the secretaries. Montalvo was middle-aged, stocky, with a shaved head that somehow did more to emphasize his baldness than conceal it. His Airport Police shirt had a stain from yesterday's lunch. The secretary looked grateful when Acevedo gave him a head check and they went outside.

They walked over by a line of parked pushback tugs, trading the usual police gossip. When Acevedo was sure nobody was looking, he slipped a thick envelope of cash from his shirt and passed it over. Montalvo hefted it briefly and then slipped it into his pocket.

"When is it this time?" Montalvo asked.

"Tuesday night," said Acevedo. "But I need something else."

"What's that?" Montalvo's tone was suddenly cautious. He liked the money well enough, but he never liked earning it.

"I need to find somebody. A man who came through here a few days ago."

"This isn't official, right? Or you'd just go through channels."

"I'd like to keep it quiet."

Montalvo shrugged. "There's only so much I can do. But come on."

They went back inside, and Montalvo led the way behind

the main counter and down a short hallway. The card on his belt opened the door to a cramped room with old, scarred filing cabinets on one side and racks of servers and Ethernet cable on the other. The place hummed with cooling fans.

Montalvo powered up a terminal at the end. "What have you got?"

Acevedo produced a photo of the woman, one he'd taken outside her place in Ocean Park. "He flew in from the mainland on the ninth. I don't know what airline. He was travelling with a woman named Melissa Simon."

Montalvo laboriously moved from menu to menu, pulling up screens. At one point he mistyped something, swore, and had to spend two minutes backtracking and starting over. This was clearly not his area of expertise.

"Are you sure about the day?" he asked at last.

"Yes, I'm sure," Acevedo said. He looked away and let out an annoyed puff of breath.

"Well, no Melissa Simon on any scheduled flight anytime between the eighth and the tenth. Could it have been a private plane?"

She'd gone to talk to her rich donors. When she came back, she brought a troubleshooter, a man whose job was to solve rich men's problems. Yes, he thought, that man might well have come in by private jet.

"Could be," he said. "That makes sense."

"Well, nothing I can do about that. If she came in that way, there's no ID check, no security. Nothing. It's just like she drove in her car."

"Damn it," Acevedo snapped. He hadn't realized how desperately he was clinging to this tiny thread. If he couldn't find the man ...

"Don't they keep a record of private planes that land here?"

"Just that a plane landed," Montalvo said. "Tail number, time of arrival. Anything else you'll have to go to someone else, and they'll want to know why."

He slapped the desktop hard. "Well, what the hell can you do?" Then he took a deep breath and gave Montalvo a conciliatory look. "I'm sorry."

"You have a picture? We can dig through camera footage, see if we get lucky. There're a lot of cameras."

Acevedo nodded. "Of the woman. Nothing of the man. But he came in with her. Anglo. Dark hair. Maybe my height. Lean build. I need a clear shot of that man. It's important, Eric."

"Okay, man, okay. If he walked past a camera, we'll find him. It might take a while, though."

Montalvo pulled the landing records, and they combed through them, eliminating commercial flights, cargo planes, charter airlines, and general aviation flights that were obviously domestic. If they came in by private plane, it would have been in a jet—a Lear or a Gulfstream. Only a handful of those had landed that day. They checked the arrival times and then went down the hall to another room where a pair of technicians helped pull up time-coded camera footage.

Acevedo showed them photos of Dr. Simon on his phone and spun them some story about a dark-haired man using her to carry drugs through the airport. Then he waited.

It took the better part of an hour before one of them suddenly called out. "Sir! I think I have her!"

Acevedo hurried over and leaned over the technician's shoulder. "Show me."

The tech hit some keys, and the screen image flashed. A couple passed under a camera. The man carried a duffel bag over his shoulder and what was probably the woman's suitcase. The woman was clearly Dr. Simon. And the man fit the glimpse Acevedo had caught of the dark-haired man at the lab. But there wasn't a good shot of his face. They walked out a pair of sliding glass doors and disappeared into a crowd on the sidewalk outside.

"That's her. What about him?" said Acevedo.

"It looks like they're heading for the cab line," said the technician. "There's another camera that should have them."

Now that they had an exact time, the technician was able to quickly pull up the footage. This camera was outside. At the far edge of the screen, Acevedo could see cars jostling for spots along the curb. The couple appeared out of the crowd, walking straight toward the camera.

It was him. Acevedo was sure of it.

"There!" he said. "That's the man. Get me the best close-up of his face you can."

The tech hit more keys, and a nearby printer started to warm up. This changed everything, Acevedo thought. Everything.

———

Branislav Skala sat on the terrace beneath a waxing moon, with the lights in his swimming pool casting rippling shadows on the wall. He sat at a white iron mesh table, with his laptop and a glass of last year's Pinot Blanc, and read his customized newsfeeds. The news was not good.

Ernst Shaller was selling his stake in Gazprom, the Russian natural gas company. Analysts said this was because he needed cash for a long-rumored takeover of a real estate development firm that came with huge holdings in London and Berlin. But Skala didn't trust that. The muscles at the back of his skull were tense, the skin vaguely tingling. That was his subconscious trying to warn him, a feeling that had saved his life more times than he could remember. Skala knew enough to pay attention to it.

Shaller sat on the board of Casse Biotech with Dorfmann

and Sir William Scott, and Skala knew they were on the opposing team. Ramirez had said as much to his partners at that lawn party when he didn't realize Skala could hear. If they'd been talking, perhaps Shaller was buying into their operation. That would be bad. That would be very bad. He needed to be in front of that.

He dashed off a quick e-mail to the investigators from Paris he'd put on retainer. "Casse Biotech—look for large cash transfers." It was the fifth message he'd sent them today. But this was a time of crisis. Significant events were coming fast. If he wanted to play in this game, he needed to be on top of them. So much was setting off that tingling feeling for him these days. He could sense things moving in the shadows.

A small window popped up in the corner of his screen. INCOMING MESSAGE, ZAJIC.

"Ah," he said out loud as he expanded it. "At last, perhaps some good news, Emil?"

HAVE HIS PHOTO, Zajic typed. SENDING NOW.

Another window popped up, and scan lines traced their way across the screen. Skala leaned forward and watched the picture take shape. He recognized the distinct angle and grainy look of a security camera shot. Gradually, a figure took shape. A man, tall and lean, well-muscled. A duffel bag over his shoulder, another suitcase in his other hand. A woman walked beside him. That one he recognized from his files. Doctor Simon of the gene bank project that had caused him so much trouble.

SGT A GOT IT FROM CAMERAS AT AIRPT.

Skala zoomed in on the face, pushing the photo's resolution as far as it would go. It was by no means high definition, but it would do. The man was identifiable. Skala studied his expression, the cast of his eyes. He zoomed back out and noted the efficient bearing of the body in motion. Yes, this man had the look of an operative. Team Kilo had sent him. It had to be them.

He pulled up what he had on Team Kilo. It was very little. He'd had to assign them the code name himself. He had no idea what they called themselves. But he knew they had great wealth and influence at their disposal. They had clashed with the group he was trying to ingratiate himself with. They would watch their enemies closely, and they wouldn't want to see someone with Skala's connections, resources, and expertise join the opposing side. And what little he knew about them showed that they struck from the shadows, with speed and ruthlessness. He had to be careful. This was a critical time.

THEY TOOK A CAB FROM AIRPT, Emil was typing. SGT. A RUNNING IT DOWN. PHOTO ALREADY OUT TO LOCAL COPS. THEY'LL FIND HIM.

And when they did, Skala thought, it would be the police who dealt with him in their official capacity. Another layer of insulation to hide the trail from this man's death back to himself. That was good.

WHEN THEY DO, I WANT YOU THERE, he sent back. YOU QUESTION HIM. I NEED TO KNOW WHAT HIS PEOPLE KNOW.

UNDERSTOOD.

What else could this man tell him? Skala had never had anyone from Team Kilo to question before, even if he was just a soldier.

I NEED TO KNOW HIS CONNECTIONS, WHO HE REPORTS TO. AND FIND OUT ALL HE KNOWS ABOUT SHALLER AND CASSE BIOTECH.

There was a momentary lull as Emil waited to see if he had any more to say. Then, SHALLER, CASSE BIOTECH. OK.

HE DOESN'T LEAVE PR ALIVE, Skala typed. LET THE COPS DO IT. MAKE SURE THEY UNDERSTAND THIS MAN HAS TO DIE.

CHAPTER 19

The next day, Crane stayed out of sight. He had tracers on their cars. It was enough for now. And every day spent following them around the Carolina region would slightly increase the chance of somebody noticing something, a little subconscious flash of recognition that would put his enemy on guard. On the other hand, every day he kept away would reduce those odds, make him safer.

So he kept track of their movements on his tablet, and he returned the Hyundai with a vague complaint about the seats not adjusting quite the way he wanted, and traded it for a blue Toyota Corolla.

He did have one rendezvous to make, though. Assuming Acevedo took his cruiser home again that night, Crane knew the route he would take. So when his shift was nearing its end, Crane drove south across town. He was getting a better mental map of the city now. He knew before the tablet confirmed it which route Acevedo would take to get across San Juan from Carolina. He merged onto Highway 17 and headed east, toward the university. Less than a minute later, Trace CR-1 turned onto the road a few miles up, headed west, straight toward him.

Crane switched on the receiver sitting in the Corolla's passenger seat. It lit up and began scanning for very high frequency, very short range burst transmissions. For a few minutes, it found nothing. Then, as the trace came closer, it started to blink and emit handshake tones. Crane kept his eyes on the road and the heavy rush-hour traffic. The receiver didn't need anything from him.

Then the receiver beeped and flashed a green light just as he saw the PR Police Taurus coming around a curve ahead. The transmitter under its front seat was obediently streaming everything it had recorded in the last twenty-four hours back to the receiver. Crane watched the Taurus sweep by, got the barest glimpse of the driver in his uniform paying no attention to one more car among the stream on the other side of the highway.

"Hello again, Sergeant," Crane muttered. "See you again soon."

The receiver gave a satisfied tone and went back to scanning. Crane switched it off. Then he took the next exit and headed north again, toward the sea and his hotel.

When he got there, he took his gear back up to his room and spread it out on the newly made bed. The housekeeping staff had left a chocolate on his pillow, and Crane let it slowly melt on his tongue as he played back the audio snippets from his bug.

Everything was time coded, so he could play it back alongside the tablet's playback of the GPS tracers. Nothing was happening in the morning. Just the occasional police call. Codes and call signs, nothing that mattered.

Crane fast-forwarded both systems, watched the red tracer pulses zip around the map at super speed. The next snatch of recorded voice blew past in a high-pitched squeak. Crane flashed back to the beginning.

It was Acevedo reporting that he was going on his lunch break. Jump.

His trace was stationary for a moment and then back on the move with another check in. Jump.

Another radio call and his reply. Jump.

Crane knew he had something even before the recording stopped, and he backed it up to play at normal speed. Even sped up, the voice sounded different. He wasn't on the radio, Crane realized. This was an incoming cell call.

"Yeah?" Acevedo's recorded voice said. A beat of silence. "Nothing. No, nothing since yesterday."

Another pause. Then, "He doesn't know shit. If he knew anything, he'd have hauled us in by now."

Crane wished he had a way to tap the phone itself. He really wanted to hear the other side of the conversation.

"Is what? Tuesday? Of course it's on ... kind of question is that? Of course we go. Nothing stops that. I—No! No, it isn't! Unless you don't want the money anymore. Fucking right. And you can explain to the Colombians how you thought maybe we should lay low for a while."

Crane took that as confirmation of what he'd already guessed. As state police officers in the district that included Luis Muñoz International Airport, the easiest way for cops on the take to make money would be to receive incoming shipments of narcotics, transfer them to the airport, and get them onto outbound flights for the US or Europe. Not the most imaginative way, but probably the easiest.

"No," Acevedo was saying on the recording, "I know. No, we don't need the van. We'll use my truck."

Crane smiled to himself. That would presumably be the F-150, also known as Trace PV-1.

"Yeah, I'll call you before then. Yeah. Bye."

Then the call ended.

Crane paused the machines and sat back against the head-board, enjoying the last hint of sweetness from the chocolate. He had them. He didn't know exactly what was going on, and he'd want to know a lot more before moving. But something—something that very likely involved smuggled drugs—was happening next Tuesday. He knew that. And he knew the F-150 pickup would be in the middle of it. The pickup with his tracer secured inside the wheel well, beaming its location to him twenty-four seven. All he had to do was follow it.

––––––––

Crane took it easy the next day. It was Sunday. There was little to do until Tuesday, when Acevedo and his cops would set off on their criminal adventure, meeting what Crane assumed would be Colombian drug smugglers. He'd find out for certain when he got there.

The only thing to do in the meantime was harvest the audio from the bug in Acevedo's cruiser, just to make sure he wasn't caught out by some change of plans. So while Acevedo worked his day shift, Crane sat out on the hotel's rear deck, in one of a long line of chaise lounges that looked out over the ocean. He didn't fit in with the other tourists scattered up and down the line. They were dressed to expose as much skin to the sun as possible, while Crane wore linen slacks and a vintage Hawaiian shirt. He was also the only one with a laptop. He was working the net, trying to sort out whom Acevedo might be working for, looking for any reason why drug smugglers would take an interest in Melissa's ecological census project. It was a fairly half-hearted search, if he was honest. He hadn't found anything even remotely useful. His plan was still to wreck the drug deal on Tuesday night and see what happened next. As he'd told Josh, shake the trees until something fell out.

So Crane enjoyed the midday sun, ignored the pair of vacationing college girls checking him out from down the line of lounge chairs, and waited.

A waiter came out with a tray of drinks for a table at the far end of the patio. On the way back, he asked if he could bring Crane anything, and Crane ordered a vodka martini. As the waiter went back inside, a hotel manager stepped out and looked over the deck. There was a nervous energy in the manager's posture, in the way he moved his hands. His eyes landed on Crane and then very deliberately flicked away again. The manager walked down the row, and Crane could sense his tension, could practically feel the beads of sweat forming on the back of his neck.

The manager glanced very quickly at Crane as he passed, and then carefully studied his shoes as he walked on. He stopped at a large deck umbrella, pretended to be dissatisfied with its positioning, and made some pointless adjustment. Then he walked down the rest of the deck and reentered the hotel through the far door.

Crane sighed and keyed a command into the laptop. The screen went blank, and the hard drive began encrypting itself with a key phrase that Crane kept only in his head. Upstairs, the tablet would be going through the same process and then shutting itself down, to be brought back to life only with a complicated password.

He folded the laptop shut and slid it under the chair. Then he got up, stretched, and took a few steps away from the chairs into a more open area of the deck. One of the college girls was staring at him with a look of frank invitation. Crane gave her a smile and an apologetic shrug. He suspected her plans were about to go dramatically off the rails.

Crane took a deep breath and let it out. And then the glass doors at both ends of the deck flew open, and the space was suddenly full of screaming police officers. Crane stood with legs apart and both hands raised as they swept toward him from both directions with guns drawn, waving back startled tourists and yelling for him not to move. The tourists screamed, covered themselves with towels, fled down the stairs to the beach. Behind them, the manager peered out from behind a door-frame, seemingly terrified by both the potential for violence and the damage to the hotel's reputation.

"Get on your knees! On your knees!" a cop screamed at Crane from ten feet away, gun leveled at him. A chorus of other cops echoed him. "On your knees."

Crane lowered himself to his knees. How the hell had they found him? The uniforms weren't PR Police, he noticed. These were local San Juan police, probably the Tourism Police unit that patrolled the upscale tourist areas like Condado. That was something, at least. However they'd found him, Acevedo had put him out to the police in general. That made whatever was going on more visible. And with all these rich tourists looking on, they couldn't get away with simply executing him and planting a throwaway gun on him. Already, he noticed, somebody had their phone out and was recording the scene. On the other hand, these men probably believed Crane had murdered a fellow officer during a traffic stop, and that was not good at all.

"Hands behind your head!" the first cop screamed, and again all the others backed him up with an overlapping chorus of commands. He crossed his wrists behind his head, and someone stepped up from behind and slapped him into cuffs. Then he was pushed roughly forward and fell onto the concrete. Hands patted him down, emptied his pockets.

The hotel guests were starting to protest now. With Crane secured, the manager apparently felt confident enough to come outside and start calming them. He pointed out to one of the officers where Crane had been sitting, and they retrieved his laptop.

A cop went through Crane's wallet and slipped the cash inside into his pocket. Then he knelt beside Crane's face, pressed his cheek hard into the concrete, and waved Crane's driver's license in front of his face. "John Crane," he said softly. "You're going to have a bad day. A really bad day. Do you understand these rights as I've explained them to you?"

Crane said nothing. He hadn't spoken since the shouting started. He didn't resist as two officers grabbed his arms and yanked him to his feet. They frog-marched him through the lobby, past gawking guests and staff. There were at least a dozen cops surrounding him, he'd been thoroughly searched, and his hands were cuffed behind his back. But most of the police still kept their guns pointed at him. They weren't taking any chances with him.

They marched him out the front doors, past the valet parking stand, to a van in San Juan police livery, and threw him unceremoniously into the back. The interior of the van was bare metal with no seats, only a metal screen separating the forward compartment and some rings with cuffs attached. Someone sat Crane up and fastened his cuffs to the wall.

Then the doors were slammed shut, and the van took off. The loose handcuffs clanked and rattled against the wall of the van as it pulled sharply out of the parking area.

Crane had to admit the cop had been right. It was starting to look like he was going to have a very bad day.

CHAPTER 20

Crane saw the daylight give way to darkness through the bit of windshield he could see, felt the van descend a ramp. They were bringing him into a police station, he assumed to a secure receiving area. Then the van lurched to a stop, and the two cops up front got out. Crane listened to the engine idling and through it the faint sound of voices. It sounded like there was some disagreement about what to do with him.

Whatever they had planned for him wasn't good. So far this had none of the elements of a proper arrest, so he assumed he wasn't going into the system. He wouldn't be able to make a phone call and bring down the wrath of Josh's high-powered attorneys. He wasn't going to see a judge and make his case for self-defense. He was on his own, and he was going to have to get himself out of this. He considered his options and waited for his moment.

The rear doors finally flew open, and someone unfastened him from the wall and dragged him out by his cuffs. He fell hard onto the concrete. At least half a dozen cops glared down at him. They hauled him to his feet. As Crane had thought, they were in an underground parking structure, but there were no cars, no other people. They could just shoot him here if they wanted.

Instead they marched him to an elevator where one of them used an override key to call the car. When it arrived, four cops got in with him, and they rode to the top of the building without stopping. They marched Crane down institutional beige hallways, past scuffed doors that led to cell wings, and through a series of security ports. Finally they passed through a door labeled "Special Holding." There were more cells here, bare cubes made of painted metal bars. Their footsteps echoed as they walked Crane to the back of the space. The cells weren't entirely empty, Crane realized. There was one man in the last cell—huge and muscled, wearing a prison jumpsuit. He looked at Crane with disinterest as the cops opened the cell and thrust him inside.

The cell door slammed shut, and then the cops turned and walked out the same way they'd brought him in. Crane watched them go. He heard the door close behind them, and Crane was alone with his new cellmate.

His arms were still cuffed behind his back.

He smiled at the huge man, who stood looking him up and down. "You having a bad day too?" Crane asked.

The other man stretched a bit and cracked his knuckles. He had a blond buzz cut and a scar on his chin. "Could be worse," he said. His accent was thick, Slavic.

"I'm Emil," he said. "You're John, yes?"

Crane assessed his tactical situation. The big man would be slow, but that wasn't much help in a confined space. And Emil looked like he was used to shrugging off punches. Punches Crane wouldn't be delivering with his hands cuffed behind him.

"You're a cop killer, huh?" said Emil. "Real tough guy."

Crane shrugged. "Don't believe everything you hear."

"Me, I never liked cops. Shoot all the bastards. Fine with me.

But they've got plans for you, so that means we have to talk before they come back."

"I see. What would you like to talk about?"

"The easy way is you draw me a map. Your contacts, who you report to, who they report to. Right up the chain. Companies, trusts, targets, the way the money moves. Don't leave anything out."

What the hell was he talking about? "Can you give me a little, um ... context there, champ?"

The punch was a roundhouse from the side opposite Crane. Emil pivoted his hips to get his body behind it and drove his fist into Crane's side, hard. Crane went over and hit the floor. He lay there gasping for a second. Great, he thought, the guy wasn't even slow.

Emil stepped closer. As he bent down to grab Crane's arm, Crane launched a kick at his knee. He felt it connect, but Emil shifted his weight and let the leg go back with the energy. He ended up dancing a few steps away as he regained his balance, but there was no serious damage.

"All right, let me get you started. Who was your contact in Bremen? The business at the Airbus plant? Who was that?"

Emil was the muscle, Crane thought. Whoever he worked for had to be the same one who had Acevedo and his cops on the payroll, the one who wanted Melissa's project killed for some reason Crane still couldn't guess. But they thought he was someone else entirely.

Crane was still trying to figure out how to use that information when Emil launched a kick that knocked him across the cell. He felt himself picked up by his handcuffs, and a stab of agony ran through his shoulders.

He tried to get his feet under him, but Emil swung him around and slammed his head into the cell bars.

"Shaller," Emil said. "Casse. Those names mean anything to

you?" He ran Crane's skull across the bars, and Crane felt blood dripping from his nose.

Then Emil dropped Crane on the floor. "You should talk to me. I'm the only friend you've got in this place."

"Yeah," said Crane, "I'm feeling it. There's a lot of love in this room."

"At least I need you alive for now."

Crane had to admit he had a point. "Okay," he said. "Tell me what you already know, and I'll fill in the gaps."

"Not how it works," said Emil, "but I'm fine with doing this the hard way if that's what you want."

He grabbed Crane's arms again and hauled him to his feet. Crane was tensing his muscles to try head-butting him when they both heard the door across the room open.

Emil hissed in annoyance. He pushed Crane away and stood with his arms crossed as a group of men walked quickly down the cells—a half-dozen cops led by a man in a suit. He looked angry.

"What the hell's going on back here?" the suit snapped. "Get this man out of here!"

A cop opened the cell door, and Emil moved back into a corner as they extracted Crane.

"You're bleeding," said the suit.

"I tripped," said Crane. "The balance is tricky with your arms like this."

The suit turned to the nearest cop. "Get those off him."

"Yes, sir."

Crane flexed his arms as the cuffs were removed, feeling the pain of returning circulation.

The suit did a head check toward Emil. "Who is that prisoner, and why is he here?"

Nobody answered.

"Jesus Christ." He turned to Crane. "Who is he? Did he do this to you?"

"Emil? Lord no, he's the only friend I've got in this place."

The man sighed. "Take him to interrogation room three."

———

They left Crane alone in the interrogation room. It was about what he'd expected. A small room with a one-way mirror on one wall. A small, scarred table and two battered chairs. There was a box of tissues Crane used to clean his face.

After a few minutes, the man in the suit entered and closed the door. "My name is Roberto Arias," he said as he sat across the table from Crane. He handed Crane a business card. Plain white stock with gold ink, a star-shaped logo. "I'm an investigator with the Special Investigations Bureau."

The SIB was a unit of the Puerto Rican Justice Department, Crane recalled. It handled organized crime, prison gangs, terrorism, and police corruption. There was certainly plenty of the latter around here.

"Your ID says your name is John Crane."

"That's right. I'm pleased to meet you, Agent Arias."

"I'm investigating a suspected criminal ring operating inside the Puerto Rico police," said Arias. "It's not pleasant, but it's the job, and I flatter myself that I'm good at my job, Mr. Crane. This investigation was going well. Then you appear, and if you'll pardon me speaking bluntly, suddenly my case turns into a complete clusterfuck."

Crane shrugged.

"The men here believe you're responsible for the killing of a PR Police officer named Hector Acosta."

Arias paused. His fingers went to his left ring finger as if to idly twist a wedding ring. But there was no ring, just a tan line where one had been.

"They believe Officer Acosta was working a case involving the theft of prescription drugs from Carolina Mercy Hospital. He was not."

Arias waited for Crane to say something, but Crane couldn't think of a thing to say that would advance his cause. On the other hand, he'd learned that if he just stayed quiet, the other person would usually fill the space themselves.

"What Acosta *was* doing," Arias continued, "was hanging around with a group of fellow officers. Sosa, Rodriguez, J., Gavilan, Rodriguez, B., and the ringleader, Sergeant Acevedo. They're up to something, but it isn't undercover work."

"What do you think they're involved in?" Crane asked.

Arias raised an eyebrow. "Nothing I can prove yet. I was hoping you might be able to help me."

"Go on."

Arias shook his head. His fingers went back to the missing ring.

"They do their patrols, they go home. Weekends they go to Hato Rey for a ball game, or fishing at Fajardo. They're men of routine. But recently their routine changed. They started spending a lot of time around a village called Benitez. No idea why. There's not a lot to do out there."

Again Crane made a noncommittal sound and waited. Arias was doing just fine without his help.

"On the day Acosta was killed, there was an incident at a research facility near there. A lot of shooting, several men from the look of it, with automatic weapons. The Carolina police recovered a great many bullets and casings. 7.62 mm Kalashnikov. According to the autopsy report, that was what killed Officer Acosta. I had a hunch. I inventoried the PR Police evidence room in Carolina. Several weapons were missing, Vietnamese AK-47 knockoffs."

Arias stopped, folded his hands in front of him, and looked at Crane with a smile. The moment dragged.

"So what do you conclude from that?" Crane asked.

"I think that, for reasons unknown, Sergeant Acevedo and his men attacked that laboratory. Acosta didn't come back. Somehow, he ended up twenty miles away, in a Cadillac belonging to the chief of thoracic surgery at Carolina Mercy."

"That is odd."

"Conclusions that follow: the director of the facility, Dr. Simon, lied when she made her statement to the police. Somebody was there when the attack happened. Somebody who was able to disarm a man with a Kalashnikov and kill him with his own gun. I don't see Dr. Simon or any of her staff doing that."

Crane grinned. "You don't know Dr. Simon very well."

Arias scowled briefly. Then a young woman in a suit came in and whispered something to him.

"You're sure?" he whispered, and glanced at Crane.

The woman nodded. Arias thanked her, and she left the room.

"Who the hell are you, Mr. Crane? Running your name and license number through the system is unusually ... unrewarding."

Crane hid his smile. That was a break. The old Hurricane Group blocks on his records must still be in place. Arias had sent inquiries and gotten something very vague and not especially helpful. He gathered Arias had seen that kind of result from a file search before and was drawing a conclusion. That was something Crane could use.

"I don't lead a terribly interesting life, I guess."

"I doubt that very much," said Arias. "Speaking hypothetically, if there were a ring of corrupt police officers in the Carolina district, what do you think they'd be doing?"

Crane let his voice take on a conspiratorial tone. He used to be an agent. He could still do a convincing imitation of one. "The airport's in Carolina. I'd think drug smuggling would prove lucrative. SIB probably isn't the only agency that would be interested in that."

Arias studied Crane for a long moment. "That's why we couldn't connect them with local drug gangs. They're not selling locally. They're transshipping them out."

"Hypothetically, of course," said Crane. "None of this is proven. But it makes your corruption case part of a bigger picture. Narcotics. Terror. The same channels could move materials, money, people."

"And that's why you're here." Arias nodded. He was filling in the picture for himself the way Crane hoped he would. "One of them's dead now. I have to settle that somehow."

"Well, I certainly didn't have anything to do with that," said Crane. "Any more than I'm discussing classified operational details with someone outside the clearance structure. Frankly, from what you've told me, it sounds like death by misadventure."

The door opened again. The same woman whispered something to Arias. He slammed his fist on the table. "Well, of course he is!"

The woman withdrew, and Crane gave Arias a questioning look. "Something wrong?"

"Your good friend Emil is gone. There's no record he was ever here. Any more than there is for you."

"You do have a problem here, don't you?" said Crane.

"I'll get you out," said Arias. "Make it clear that you're off limits. If I push things, I could put half the cops in this station away and suspend the rest without pay. They know it. The moment I showed up, you should have seen them jump." He shook his head. "There really are some good cops on this island."

"I believe it," said Crane.

Arias got Crane's effects in a plastic bag. There was just his wallet—with the cash missing—and his room keycard. Crane slipped them back into his pocket, and they left the room.

All eyes were on them as Arias walked Crane through the station and out the front doors. But only from an angle. Whenever Crane tried to make eye contact with someone, they quickly looked away and made themselves busy with something. Crane was fine with that.

"Do you know anything that would explain why they decided to attack a non-profit lab doing botanical research?" he asked as they walked.

"No," Arias admitted. "That still doesn't make any sense to me."

"Me either. Now Emil."

"Your only friend?"

"He's not a cop, and he's not from around here. Eastern Europe, from the accent. That suggest anything to you?"

"We've got some of them around," said Arias, "but the Ñetas control the drug action here. They don't leave a lot of room for competition."

"Would they work with cops?"

"Doubt it. Anything's possible, though."

Crane waved at a taxi, and it pulled up to the curb. "I'm glad you came by when you did, Agent Arias. I've got your card. Sorry I can't give you one of mine in return. But if I find anything that will help nail your dirty cops, I'll give you a call."

"I'd appreciate that."

They shook hands, and then Crane got into the cab, and it slid smoothly away.

In the back seat, Crane closed his eyes, let out a long breath. That could have gone very badly. He'd underestimated his enemy, and he'd failed to adjust to his new reality. He was a lone wolf now. If Arias hadn't been on the case, he might not have made it out of there. As it was, if Arias pushed hard enough to confirm that Crane was really the government presence he'd let him believe ...

Crane had the feeling he was wearing out his welcome in Puerto Rico.

CHAPTER 21

Emil was going to interrogate the man from Team Kilo, and Skala was very eager to hear what he had learned. But that was a short-term issue. His meeting with the Moravian Development Bank was a key part of his longer term strategy for growing the estate, commercializing the vineyards, and ultimately for raising his profile. So rather than postpone it, he took his laptop with him. He carried it into the bank and held it tightly against his body as they escorted him up to the top floor and into a wood and glass conference room.

There were four people on the bank's team. The older man was clearly the one in charge, with his graying temples and the more expensive suit. He wore diamond cufflinks, and his card called him the Director of Strategic Partnerships. Then there were two younger men and a slender woman with blonde hair and a pencil skirt. Skala sat across from them with a hard copy of their PowerPoint slides and a notepad with the bank logo. His laptop blinked silently beside him.

One of the junior men presented the details of a financial package that would enable him to build his estate from a small, regional vineyard into one of the leading wine producers in Central Europe. Skala liked what he was hearing.

Then the laptop pinged softly beside him, and Skala raised a hand to stop the young banker. Everyone around the table turned their eyes toward him, but Skala's world had shrunk down to the size and shape of his laptop.

"Forgive me," he said. "Do you have someplace I can take this?"

"Of course, Mr. Skala, of course," said the Director of Strategic Partnerships. "Anuska, show Mr. Skala to one of the guest offices."

"Come with me, Mr. Skala," the woman said. She led him down the hall. He watched her calves flex with each step of her high heels. She took him to a small office with a desk and a bookcase and a nice leather chair. A secretary brought a glass and a pitcher of cold water on a metal and leather tray. Then they left him alone, and the woman closed the door. He sat looking out the glass panel beside the door. Across the hallway was a maze of cubicles. He saw heads above the dividers, with telephone earpieces, their lips moving noiselessly.

He opened the laptop, keyed in his passwords, and brought up Emil's channel.

WHAT DO YOU HAVE FOR ME? he typed.

BAD NEWS, Zajic sent back. HE GOT AWAY.

Skala took in a sharp breath and forgot to exhale. He had escaped? How could that be?

HOW IS THAT POSSIBLE? I THOUGHT COPS ARRESTED HIM.

Zajic quickly related the highlights of what had happened. The cops had brought the man in. They'd given him to Zajic, who had been doing what he'd been told to do. Then someone new arrived, someone who brought the cops to heel in short order and pulled the man out of the cell before Emil could get much of anything out of him.

THIS MAN WHO RESCUED HIM, WHO WAS HE?

THEY SAID HE WAS SIB.

What the hell did that mean?

WHAT IS SIB?

LIKE GIBS.

The GIBS was the government watchdog agency that investigated police corruption. This was bad, Skala realized with growing horror. This was very bad, indeed. He had turned out every cop on the island to find the stranger, and they'd done it! They had put him in a cell with Emil. Emil would have pried the truth out of him, and then the cops would have made him vanish forever. But within minutes, an agent from the fucking state security police swooped in and plucked him out of the cell. Only Team Kilo would have that kind of pull. This was even worse than he'd feared.

"Fuck," he said out loud. His anger and fear fed off each other and grew. "Fuck!" His voice grew louder as he rose out of the chair until he was shouting, "Mother fucking son of a bitch!"

He swept the pitcher and water glass off the desk in a rage. They shattered against the near wall and sprayed water everywhere. Outside in the cube farm, worried faces turned toward the window.

DOES HE KNOW WHO YOU ARE? he typed, trembling with rage to the point that he was barely able to find the keys.

NO.

Maybe Emil was right about that, Skala thought. But maybe he wasn't. So far, Team Kilo seemed to know everything. If they connected Emil to him ...

The door opened, and the woman leaned in. "Sir, is everything all right?"

Behind her, the cube workers had risen and formed a group in the hallway, looking on like they'd look at a wrecked train.

"No, it's not fucking all right!" Skala bellowed, advancing to the door and driving her back in alarm. "Get the fuck out!" She turned and fled down the hall. He glared at the knot of junior employees gawping at him.

"Get back to work!" he shouted. "Get the hell away from me, or you'll find your fucking kids in the river."

Then he slammed the door so the glass rattled in its frame.

I'M PULLING THE PLUG. NO MORE. IF YOU SEE HIM AGAIN, KILL HIM.

He typed quickly and waited for Emil's reply, watching his fingertips shake above the keyboard.

UNDERSTOOD.

MIGHT HAVE TO BRING YOU HOME. STAND BY.

Then he closed the laptop and gathered it up. When he stepped out into the hallway, the Director of Strategic Partnerships was striding toward him with his two junior executives in his wake.

"Mr. Skala, you're very upset. Let me—"

"You've never seen me upset!" he snapped as he brushed by them. "Meeting is cancelled."

They followed after him as he hurried out to the elevators and punched for a car.

"Yes, I think it's best if we reschedule for a time when you're calmer," said the Director of Strategic Partnerships. "We owe our employees a professional en—"

"Where is the fucking elevator!" he screamed in the man's face. All three of them recoiled.

A moment later, the elevator chimed, and the doors slid open. Skala stepped in by himself and punched for the lobby without a word.

This was a disaster, he thought as the doors slid closed. All he'd done was focus Team Kilo's attention on himself. He needed to think. He needed time to think. About what to do and how to defend himself if they managed to follow the trail back to Brno. He needed to get back where he was safe, out of the city.

He would go back to his estate. And if anything moved that he didn't like the look of, it would get its goddamn head blown off.

CHAPTER 22

Crane sat on his bed in a cheap motel outside Carolina. It was a significant step down from the Vanderbilt, where he'd checked out as soon as he got back from jail. It was best all around. The hotel was relieved to get rid of him without the unpleasantness of evicting him, and Crane wanted to drop off the grid. Agent Arias had said he'd keep the cops off his back, but Crane couldn't rely on that. Arias' job was dealing with cops who didn't do what they were told.

So he'd found a struggling motel on a side road off the main highway. He'd changed rental cars again and parked the new one behind the building, out of sight from the road. He'd identified a couple of the ubiquitous roadside bars called *chinchorros* within walking distance that offered good food and cheap beer, and he'd gone to ground.

But now it was Tuesday, the sun was setting, and it was almost time to move. Crane had spent the last couple days in ratty cargo shorts and T-shirts, walking down the highway in flip flops for meals, and generally blending in. But now he'd changed into his operations gear. Black, plenty of pockets. He looked like a Hurricane Group agent again. He let that brief moment of nostalgic regret wash over him. He'd worked incredibly hard to become a field agent, but Hurricane was gone now. It wasn't his fault, and there was nothing he could do about it. But he could still do good here, with Hurricane or on his own.

He'd set an alarm on his tablet to alert him if Trace PV-1—Acevedo's F-150 pickup—moved. Now it was beeping insistently. He watched the truck roll out of its local neighborhood and onto a crosstown expressway, headed in his direction.

It was time to go.

Crane doubted he'd be coming back here. He'd already packed his duffel bag, and now he loaded it into the trunk. He re-checked his mission gear, just as they'd taught him at Hurricane. He dropped the room key on the nightstand and left the room behind. Five minutes later, he was driving east on 66 in the twilight, moving slow in the right-hand lane and watching his tablet as the F-150 gradually overtook him on Highway 3 to the north.

It passed him near Bartolo, just before 66 merged into 3 and deposited Crane onto the same road, a couple miles behind the truck. This would do, he thought, and maintained speed to keep his distance as they headed east into the night.

Crane had concluded they were going to Fajardo well before the F-150 exited the highway and took to side roads. Fajardo was at the very northeastern tip of the island. From his reading, Crane remembered there were some tourist spots there, a lagoon, and some high-end resorts with private beaches.

He followed the truck through a small town called Soroco and on toward the coast. He had the truck in sight now. His headlights would be visible in Acevedo's rearview. At some point, he expected the truck to go somewhere where a vehicle following would become obvious. He zoomed in the tablet's map. They were running out of roads, fast. There was a small cluster of winding side streets coming up on his right, pressed against the south end of a nature preserve. In the middle of the preserve was a large, round body of water. The map called it Laguna Grande, or large lagoon. That seemed a bit literal to Crane. On the other hand, along the lagoon's western edge, a narrow spit of sand separated it from the Bahia las Cabezas, or Bay of Heads. Crane had no idea where that name had come from. Perhaps less imagination was better in this case.

A narrow dirt road cut off to the left and headed up into the park along the narrow strip of land between the lagoon and the sea. The F-150 braked and turned down that road as Crane suspected it would. Crane had followed as far as he could. He continued on past the turn and passed a trio of cars parked on the narrow shoulder. He'd seen two of them before, the Charger and the silver Mustang.

"The gang's all here," he murmured. He took it slow into the neighborhood and found signs telling him where to park for the "Bioluminescent Bay." He passed a truck pulling out, towing a trailer stacked high with plastic kayaks. Ideas started forming in Crane's mind. He had thought he would need to walk down the road after Acevedo, but perhaps there was a better way to approach the scene.

He parked in a nearly empty lot and got out. The place looked like it would be packed during the day, but it was well after midnight now. Most of the food stalls and souvenir shacks were closed, but there was still a party atmosphere about the place. Lights were strung between the palm trees. Salsa music drifted on the cool night breeze off the water. Small knots of tourists stood around wearing life jackets or carrying backpacks. Across the lot, a group was lining up to board a shuttle bus back to one of the area resorts. Near a still-operating food truck, a couple danced to the music while others talked animatedly about the adventure they'd just had.

Crane checked his GPS, confirmed where he needed to go.

He strolled down the beach that circled around an inlet shielded from the open sea. The water was studded with the ghostly white hulls of anchored sailboats. Beyond them was darkness so deep it looked almost solid. The nature preserve. Even in the middle of this developed, crowded tourist area, it offered a nearly impenetrable veil of trees and vines that could hide nearly anything.

The beach was lined with clusters of kayaks belonging to the various tour companies that worked the lagoon. A few guides lingered about, making sure to collect all the life jackets they'd handed out, or picking up discarded glow sticks. But farther down, Crane found a group of a dozen or so unattended kayaks roped together into a line.

Crane looked around, made sure no one was looking his way. Then he quickly cut one of them loose and pushed it out into the gentle surf. He moved his pack around to his chest, climbed into the kayak, and set out across the small bay.

In almost no time, he was well away from the beach, paddling among the darkened sailboats that rocked gently in the swells. On the other side of the bay was a small channel through the mangroves that let the lagoon drain into the sea. There was no moon, and Crane could barely make out the tree-line against the sky. He had no idea where the channel mouth was. But between his GPS and the night vision goggles in his pack, he would find it.

He paddled on through the flotilla of sailboats and headed into the wall of utter darkness ahead.

He didn't see a figure lying on the deck of one boat, watching him as he passed. After he left the boat behind, Crane was looking intently for the mouth of the channel up ahead, and didn't notice the glow of a smartphone screen.

———

Acevedo pulled his truck off the road, as far back into the belt of trees as he could without getting stuck, and killed the lights. The engine slowly ticked as he got out and let his eyes gradually adjust to the dark. There was water on both sides of him. The lagoon was just away to his right through the trees, the beach and the Bahia las Cabezas across the road to his left. It was a place Acevedo always found foreboding, even with its beauty.

"Over here," came Sosa's soft voice from the trees. The others had parked down on the paved road and walked up. They'd be at the lagoon to meet the Little Russian. Zajic lived aboard one of the boats on the other side of the lagoon—Acevedo supposed he wanted to be close to where his business took place. And he always insisted on taking his dinghy up the channel and across the lagoon. Whatever. As long as he was here.

And he was, Acevedo saw as his eyes adjusted. Zajic was pulling the dinghy out of the lagoon, up onto the sandy spit. Then he took a canvas bag out of the small boat and walked toward them. Acevedo's men clustered around him. One less this time. The Little Russian looked grim, Acevedo thought. The omens were not good for this deal.

"Everything ready?" Zajic asked gruffly.

"Sure. We're fine," he said. "What happened with the guy who killed Hector? Did you deal with him?"

"Shut up about that," said Zajic. "Nothing to the Colombians, either."

Acevedo wasn't stupid. Of course he wasn't going to tell the Colombians his problems. But he could tell it had gone badly. Zajic was being even more of a prick than usual. That meant things weren't going to plan, and it was gnawing at him.

They walked back up to the treeline, maybe twenty yards ahead of the truck, and looked out across the bay. He couldn't see anything in this darkness, but he knew the Colombians' boat would be out there somewhere. It would be running without lights, moving dark and quiet, swerving in close to shore, but ready to vanish like a ghost if things went wrong.

Zajic opened his bag and took out a tripod and a battered directional antenna. He used a compass to orient the antenna out to sea, and then plugged in a little Motorola Family Radio handset, like the ones the tourists used to keep track of their kids at the beaches. Boosting it with an external antenna that way was illegal, of course, but that hardly mattered under the circumstances.

"Here, hold this where I can see it," Zajic said to the nearest man, Fat Rodriguez. He handed him a notepad and then held a penlight so he could read it. He thumbed the mic on the little Motorola and read off a sequence of numbers.

They waited. The handset hissed with static. Zajic swore under his breath. He keyed the mic and repeated the numbers. A moment later, the handset crackled, and a voice read back another sequence. Zajic didn't bother to check it, Acevedo noticed. That made sense, he thought. Who else would be out here reading off numbers on the Family Radio Service band in the dead of night?

Zajic snatched the notepad back from Rodriguez, put it and his penlight back into his pocket, and started to break down the antenna.

Somewhere out there in the darkness, Acevedo knew a black zodiac was being lowered into the water, loaded with armed men and illegal narcotics. He always had a wild fantasy of arresting the Colombians when they came ashore. It would be a huge bust. He'd be in the papers. He'd be a hero.

He smiled to himself. Well, until they killed him, anyway. No, that path was closed to him now. Nothing to do but wait for the zodiac to hit the beach, load the drugs into the back of his truck, let the Little Russian sign off on everything and pay everyone.

Except the Little Russian was looking at his phone.

"Fuck me," he said. He looked out to sea nervously and then back at his phone.

"What's wrong?" Acevedo asked.

"I have to go."

"What the hell?" Acevedo hissed. "Now? You got somewhere else to be now?"

"Trouble. Stall them. Tell them I'm getting the money or something. Shit, shit, shit."

Zajic dropped the antenna. He reached into his bag and pulled out an assault rifle. Then he was running down to his dinghy in the lagoon and dragging it out into the water.

"I see them," said Old Rodriguez quietly, peering out into the bay. "They're coming."

"Shit," Acevedo said under his breath. This just got worse and worse. Acevedo led his men down to the beach.

"Let me do the talking," he said, trying to sound like he knew what he was going to say.

CHAPTER 23

Crane found the mouth of the channel and steered the kayak into it. It was perhaps twenty feet wide, only a few feet deep—anything with much more draft than his kayak wouldn't be able to clear it at all. Thick forest lined both banks, the branches interweaving above to form a tunnel of trees and vines. The night air was cooling, and the channel was still. He was paddling against the outflow, but it was so gentle he barely noticed.

On a moonless night like this, it was pitch black inside the tunnel. Crane fished in his pack for the night vision goggles and put them on. As he flipped the switch, the channel lit up in a pale, ugly green. Crane had always hated night vision green, but at least he could navigate by it. He moved up the passage, listening to the sounds of frogs and the soft noise of his paddle blades slicing into the water.

The goggles were giving him strange traces off his paddles, he realized after a few dozen strokes. He tapped them a couple times, to no effect. Then something moved ahead of him. A large iguana hunting at the channel's edge startled at Crane's approach and tore up out of the water and into the cover of the trees. The water around it boiled with light. What the hell was that?

Crane switched off the goggles and lowered them to his chest. Then he almost laughed. The water still glowed. He took another stroke, and the water glowed as it swirled around the blade. Bioluminescence! There were millions of microorganisms in the water that gave off a faint glow when something disturbed them. That was what the tourists came to see, and now Crane understood why. There was something eerie but delightful about the water's glow as he swirled his hand around in it.

He took a few more paddle strokes and then reminded himself he wasn't here for fun. And he needed to see more than just the water. He put the goggles back on and started off up the channel again.

The passage took a sharp left and then turned back to the right in a long, sweeping curve, but he was moving more or less straight north overall. After one last turn to the left, the channel led straight out of the tunnel and into the lagoon itself. The lagoon was large, roughly rectangular, and ringed by forest. The visibility was slightly better here, out from under the tree cover, but not much on a night this dark. It was a perfect night for smuggling. Crane scanned the shoreline but couldn't make out anything.

He moved farther out into the lagoon. The water still glowed around his paddles, and he could see pale, gauzy clouds of light beneath him. Schools of small fish were feeding.

Then there was a bright flash ahead. The bullet plowed past him before he heard the crack. The second actually hit the bow of the kayak with an alarming snap. Then there was a third. Crane ducked down to lower his profile as much as possible. Then he dug the paddle into the water and rowed like hell. There was no cover here, nothing but still, open water. His best chance was to be a moving target.

More bullets slashed through the air around him. The flashes were coming from out on the water itself. A boat. There it was. A small inflatable. One figure inside, rising to fire a rifle. Crane ducked low, and a three-shot burst passed behind him. The shooter didn't have night vision, he realized. He was mostly shooting at the luminosity Crane stirred up as he moved. Bad tactical decision. But that would be little consolation if he got a lucky shot.

Crane took off the goggles and stuffed them back into his pack. He slipped the pack off and set it carefully on the kayak's prow. The shooting had stopped, for now at least. The shooter had realized he was firing blind and wasting bullets. But he'd be on the move. Crane scanned the water. He thought he saw a low dark shape in the distance and the dim line of its luminescence as it moved through the water. He slipped his legs out of the kayak, careful not to dump his pack into the lagoon, and then edged into the water. It was cool but not uncomfortably so. It glowed faintly around him as he moved. There was nothing he could do about that.

Crane moved his pack into the interior of the kayak just as the gunman decided to try another shot. This one slapped hard into the side of the kayak. He was getting luckier, or else just closer.

There was a cord tied to the kayak's prow. Crane took it and dove beneath the surface, towing the kayak behind him as he swam. Every stroke created a bright cloud around him. This was no good, he realized. He'd be visible from the surface.

As if to confirm his fears, a bullet drilled past him like a comet. Then another and another, straight lines of bright light lancing through the water around him. Crane went still and let himself sink deeper, trying to not stir up any more light than he had to. He hit sandy bottom and let himself sink into a crouch. He guessed he was maybe twelve or fifteen feet beneath the surface. He knew this wasn't something he could keep up. He'd been trained to hold his breath longer than most people could, and remaining still would help conserve his oxygen as well as reduce his glow. But he couldn't stay down here forever. He was already feeling the lack of air.

Above him, he saw the angry boil of light that was the other boat's wake. It was an inflatable dinghy. From the way it lit up the surface, he guessed it had an electric trolling motor. He hung still, his arms and legs limp. He heard the muffled sound of another burst from the rifle, but this time the bullets didn't light up the water around him. They'd been aimed at the kayak itself. The shooter was confused. He'd lost his target. He'd be wondering if he'd hit Crane after all. Was his body slumped down in the kayak, invisible in the dark? Or was he just playing dead there, waiting for his chance to shoot back?

The angry glow calmed as the shooter turned off his trolling motor. The boat slowed as it glided toward the kayak. Crane urged him to hurry as his lungs screamed for air.

Then he felt a gentle tug on the cord in his left hand. He pictured what must be going on above. The dinghy bumping into the abandoned kayak. The shooter putting down his rifle, leaning over the side to pull it alongside and see what was there. The dinghy tipping slightly with his weight.

Crane pushed off the bottom with all his strength, exploding up toward the surface, toward air, toward the barely visible outline of a black rubber boat on a dark night.

The boat was formed from a single pontoon, folded more or less in half to form a wedge-shaped hull. It had a vinyl floor and a transom at the rear to keep the water out. Crane hit one side of the pontoon hard and felt the boat nearly flip. He felt the weight of the body inside it propel out over the side. He heard a man's scream, as he burst into the night air and let his breath out in a great roar and then breathed fresh air back in. The other man struggled to get his body oriented and under control, and the water lit up around him as he thrashed. In an instant, Crane recognized his friend Emil.

Emil stabilized himself by grabbing the side of the kayak, managed to tread water. He saw Crane and bellowed in rage. Crane pulled his boot knife from its sheath and swam for him.

Emil saw him coming. As Crane thrust with the knife, he managed to slam his forearm into the inside of Crane's wrist and knock the knife away. Even in the water, his strength was remarkable. But all that muscle was heavy. Crane took a deep breath and held it as they sank beneath the surface again. Emil clawed at Crane, and they grappled as one large, thrashing shape while the water boiled and burned around them. Emil had size on Crane, and he was even fast. But here those qualities worked against him. The water muted his strength, and his mass was dragging him down.

Crane didn't fight back; he clung to Emil like a tired boxer, preserving his energy and letting Emil exhaust himself. He moved only to defend himself.

They sank deeper and deeper. Crane could make out Emil's face in the bioluminescent glow, could see him start to panic. Emil tried to disengage as they hit bottom, but now Crane counterattacked. He delivered a hard, fast punch to Emil's abdomen, pushing up against the diaphragm, forcing out the air he was fighting so hard to hold inside.

Emil exhaled a cloud of glowing bubbles and breathed in water. He looked at Crane in terror. He tried to push away and head for the surface, but he couldn't shake Crane. His struggles grew weaker. At last another stream of bubbles came from him and then stopped. His limbs went limp. Crane released him and let him sink down to the sand. Then he pushed off and broke the surface with a deep breath.

He was beside the dinghy. He pulled himself up onto the

pontoon and collapsed there, breathing hard. He looked down into the water. It was still and dark below. Nothing glowed in the darkness there. Nothing moved.

Finally he pulled himself the rest of the way into the boat. Emil's assault rifle was still lying in the bottom. It was a Czech CZ-805. He found three more magazines in a plastic box secured under the dinghy's aluminum seat.

Crane pulled the kayak over and recovered his pack full of gear. Then he turned on the electric trolling motor and headed back across the lagoon. This wasn't finished yet.

CHAPTER 24

The zodiac hit the beach, and the Colombians leaped over the side into the calf-deep surf and hauled the boat up beyond the tide line. There were six of them, each in black, each with a submachine gun. Acevedo thought they looked like a squad of action movie commandos.

The first man up the beach was balding and missing two fingers on his left hand. That was Vasquez. He was always the man in charge. He might have seen one or two of the others before. They didn't matter. Vasquez would do all the talking.

"Good evening," said Acevedo, offering Vasquez his hand. Vasquez ignored it. He looked over Acevedo's men standing in a rough line behind him.

"Where's Zajic?" he said.

"He's coming."

Vasquez looked displeased. "He did the radio check. Where is he now?"

The other Colombians were still back at the boat. They'd started unloading boxes onto the beach, but Vasquez made a gesture and they stopped. They moved up behind their leader, scanning the trees.

"It's okay," Acevedo said quickly. "Everything's fine. He's checking something out, and he'll be right back. He wants to make sure everything goes right. That's all."

This was bad, he thought. Very bad. Zajic was the guy with the money. The guy the Colombians were here to do business with. He and his men were just cops. He kept his hands out away from his sides and hoped to God the others had the sense to do the same.

"We're all here to do business, right? He'll be here by the time you're unloaded."

Vasquez looked uncertain. He had his good hand on the receiver of his gun. The others were taking their lead from him.

"We don't touch anything until he comes back and pays you," said Acevedo. "Then you can be gone and we'll load. That's our risk."

Vasquez made eye contact and held it, sizing him up. If they made it through this, Acevedo decided, he was going to kick the Little Russian's ass, and to hell with him and his boss.

Vasquez relaxed his posture, took his other hand off the gun. Acevedo felt the tension easing slightly.

Then there was the crack of Zajic's rifle from somewhere out on the lagoon.

The Colombians freaked. Everyone had their guns out now, leveled at him and his men.

"Whoa! Whoa!" Acevedo held his hands up. "It's cool, it's all cool. That's him! He's taking care of it. He'll be back with your money."

"You keep still," said Vasquez. He gestured to his men, and two of them ran wordlessly across the road toward the shore of the lagoon. The others kept Acevedo and his men covered. A short burst echoed from the lagoon, and then another.

"Everybody just stay calm, all right. Someone was poking around before. Zajic's taking care of it."

There were more gunshots.

"What have you got?" Vasquez shouted to the two men on the bank of the lagoon.

"Flashes on the water," someone shouted back. "Too far out to see."

"That's him," said Acevedo. "He's taking care of it. Everything's going to be okay."

Vasquez ignored him. He paced in a tight circle in the sand, weighing alternatives, muttering to himself.

Finally he turned and shouted toward his two men at the lagoon. "Pablo, Chivo, get back here!"

Acevedo's instincts told him to get out of there. He took a step sideways, away from Vasquez, and then another.

"Deal's off," Vasquez said. "Clean up."

"No!" Acevedo shouted and dove for the sand. There was a flash of light from Vasquez's weapon, and he felt the bullet rip through his abdomen. Acevedo hit the sand and lay there, stunned as a firefight erupted around him. Two of the Colombians opened up with their little machine pistols, spraying bullets everywhere. He saw Fat Rodriguez go down in a spray of blood. Sosa managed to get his pistol out of his belt, but another burst cut him down before he could get a shot off.

Old Rodriguez had managed to get behind a palm tree. He fired two shots from behind it but hit nothing. Bullets slammed into the tree trunk, shredded the bark.

Acevedo felt the pain begin, a burning in his gut that kept getting worse when he thought it hurt as badly as it was going to. His luck had finally run out, he thought. No house by the sea. No fishing boat for him. He was going to die here, and Emilia would have to raise the children alone. She would know what he had been.

Old Rodriguez always was a tough son of a bitch. Acevedo saw him get hit, but he kept shooting back, swearing at the top of his voice. But he only had so many clips, and there were six of them. Already they were moving to outflank him. In a few more seconds, they'd have him. It was one more thing for Acevedo to take to his grave. He'd gotten all his friends killed for nothing.

Then two of the Colombians went down, one right after the other with two short bursts. The others looked around for the new enemy.

Acevedo saw him first, a tall man striding through the trees with an assault rifle. The gun flashed, and another of the Colombians went down. The others scattered, looking for cover. Vasquez fired back, but the man wasn't where he'd been a moment before.

Acevedo knew instantly who he was. This was the man who had killed Hector. The man he'd fired at and missed back at the lab. The man everyone was so scared of.

Acevedo felt his consciousness starting to fade. He was losing blood fast. He heard the gunshots as a single, long roar that sounded like it was coming from a distance. The night lit up with muzzle flashes like fireworks. Acevedo saw the dark-haired man turn, fire, move, fire. He heard someone—one of the Colombians?—calling for someone named Ana. He looked for Old Rodriguez and saw what he thought was his body slumped in the sand near the shredded tree.

Acevedo felt the darkness swallow him, and everything went quiet.

When he woke, he was sitting up against a tree trunk. The dark-haired man was squatting beside him, pressing somebody's shirt into his wound.

"Hold this here," he said.

Acevedo looked at him in mute incomprehension for a moment. Then he carefully moved his hand to hold the bloody shirt against his side.

The dark-haired man pulled a field bandage from a pocket

on his thigh. The paper packaging was soaking wet. The man tore the soggy wrapper away and peeled off the plastic backing. He looked down and realized Acevedo had let the shirt fall away from his side. Blood pulsed weakly out to soak his clothes.

He was trying feebly to put the shirt back in place when the dark-haired man moved his hand away and pressed the bandage into place.

"That won't save you," the man said. "Another hour maybe. You can die here with your friends or I can call for help. If you make it, you'll spend a long time in prison. It's your call. What do you want me to do?"

Acevedo couldn't help laughing, even though it caused stabbing pain in his side. He was being given a choice of whether to live or die. That was unexpected. It was funny because he'd probably screw it up. He'd been making a lot of bad decisions lately.

———

Crane stood on the beach, surrounded by the dead. There were four cops from Acevedo's ring. The smugglers had taken them out, and that wasn't surprising. The smugglers had submachine guns, H&K MP-5s mostly, though one had actually been carrying an honest-to-God KRISS Vector, mainly for its looks, Crane suspected. The cops, on the other hand, were mostly armed with semiauto pistols. A Glock, a Smith and Wesson. The one who'd managed to get off most of the shots for his side had an old Army .45 M1911. It had been a one-sided fight.

He surveyed the scene. There were ten bodies, shell casings and guns everywhere. A boat and a pile of drugs down by the waterline. It was one hell of a crime scene. Agent Arias would have a field day.

Then Crane heard a faint groan behind him and turned to see Acevedo quivering on the sand. One was still alive, anyway.

He rolled Acevedo onto his back, pulled him over to the nearest tree, and leaned him up against it. Acevedo mumbled something as his head lolled on his shoulder. Crane found a Glock in his belt and tossed it away. Then he checked his wounds. One shot, through his intestinal cavity. He'd be bleeding and oozing fluids internally. Without serious medical help, Acevedo was going to die.

Crane considered leaving him to his fate. This man had tried more than once to kill him. But no, that fight was over. Acevedo was no longer a combatant. Besides, he might know something useful, and Crane was out of people to question.

He cut a black T-shirt off the nearest body and pulled Acevedo's own bloody shirt away from the wound. Acevedo raised his head and looked at him in confusion. He pressed the balled up shirt into Acevedo's hand and pressed it against the wound.

"Hold this here," he said.

Acevedo nodded and weakly pressed the shirt against his side. Not nearly hard enough, but that was no surprise in his condition.

Crane pulled a field dressing from a side pocket, tore away the soggy wrapper, and peeled away the backing.

He moved Acevedo's hand away and pressed the bandage into place.

"That won't save you," he said. "Another hour maybe. You can die here with your friends or I can call for help. If you make it, you'll spend a long time in prison. It's your call. What do you want me to do?"

Acevedo looked at him blankly for a moment, and then he started to laugh. Crane raised an eyebrow.

"I know who you are," said Acevedo. "Who else could do all this? You're the one they're all so scared of. Team Kilo."

"No idea what you're talking about," he said. He patted Acevedo down, found his cell phone. "You want me to make the call or not? Think it over. Might be a tough decision."

"No, no," said Acevedo. "Make the call. When death himself saves your life ..."—he coughed and winced at the pain—"he must have a reason."

"I do. You want me to call help, you tell me what you know."

"We take the drugs to the airport," Acevedo began.

"I know that. This is the delivery, you get them into the airport, you've got people there to get them onto the planes. That's not what I'm after. I want to know about the gene bank in Benitez. What the hell was that about?"

"I don't know," said Acevedo. "That was bullshit. They weren't doing anything. Orders from the Little Russian and his asshole boss."

Crane sighed. Of course the cops had no idea why they'd been turned loose on a harmless research project. They were just following orders.

"The boss have a name?"

Acevedo coughed again and winced. He was silent for a long moment. "Just the boss."

"The Little Russian. Is his name Emil?"

"Zajic. He lives on a boat over in the bay."

That explained why he'd come in a dinghy instead of driving like everyone else.

"But you killed him, didn't you?" Acevedo said around a wet cough.

"What's the boat called?"

"*Lucky* something. *Lucky Break*?"

Maybe there would be something on Zajic's boat that would point to his boss. And maybe not, but Crane had all that Acevedo could give him.

He powered up the phone and made the call. He told the

dispatcher how to find the narrow road between the lagoon and the sea, and gave them Acevedo's name. They assured him they'd have help there within minutes.

Crane slipped Acevedo's phone back into his shirt pocket.

"Help's coming," he said. "It's going to take them twenty minutes, anyway. That's what I can do for you."

Acevedo nodded.

As Crane turned away, Acevedo said, "You going after the boss?"

"That's right."

"You find that son of a bitch, shoot him for me."

"Get in back of the line," said Crane. He bent down to pick up a discarded Glock and checked the magazine. Then he walked back to the lagoon, pulled the dinghy out into the water, and set off into a nebula of luminescence.

CHAPTER 25

The name of the boat turned out to be the *Lucky Strike II*. Close enough, Crane thought. He steered up to the stern, climbed aboard, and tied the dinghy to the rail. *Lucky Strike II* was a thirty-six-footer, all white, the sails secured against the mast in a navy blue cover. The boat was dark and silent. Crane heard only faint voices across the water from one of the other boats anchored all around. The sea slapped gently against the hull.

Crane kept the Glock down alongside his thigh in his left hand as he opened the door that led below the deck. He stepped down into darkness and stooped so his head would clear the ceiling.

"Emil? Is that you?"

A light came on, enough to see by. There was a small galley to his right, a seating area to the left. Clothes and various belongings were scattered on the floor. The voice came from behind a curtain ahead of him. Then it was pulled aside, and a woman looked out from a V-berth in the bow.

She gasped and ducked back behind the bulkhead. "Don't hurt me!"

"I won't," said Crane. "You're Emil's girlfriend?"

She said nothing. Crane opened a cabinet, found only dishes and some supplies.

"I'm afraid Emil won't be coming back."

He turned to the small seating area, found a few scraps of paper on the table, but nothing that caught his interest.

"You should also know that the cops are going to be swarming this boat in a few minutes."

"Shit," he heard her say. "Oh shit, shit, shit." Then the sound of her scrambling across the bed, opening a locker. Crane put the Glock away and then pulled the curtain back. She froze in the act of stuffing clothes into a duffel bag. She was young, dark haired, wearing lacy shorts and a baby doll tee. Crane tried to look reassuring. After a moment, she went back to furiously cramming her things into the bag.

Crane sank to his knees and looked under the berth. There was a safe tucked in beneath it, with a combination keypad.

"You know the combination to this?"

The girl swallowed, shook her head. Then she said, "I know where he keeps it," in a voice that was barely above a whisper. She pointed to a drawer in a wooden desk forward of the galley.

The drawer was locked, so Crane found a carving knife in the galley and forced it. Inside were some keys, a notepad, the usual loose junk, and a business card with what had to be the safe combination in pencil on the back.

The card was from a company called Deštnik Biologicka, with an address in Brno in the Czech Republic. It identified Emil Zajic, in both Czech and English, as "Director, Mergers and Acquisitions."

Crane had a hard time imagining Zajic as a business executive.

He pocketed the card and returned to the safe. The girl had

finished packing everything she could reach and had pulled on a pair of jeans and a more substantial shirt. Now she sat on the bed, pressed as far back into the bow as she could get with the bag in front of her.

She watched Crane kneel at the foot of the bed and punch numbers into the safe's keypad.

"What happened to Emil?" she finally said.

"He tried to kill me."

She accepted that in silence.

The safe's locking bolts snapped back with a solid, metallic sound, and Crane opened the door. Inside were several bundles of hundred dollar bills, a CZ-75 pistol with a suppressor, a watch that proved to be a Breitling Navitimer, and a black Moleskine notebook. Crane flipped through the notebook, but it was in Czech, which he didn't read.

He tossed the cash to the girl, and it quickly vanished into her bag. He pocketed the notebook; Josh would be able to find someone to translate it. The watch was far too nice to be abandoned to some evidence locker. Crane put it on his wrist. The silenced pistol might come in handy as well, he decided.

A quick search of the boat didn't reveal anything else, and Crane didn't know how far behind him the authorities might be if Acevedo had lived to tell them where he'd gone.

He held his hand out to the girl. "Come on, I'll take you to shore."

She didn't take his hand, but she did follow him up onto the deck and let him help her over the rail into the dinghy. She sat in silence as he steered them to land and pulled up near where the kayaks had been beached earlier in the night.

They stood at the waterline for a moment, looking out at the boats, lit by the strings of lights in the trees behind them.

"He was good to me," the girl said at last.

"I'm sure he was," said Crane.

Then she shouldered the duffel bag and walked away into the night, and Crane made the call to Agent Arias of the SIB.

———

It was mid-afternoon the next day when Crane pulled up outside the little guest house in Ocean Park. Melissa's Jeep was parked down the street.

A middle-aged man in shorts and flip flops opened the door and called Melissa down. Then he disappeared into the backyard and left them in the living room. Melissa seemed unable to settle herself. She offered Crane a drink. When he declined, she went into the kitchen, anyway, and Crane heard her rattling around in the cabinets and drawing water. He wandered the room, looking at the owners' personal photos and the decorations.

Melissa eventually came back with a pitcher of ice tea and a couple glasses. Crane took one, since she'd gone to the trouble.

"Is everything okay?" he asked.

"I guess that's what I'm supposed to ask you," she said. "You kind of went dark for a while, and now you're here. Has something happened?"

"I wanted to let you know I think it's safe to start rebuilding your facility. Getting in new equipment and so on."

"That's going to take a while."

"I know. This isn't over. I still don't know who was behind it or why they went after you. But they've got bigger things to worry about now. I'll talk to Josh."

"It's the thing at Fajardo, isn't it?" she said. She sipped her tea and put it back down on the tray. "It's all over the news. Those cops working for the cartels. Something told me it was the same cops. It was them, wasn't it?"

Crane nodded. There were nine dead, according to the news,

and one in critical condition. So Acevedo had made it. He could see her wanting to just ask him straight out if he'd killed all those men. But she didn't. Instead she bottled up that fear, layered over it with the good news that she could begin her project again. But the undertone of playful attraction between them was gone. A part of her was afraid of him now.

"Do you think you'll be able to get another of those gene sequencer things? The ones that come ten at a time?"

"The high seek? God only knows. I know some people who wanted to be in the batch last time. Maybe they're still looking. I don't know. And that's just one thing. There's so much to do."

He got her talking about her Christmas list of lab equipment, and her excitement gradually overcame her discomfort.

"What will you do now?" she asked when he rose to leave.

"Whoever put all this in motion is still there," said Crane. "I need to find them and find out why. That's when it will be finished for good. I've got some leads. I'll be leaving Puerto Rico."

She grabbed his arm in the doorway. "Thank you," she said. "I'm not sure if I've said that before. I know I've been a pain in the ass."

"Not at all."

"And I know you've done a lot to help me," she continued. "I want you to know how much it matters. If it wasn't for you, I would have lost everything."

"You're welcome," said Crane.

"Do you think you'll be back this way?"

There was something in her voice that made Crane pause and meet her gaze. He could sense the ambivalence there. As much as she tried, as much as part of her wanted to, she couldn't quite forget the blood they'd cleaned off the floor of her lab or all those bodies on the beach at Fajardo.

Crane smiled. "It could happen."

"Well, call me if it does. We'll go back to Rosa de Triana, have some sangria, and catch up."

"I'd like that," said Crane, knowing it would never happen.

Then he turned and walked away down the short stone path to the street. Melissa watched him go from the doorway, but when he glanced back from the sidewalk, she had closed the door.

CHAPTER 26

Prague, Czech Republic

Nine days later, John Crane stepped off a British Airways 777 and into a carefully crafted persona. This Crane wore a navy Brioni suit with a very subtle gray pinstripe and carried a Dunhill grip bag. This was a man who took his importance for granted and expected others to recognize it. After he cleared Czech customs and border control, he followed the flow of people into the arrivals terminal. There he met a woman in a chauffeur's uniform, holding an iPad that displayed "Mr. Crane" in large type, and followed her to a Mercedes sedan. Crane sat in the back and reset the Breitling he'd taken from Zajic's boat to Central European time.

They drove around the perimeter of the airport and parked next to a private aviation hangar. Crane got out and looked around. It was cold here, especially after Puerto Rico, and the solid overcast sky threatened to spit rain. The temperature was somewhere in the fifties. The landscape was flat and industrial, with the distant roar of jets in the background. The driver handed Crane his bag and then unlocked the hangar's side door.

"Trouble getting anything into the country?" Crane asked.

"No, sir," she answered. "The car's ready, and your things are in the trunk." She handed Crane a car key. "Mr. Sulenski sends his regards and wishes you good hunting."

Crane watched the Mercedes drive away, leaving him standing alone in a plain of concrete and rust. He breathed in the air and watched tractor trailers with faded paint roll steadily past on the highway in the distance. He stood there for perhaps a minute, just soaking in the reality of this new place. Then he walked into the hangar and locked the door behind himself.

Parked in the middle of the hangar, looking simultaneously ominous and very expensive, was a black Audi R8, the Anderson Germany Hyper-Black edition, its V-10 tuned for even greater horsepower and its weight reduced with judicious use of carbon fiber. Crane allowed himself a moment to be awed by it, and then reminded himself that his character would take this car for granted. More than that, it wasn't here for Crane's enjoyment. It was a tool, meant for dangerous work, something to be taken seriously.

But that didn't mean he couldn't enjoy himself along the way, he told himself.

He opened the trunk and found two matching suitcases, dark blue with brass fittings and black leather straps. The first contained clothes, a shaving kit, the basic travel gear. The second was more interesting. Inside were Emil Zajic's assault rifle and silenced pistol—chickens coming home to roost, Crane thought to himself—along with several fresh magazines for both. Below those was the rest of the radio and electronic gear Crane had ordered in San Juan, the pick gun and some other specialized burglary tools, and a few new goodies generously provided by Josh. In his previous life, the US government would have gotten these things into the country using back channels with the Czech government. He had no idea how Josh had done it, but apparently being a multi-billionaire opened a lot of doors.

Crane got into the Audi, a cocoon of black and orange leather and carbon fiber panels. The engine started with a restrained growl. A remote on the passenger seat opened the main sliding doors. Crane tapped the button again to close them and then dropped the remote out the window and drove out through the doors as they slid shut. The Audi accelerated smoothly out onto the road, and Crane steered it onto the E50, headed southeast for Brno.

Josh's people had dug up what they could about the company on Zajic's business card. It wasn't much. Deštnik Biologicka was a small biotech startup that did something involving protein folding. Josh had promised a more complete briefing, and Crane assumed it was inside a manila envelope he'd found in one of the suitcases. The company was apparently part of a government-funded biotech incubator called Jižni Morova BioKapital—South Moravian BioCapital—that provided seed funding and office and lab space for a dozen similar startups.

Josh had seized on that angle immediately, especially when he found out that the incubator would be participating in a Czech biotech fair at the end of the month to connect its fledgling companies with investors and industry mentors. "The best way to get inside a startup is to be an angel investor," he'd said. "You can pluck them out of obscurity and make them instant millionaires. Or not. Who knows what motivates you? What will make you shower them with favor or drop them back into the abyss? They'll roll out the red carpet, show you the labs, open up their books. Anything. It's perfect."

And so Crane was now a high-rolling principal of The Scorix Group, an entirely fictional investment fund that specialized in securing enormous returns by betting early on promising startups in biotech and pharmaceuticals. Josh had known exactly what to do to instantly create Internet credibility for the imaginary firm, and that had opened doors as quickly as Josh promised. Tomorrow morning, Crane had an interview with a Klement Novak, who was Deštnik's CEO. Crane was supposedly in Brno in advance of the fair, like the early bird at a garage sale, to scoop up the bargains before the crowds picked everything over. Josh's people reported that Novak was almost pathetically eager to meet with a representative of Scorix and had promised him full access.

As the sun set, Crane sped through the outskirts of Brno, zipping around slow-moving trucks and getting used to the feel of the car. Clearly something was going on at Deštnik besides protein folding. Hopefully tomorrow, he'd get a better idea of just what.

A wiry, red-headed man in a battered old army jacket leaned against the wall of a building across the street from the Brno Palace Hotel on Husova, just inside what had been the city wall back in the Middle Ages. He tossed his cigarette butt onto the sidewalk, pulled a pack of Moon Special Blends from his pocket, and lit another. He was very bored, but work was work.

Then he perked up as a black Audi pulled up in front of the hotel and was rushed by the front reception crew. A tall man with dark hair got out and spoke briefly with the valet. He wore a suit that looked like it cost as much as his car. After a moment, he gave the valet the keys. Two bellboys unloaded a couple suitcases and a carry-on bag from the trunk onto a luggage cart and hurried it inside.

The redhead pulled out a cheap smartphone with a clip-on zoom lens and grabbed a couple shots of the car and the driver's face. Then the camera quickly vanished back into his coat. The valet took the car to the parking garage, and the driver looked around the square and then strode into the hotel.

Maybe the day wasn't a total loss after all, the redhead thought as he pushed off the wall and walked away, whistling an old tune his mother used to sing when he was a boy.

———

Anton Kucera hung up the cell phone and tossed it onto the table with the others.

"Andrei," he shouted, "another beer!"

"Coming, boss!"

Kucera had been holding court in a back corner booth in this rundown tavern for weeks now. The regulars had long since accepted that the back corner was off limits, and nobody sat anywhere near him. The battered and scarred tabletop had four cheap phones and a couple notebooks spread across it, with Kucera's empties stacked at the far side.

This was basically his office now. He'd had Skala's old office refinished to perfection. It was spotless. There was nothing left to show that his man Lubor had gotten his brains blown all over the carpet. But Kucera hadn't moved into it after Skala went off to his vineyard in the country. He left it there like a tomb.

This booth was at least closer to the street. Kucera had no interest in being a respectable businessman. He was a thug and felt no need to rise above that. He just wanted to be the top thug. Skala had gotten too far from his roots. He wouldn't make the same mistake.

And yet. Somehow since he'd taken over Skala's operations, he couldn't shake the feeling that he'd been played. He spent all his time coordinating among everyone who now reported to him. He settled disputes. He took reports from his underlings and sent them off on errands. It felt like he'd been promoted into middle management.

The whole thing wasn't what Kucera had expected. He'd just been on the phone with Novotny again. Novotny had worked out some kind of special deal with Skala like twenty years ago to save face. He worked for Skala, but he didn't admit that he worked for him. And Skala was responsible for keeping his people out of Novotny's way, so now Novotny expected that to pass down to Kucera. And so whenever the skinheads got in Novotny's hair, putting pressure on the little shopkeepers who paid him, it was Kucera who got the call. Whenever any petty crook in Brno got kicked in the balls over something, Kucera had to feel it too. It wasn't what he'd imagined at all.

The bartender brought him another Black Mountain, with no glass. It had taken him a couple days to figure out that Kucera preferred to drink it straight from the bottle, but he had it down now. Kucera nodded and waved him away.

As soon as he put the bottle to his lips, one of the phones buzzed and rattled on the table. A text message from one of his loan sharks saying a big debt wasn't being paid on time. What should they do?

What the fuck did they think they should do? Go around and break some damn kneecaps. It wasn't rocket science. But of course, it was never that simple. He texted back, fully expecting them to come back with some reason why they couldn't or shouldn't damage this particular mark.

The door opened, and one of his runners came in. The scruffy-looking redhead in the dirty army jacket. Kucera couldn't even remember his name.

He came up to the table and nodded at Kucera. "Got something, boss. At the Palace."

He handed over his phone, and Kucera thumbed through the photos of new arrivals. The most recent did indeed look promising. The car was an Audi R8, some kind of special tuner version. It looked expensive as hell, like nothing he'd actually seen in Brno before. The driver was Western, English maybe, more likely American. His suit looked expensive too. Kucera wondered what he had in those suitcases.

"Good job," he said to the runner. He thumbed up a menu and mailed the photos to his own phone. He'd distribute them to his people and figure out whether to rob the American's room or maybe go for the car.

"Spread a little money around the hotel," he said. "Find out what you can. Let's figure on going for his room tomorrow night. Get your crew ready."

"Will do, boss," said the runner. He took his phone back and hurried back out of the bar.

Kucera sipped his beer. He needed to get out there and actually do something criminal or he was going to explode.

CHAPTER 27

The next morning dawned cold, though the sky was clear and the day promised to be more comfortable once the nighttime chill burned off. Still, it was a warning to Brno's residents that autumn was setting in and winter not far behind it. Crane wore a light overcoat as he waited for the valet to bring the Audi around. He watched the streets, thick with traffic, bicycles, and pedestrians. An electric tram went by and stopped down the street.

When the Audi arrived, Crane steered into the morning rush and made his way carefully across town. He quickly realized that the Audi's ridiculous performance was wasted at the moment. Brno was an old city, built long before traffic was an issue. The streets were narrow and twisting, and Crane suspected he'd move faster on foot.

Outside the city center, he made better time. Deštnik Biologicka a.s. was in a research campus on the outskirts of the city, along with a collection of other startups, all of them funded by South Moravian BioCapital. Crane pulled in only about five minutes late. The campus sprawled across a gently rolling piece of land that looked like it had been pasture a generation ago.

The buildings were modern and low slung, with alternating bands of reddish stone and dark glass windows. Single stories around the outer band of the complex, three stories nearer the center. The place was shot through with meandering footpaths and greenery and studded with small parking lots.

Crane found the building he needed—realizing how confusing the layout was to visitors, the designers had put enormous numbers on the buildings—and pulled into a visitor parking space near the doors.

A small entourage was already lined up outside waiting for him. The man in the center of the line broke free as Crane approached and strode up to him with a huge smile and an extended hand.

"Mr. Crane, how wonderful to meet you," he said in good, if strongly accented, English. "I am Klement Novak, CEO. So happy to have you here!"

They shook hands and traded business cards. Then Novak introduced Crane to the senior staff lined up behind him. They were all young; Novak might have been Crane's age, but he was easily the oldest of the group. They all looked very much like struggling young doctoral students. Emil Zajic couldn't have stood out any more here if he was a kangaroo.

They headed inside where more staffers fawned over Crane. They took his overcoat, brought him sweetened tea, and sought desperately to gain his favor. Klement led him to a conference room, prepared as if for a state dinner, with water glasses and leather binders. The digital projector threw the company logo up onto a screen.

"So excited to talk about what we've been doing," Novak was saying. "And I have to say, it's such a reassurance to have you take an interest, Mr. Crane. As researchers, we get so close to our project that sometimes it's all we can see. So for us, your interest is the confirmation we need that our work has commercial potential and isn't just interesting from a scientific standpoint. You prove we aren't just indulging ourselves. So thank you."

Crane could see he was expected to say something equally complimentary.

"Thank you, Mr. Novak," he said. "I'm very glad to be here. At Scorix, we know that there are breakthroughs happening all the time in labs like this one all around the world. Our job is to find them and help them move beyond the lab so they can benefit the world. And we're very excited by what you're doing here. I look forward to learning more."

That part, Crane admitted to himself, was a lie. Even after reading the thin dossier Josh's people had been able to put together on the company and its work, he still had no idea what they really did.

Novak launched into his presentation, and it was heavy on science that was miles over Crane's head. There were terms like "random coil" and "co-translational" and "n-terminus." The accompanying slides were full of complicated diagrams made of dots and lines with arrows pointing from one to the next.

As far as Crane could follow, long chains of molecules called polypeptides somehow turned themselves into complex 3-D protein structures that were vital to life and also could have a wide range of medical applications. The question was, given the astronomical number of possible ways a molecule might fold, how did they consistently manage to turn into the same useful proteins instead of just useless chemical junk? Crane pictured a million monkeys with typewriters producing Hamlet. Except with molecules.

Novak was talking about existing computer simulations and "chaperone molecules" that guided the fold along a few standard paths instead of leaving everything to chance. It sounded like this part was existing science, so a VC investor wouldn't have been all that excited by it. Even so, Crane had seldom felt so stupid. He consoled himself with the thought that Emil Zajic would probably have lost his temper and punched somebody by now.

Then Novak got to the payload. Deštnik was working on the principles that nudged the proteins along a particular path and learning to steer them more specifically. Once researchers had designed a desired protein on a computer, Deštnik's methodology would let them build it out of common "starter" proteins by introducing particular chemical tools to produce the right folds in the right sequence.

"We'll eventually be able to practically 3D print any desired protein structure from the ground up," Novak concluded. "We're looking at a significant savings in time to research new molecules and bring them to trial, as well as a huge reduction in cost with the corresponding upside in gross profitability."

He looked very proud of himself. Crane realized it was time for tough questions. Novak knew he was no scientist. He'd be trying to gold plate everything, and Crane the venture capitalist would push back. Besides, Crane wanted him off balance.

"That sounds great," said Crane. "Define 'eventually' for me."

"We're making strong progress," said Novak. "A lot of that depends on funding, obviously. That's why we're so excited to get Scorix on board. As you said, it takes money to get these advances out of the lab."

"So not six months?"

Novak sputtered. "I'm not sure I can be that precise," he said. "Certainly we're moving as fast as we can toward practical applications."

"It's just—I have a confession to make," said Crane. "I've heard about your work before. I was talking to Emil Zajic at a conference recently, and he was confident you'd have a tech transfer package ready by first quarter next year."

Novak looked blank. "I'm sorry, who were you speaking with?"

"Emil Zajic? Your Director of Mergers and Acquisitions?"

"I'm sorry, Mr. Crane, you must be mistaken. I don't know anyone by that name, and Deštnik's in no position to be looking at M&A right now. We're hoping for angel funding to get our process nailed and documented. After that, our strategy is to partner with a larger firm that would acquire the intellectual property for their own R&D."

Crane smiled. "My apologies. I talk to so many people at these conferences. I must have confused Mr. Zajic's company with yours. Can I see the lab? I'd like to see this process in action."

Novak stood up and beamed. "Of course! We've got a tech demo set up for you."

They took Crane through the labs and showed him everything. He nodded in the right places and asked the occasional obvious question. At one point, he mentioned that Scorix was investing heavily in gene sequencing and asked about their solution's applicability to that. Novak pivoted fast and came up with something, but Crane could tell he was blindsided by the question. He was furiously bullshitting an answer as best he could. Their work had nothing at all to do with Melissa Simon's gene bank project.

When it was done, they ended up back in the main lobby and everyone said the polite things and there was a lot of shaking of hands all around again.

"I'm here for a couple days," Crane said as Novak walked him back out to his car. "I'd love to talk more outside the lab environment."

"I thought you might want to sample the nightlife while you're here," said Novak. "I reserved a table at Borgo Agnese. It's the best restaurant in town."

"That sounds great," Crane said as they shook hands one last time. "I look forward to it."

As he drove back into Brno, Crane considered what he'd seen. Nothing suggested that Deštnik was anything more than a struggling tech startup. They'd eagerly shown him everything, just as Josh said they would. Nothing looked out of place or suggested any criminal connection. Crane wasn't ready to make a final call yet, but his gut feeling was that Novak didn't know anything. He was just a guy trying to sell his company and get rich.

But then there was Emil Zajic, with his business card for a position that didn't exist, at a company that had never heard of him. If he didn't work for Novak, then whom did he work for? What the hell was going on here?

———

Branislav Skala paced the polished marble floor of his ballroom in a paisley-trimmed silk bathrobe and slippers. The room was something out of Versailles. There was an enormous pastoral mural on one wall, with fauns piping and half-naked nymphs dancing among the trees. The opposite wall was a row of tall, arched windows, black with the darkness outside. The place was designed for parties of a hundred or more, but tonight Skala wandered the huge space alone, except for two muscular body-guards in suits and shoulder holsters near the door.

Skala found the room calming. He liked to come here when he was upset, and he was very upset this evening. The blown deal with the Colombians would have ripple effects well beyond the loss of the drugs themselves. The Colombians were furious, smelling betrayal. But he'd lost as much as they had. When Emil wasn't found among the dead on the beach, Skala entertained hopes that he'd gotten away, that he was holed up somewhere and would report when he could. But a few days later, they'd found his body in the water nearby. Apparently Emil had simply drowned. But then why was his dinghy found more than a mile away, beached on the other side of the bay?

The authorities weren't saying what happened to him, and Skala couldn't push for more information without raising more questions. But he sensed the hand of Team Kilo in this. Everything had gone wrong since their man appeared in Puerto Rico. He thought he'd convinced the Colombians that they'd both been ambushed by some third party, but it would take a long time to repair the damage to their business relationship.

The phone in his pocket chimed quietly. Skala checked the screen. It was his man at Jižni Morova BioKapital. One of the firms he had enrolled there was attracting interest from an American investment fund, and he'd asked for a report. Perhaps this would finally be some good news at last. If the Americans bought Deštnik, he could just move the parts of his operation it concealed to other startups on the campus. That was no problem. And it would bring him a great deal of money—legitimate money—and raise BioKapital's profile in the European pharma community. A win for him all around.

The phone chimed again, and he answered. "How did it go, Dalibor?"

"The American was here today, sir," said his man. "Novak said it went well. He made the presentation, showed him the lab. Right now he's taking him to dinner."

Novak was smart enough, to be sure, but Skala didn't like the idea of trusting a deal this big to his social skills. For a moment, he wondered if he should send a girl to the American's hotel. But no, he decided. Go with the class approach.

"I've sent Novak's report to your secure account," said Dalibor, "along with what we could find on the American and his company. It's not much. They keep their cards close to their chest, these guys."

"That's fine," said Skala. "Let me know if you get anything else."

He hung up.

Skala's laptop was on a rococo gueridon near the doors, next to one of his bodyguards. He gestured impatiently, and the guard brought it to him, and then held it out on his outstretched forearms as Skala woke it up and swiped his fingertip across the reader.

Dalibor's upload was there. He opened it and skimmed through the brief report on the American company. What little there was read as though Dalibor had pulled it from their website. He scrolled through to copies of e-mail traffic, setting up an appointment with their representative, a Mr. John Crane. Again, nothing very interesting.

There were some photos attached, taken by the security cameras at the campus. Skala opened the first and physically recoiled. The bodyguard looked with alarm over the back of the laptop.

"Are you all right, sir?"

Him! The clothes were different, but there was no question about it. It was the same man from the airport photo in San Juan. The one who had wrecked everything there, the man who must have killed Emil. He was here!

"Sir!" the bodyguard said more urgently. "Is something wrong?"

"Double the perimeter guard."

"Sir?"

The man stood there awkwardly, unable to act with Skala's precious laptop perched on his forearms. Skala grabbed the computer and slammed the lid shut.

"Do it!"

The bodyguard hurried away. At the door, he gestured to the other one, who moved closer to Skala and hovered there nervously.

"This way," Skala snapped, and stormed off toward his apartments at the rear of the house. Something was very wrong, indeed. He had to deal with it quickly and decisively, because the consequences if he failed made Skala's blood run cold.

CHAPTER 28

After an excellent ossobuco ravioli and a bottle of Gaja Barbaresco, Crane drove the Audi back to his hotel through the narrow streets of Brno's old town and tried to size up Klement Novak.

It was difficult to imagine the man as a gangster, someone who might send Emil Zajic and a pack of dirty cops out to destroy his enemies. That was assuming there was even a reason for him to take offense at a biological research project in the Puerto Rican rainforest—which there wasn't. Throughout dinner, Crane had studied and picked at the persona Novak presented. He couldn't find a hint of anything but an eager scientist and entrepreneur, someone who sensed a shot at the big time and was trying desperately to grab it. Crane actually felt bad for deceiving him. Novak would be devastated when the Scorix Group evaporated, along with their money and industry connections. Perhaps when the real biotech fair came along at the end of the month, some other investor would pick up Deštnik.

He realized his train of thought implied that he'd accepted the idea that Novak simply wasn't the enemy he was looking for.

Novak truly had never heard of Zajic, or of Melissa Simon, and knew nothing about the whole affair.

So where did that leave things? Who was behind it, and why had Zajic been provided with fake Deštnik business cards?

He tried another angle. Why would Zajic want to pose as an Deštnik employee? He was hardly one to go to biotech conferences or take meetings with scientists. If he needed a fake cover job, why that one? Why not a private security consultant? That would be more believable. Or a music promoter or a construction engineer—pretty much anything but a biotech executive. For that matter, why use a real company at all, giving himself an identity that would fall apart the moment someone called Deštnik's front desk?

A thought occurred to Crane, and at the next light, he checked Zajic's card against Novak's. The mailing address and the e-mail domains matched, but the phone numbers didn't. Zajic's card gave what looked like a Brno number, but the exchange was different from the number on Novak's card. Deštnik would have an internal PBX, or more likely a virtual one these days, with its own exchange number. All company phone numbers should have shared that exchange. But someone with Zajic's card, someone calling to check him out, wouldn't get to Deštnik at all. They'd go someplace else, no doubt to someone who would be all too happy to confirm Mr. Zajic's credentials with the company.

But the e-mail address did match Novak's. Now that was interesting. If Zajic wasn't really an employee, the emil.zajic@Deštnikbio.cz address wouldn't exist. If someone tried sending a message to it, it should bounce. Were they just assuming nobody would try to e-mail Zajic? But why take that risk? Especially when it would be easy to set up their own domain that they could control?

No, Crane's instincts were telling him that e-mail address

wouldn't bounce at all. And that meant that whoever sent Zajic off to Puerto Rico hadn't just gone to a print shop and run off some fake business cards. They were connected to Deštnik somehow, hiding behind it. They'd wormed their way deep enough into the company to have control of its e-mail servers and set up a hidden address for their muscle in Puerto Rico.

Who could do that without Novak being any the wiser? Did one of Novak's employees have something going on behind the scenes? Who handled their IT infrastructure? That was worth finding out.

Crane pulled up in front of the hotel and gave the Audi to the valet. The Brno Palace was bathed in spotlights, its old white stone and its new glass panels gleaming in the night. A few couples out for a late night stroll wandered the plaza out front. Something in the back of Crane's mind sent up an alert as he watched the Audi's taillights disappear around the corner of the building.

There. That man across the street, the redhead making a phone call. He'd seen him before. Crane had only been in Brno for a little over twenty-four hours, and that figure was starting to become familiar. It could be nothing, but Crane had been trained to notice details like that, in case they proved important. The redhead in the army jacket was appropriately filed away in Crane's mind.

He strolled into the hotel's huge, glass-roofed interior and took the elevator up to his floor. The moment he opened the door to his room, he swung back against the hallway wall and his hand went to the pistol inside his jacket.

The room had been torn apart. Crane checked the hallway; it was empty. He listened but heard nothing from the room. He swept the door back hard and fast to hit anyone hiding behind it, and went inside, crouched low, leading with the gun.

The room was empty. He checked the bathroom, the closet,

under the bed, anywhere big enough to hide a person. They were gone. But they'd cleaned the place out. His suitcases were gone, and clothes lay scattered around the room. The dresser drawers had been tossed onto the floor. There was nothing subtle about it, but they'd been thorough. Anything that Crane hadn't stowed in the Audi was gone, and that included most of his gear.

Presented with a situation like this, John Crane of the Scorix Group would complain to the hotel, file a police report, go through the official channels. Crane sighed and double-checked the room for anything remaining that didn't fit his official persona. It would have to go down in the Audi, along with his pistol, before he started raising hell at the front desk. But his guests had left very little behind.

He checked the door on the way out. There were no signs it had been forced. So they had managed to open the coded electronic lock. That wasn't hugely surprising. Crane had done so himself on more than one occasion. But it did speak to a level of preparedness on their part. He took the elevator down, stashed his gun in the Audi, and practiced looking outraged as he walked back around to the lobby.

The redhead in the army jacket was gone from his post across the street. He could have nothing to do with this. But Crane wasn't a big believer in coincidence. He walked back inside and made a beeline for the front desk to ask loudly what kind of hotel this was, demand that the police be called, and remind everyone in earshot that he was a wealthy American and not to be treated this way. It was embarrassing, but it had to be done.

It was almost 1:00 a.m. by the time Crane got back to his room, and he was tired of playing the jerk. He'd made a scene in the hotel lobby until the night manager had called the general manager out of his bed and urged him to come in. Both of them had fawned over their valued guest and expressed suitable shock that something like this could happen at the Brno Palace. Then Crane had played the aggrieved and entitled American for the police, demanding immediate action and bemoaning how this sort of thing would never have happened in the United States.

The officers had taken a look through the room but found nothing useful to their investigation. They dutifully took Crane's report and an almost completely false inventory of what had been taken. But they admitted they could offer little hope for the recovery of his things. Gangs of thieves targeted wealthy visitors, they told him. They would check local pawn shops, but the clear implication was that this was a pointless task meant more to get him off their backs than to actually catch the thieves. After his performance, Crane was certain they weren't going to go very far out of their way to help the obnoxious American who—as he had helpfully pointed out—made more in a week than they made all year.

It was what he had to do, of course. The last thing he wanted was the police actually turning up his esoteric surveillance gear and wondering what he was doing with it. But he still felt bad.

He took a few minutes to clean up the worst of the mess. He'd deal with the rest tomorrow. He undressed and got into bed. He switched off the light and was asleep in minutes.

———

Anton Kucera tossed his pen across the bar and closed his note-book. The pen ricocheted off a framed photo of some football club from the old days and fell behind the cigarette machine beside the door to the bathrooms. Someone at the bar looked over his shoulder at the sound but quickly turned back to his beer.

That was it for tonight. The books were sorted out. Until tomorrow, of course, when the protection money would come in and the whole thing would start over again.

Eventually, he told himself, he would be able to hire people to take care of this shit for him. God knew he had money enough. But Skala's operations were all new to him. He had to understand how they worked, who did what, how the money moved. If he didn't, he'd be robbed blind, and then someone would decide he was weak and could be taken down and replaced. So for now, he did it all himself.

He sat back and drained his bottle, the beer warm and flat now. He glanced over at the bar but didn't shout for another. No, he needed to move. A walk home and some clear air. He could call Radek and have him send a girl around to his place. But no, he didn't even want that tonight. Christ, what was this doing to him?

Two figures moved into his field of view. The red-headed runner whose name he still couldn't remember and another one whose name he was pretty sure he'd never heard. They stood there, nervously shuffling from foot to foot, until Kucera grunted, "Well?"

"Boss, we've got ..."

He just trailed off and let it hang there. Kucera sighed.

"What? A problem?"

"Not exactly. I don't think so. It's just weird. We hit that guy's room like you said. Everything went fine. It's just, his stuff. You should come take a look."

Christ. Nobody could handle anything themselves. Not even something as simple as rolling a hotel room. He slid out of the bar, and they led the way through the doors to the bar's rear storeroom. A pair of suitcases were laid out on a side table. Kucera sized them up.

"They look worth something."

"Take a look inside," said the redhead.

Kucera did and let out a low whistle. The bags were full of ... things. Kucera recognized a pair of night vision goggles, a couple small cameras with interchangeable lenses, radios, a lockpick gun, at least a dozen black boxes that looked hand built for purposes he could only guess. It all looked salable. It looked like a damn good haul, in fact. But still ...

"Who the hell is this guy?" he murmured to himself. Then something made him ask, "Any weapons?"

"No," said the redhead. "We looked. No cash, hardly any clothes. Just all this stuff."

He let out a breath and walked around the table. He checked the bags for tags, but they were blank.

"What do you want us to do with it?" asked the redhead.

Kucera pulled a sheaf of bills from his pocket and handed them to him. They instantly vanished into the redhead's jacket.

"Leave this here," he said. "I'll figure out what to do with it. And put some guys outside the Palace. I want to know what that guy's up to. Keep a tail on him."

They nodded and started to leave.

"Keep your distance," he called after them. "And switch up guys. At least a couple times a day. I don't want him making you. Anything he does, you let me know right away."

They left on a cloud of promises to do just as he said, and then Kucera was alone with the gear. He picked up a thin plastic box the size of a cigarette pack with a battery door on one side and a recessed slider switch. He had no idea what it did.

Then the phone in his pocket rang, and Kucera closed his eyes. Only one person had that number.

He pressed accept.

"Yeah?"

"We have a problem," said Skala. "A big problem. I'm coming into town now. I'll meet you at the office in half an hour."

"I'm not at the office."

"Well, get—"

"Meet me at Rebel Bar. You know it? In your old neighborhood."

He could hear Skala's irritation through the line noise, but at last, "Fine. I'll be there."

"What's the big deal, anyway?" Kucera asked.

"Someone's just come to town," said Skala. "Someone very dangerous. To both our interests. We need to deal with him fast."

Kucera looked over the suitcases, the piles of high-tech equipment, and a cold feeling came over him.

"This guy," he said, "he wouldn't be staying at the Palace, would he?"

CHAPTER 29

It was almost 1:00 a.m. when the doors at Rebel Bar flew open and two of Branislav Skala's men quickly swept the place. Kucera had been up too long; he'd been doing what amounted to bookkeeping. He was in no mood.

The bar was empty. They'd chased out the last of the drunks after Skala's call. He'd sent the bartender home, and one of his own guys was quietly polishing glasses behind the bar with a weapon ready. Skala's people would expect that. They took up their own positions flanking the door, and a moment later, Skala himself entered, looking grim. Kucera beckoned him over to his booth in the back.

The bar was grimy and smelled of beer and cigarettes and piss. It was a world away from Skala's gleaming corporate office with his long-legged secretary and his fancy furniture. Kucera insisted on meeting here mainly to piss Skala off. But he could see from Skala's grim expression that it wasn't working. Skala was too worked up about something to get the full effect.

The old man swung into the booth across from Kucera. "Can that guy really make a drink? I need a strong one."

Kucera gestured to the guy at the bar.

"What's got you up so late?" he asked. "Away from your castle on a cold night?"

Skala wasn't taking the bait. "What did you mean," he said, "when you asked 'is he staying at the Palace?'"

Kucera shrugged. "A rich mark showed up at the Palace yesterday. I sent some guys to hit his room. Usually that means cameras, laptops, watches, some cash. Not this time. It's in the back room there."

"Show me."

So he took Skala into the back room and showed him the expensive suitcases full of unlabeled electronic gear. Skala picked through the stuff, trying to figure it out. He noted where something plugged into something else. He almost switched something on but stopped himself. The old man looked like he'd seen a ghost.

"I knew it," he said, more to himself than Kucera. "I knew it. This proves it. The son of a bitch is Team Kilo, and he's here."

"What are you talking about? Come on out and have a drink."

Skala spent another thirty seconds sorting through the equipment as if there was some clue there that he'd find if he just looked a moment longer. Finally he nodded and followed Kucera back out to the booth. The bartender had left a couple shots of vodka on the table. Skala picked his up and knocked it back even before he sat down. Kucera didn't know what the hell was going on, but the old man was rattled. Right to his bones, he was rattled. He tried to decide if that was a bad thing or a good one. It didn't work. He couldn't figure it out.

"What the hell's got into you?" he asked as he sat down and picked up the other shot glass. "What's Team Kilo?"

"They're an enemy," said Skala. "Not crooks like us. Something worse."

"So what? Cops? Government? Come on, it's late. Make

sense."

"It's what I've been trying to make you see for a while now," Skala said with a sigh. "When I was a poor kid on the street, I saw the gangs and I thought, that's power. They don't take shit from anybody. So I became a gangster. And when I made it to the top of the gangs, I saw rich men with real businesses and legitimate money, and I thought, that's the real power. They just take what I had to fight for. They don't have to look over their shoulder all the time. They send their kids to college, and their kids don't have to do what I had to do to get here. So I became one of them. I didn't run for office because look at me. But I saw government, and I got my hand in there because that was how you used power to protect yourself and get what you want."

Kucera let out a very conspicuous yawn, but the old man ignored him.

"So I thought, okay, I made it. I'm at the top. But once I got there, I started to see it's not really the top. Governments come and go. We used to be ruled by communists. We used to be Czechoslovakia. There's another world beyond governments, Anton. That's what I'm trying to tell you."

He drew concentric circles on the tabletop with his fingertip. "There are people beyond all that. They make the world what they want it to be. Cops and governments can't touch them. Not so different from us, really. They have their alliances and their rivalries. They spy on each other, and they have their betrayals and their wars. But they're pure power. We can't even see them from down in the gutter."

"You're so full of shit," said Kucera. "You sound like old Havel the Nazi. You remember him? Is it the Jews you're talking about?"

"This is real!" Skala slapped the table, and Kucera saw a bit of the old Skala rising in him, the man that terrorized Brno for decades. "I gave you Brno to run for me because I wanted to break into that world, Anton. And I'm doing it. I found a group with a problem I know how to solve. And when I solve it, they'll see they need me. And then I'll be one of them. Before long, I'll own them. But they have enemies."

"Enemies called Team Kilo?"

"They don't have names. They all keep their secrets. It's hard figuring out who's in bed with who, whose toes you're stepping on if you make a move. I keep my eyes and ears open. There are plenty of factions out there in the shadows. Alfa, Bravo, Charlie, Delta ... these are Kilo. They're the ones to be scared of."

"And this man's one of theirs."

"Has to be. The things he's done ... He's got to be. And now he's here. And you robbed his fucking room! Now he knows we're on to him!"

"Wait a second," Kucera snapped. "We weren't on to him. We robbed his room because he's fucking rich. That's what we do. It doesn't tell him anything."

"We can't assume that!"

"Whatever. So what do you want to do?"

"I want you to kill him!" Skala snapped. "You know where he is now. Kill him! Send Janda or Krall! Now, before he goes to ground."

"Fine. I'll send Krall."

"It can't look like we took him out. Tell him. It has to look like an accident. A suicide."

Kucera sighed as he took out his phone. "Of course it does."

———

After giving Krall his orders and getting Skala bundled back into his limousine, Kucera finally made his way back to his rooms. He lived in an old row house he'd gotten ownership of years ago through a combination of loan sharking and outright extortion.

It was his fortress, lined with alarms and intrusion barriers. He could fight a war there if he had to, with guns and ammunition stashed in the walls. It was the one place where he truly felt safe.

Someone was sitting on the front stoop, he realized as he walked up. A girl, with long, bare legs and electric blue hair. She wore a micro skirt and a tight top that barely contained her breasts. She stood up as he climbed the concrete steps, and looked at him shyly through her blue bangs.

"What are you doing here?" he asked with a smile.

She smiled back. "Mr. Novotny sent me." She gestured through the outer door to where Jozef sat stone-faced at the security post. "But he made me wait out here in the cold," she added, her voice soft and flirtatious.

"Well, that's his job," Kucera said. It occurred to him that there were some advantages to Novotny needing his help. And that perhaps he wasn't as tired as he'd thought. "But why don't you come inside now, and we'll see if we can't warm you up."

He waved to Jozef, who buzzed him through and then raised an eyebrow at the girl as they passed. Kucera winked and slapped her ass to make her giggle.

"What's your name, then?" he asked as they went up the stairs.

"Tonight, I'm whoever you want me to be."

————

Later, Kucera lay spent in the tangled mess of his bed, the blue-haired girl lying naked at his side, breathing softly against his bare skin.

Novotny had been holding out on him, he decided. He was going to keep this one instead of sending her back. There was a mix of doe-eyed submission and voracious appetite in her that drove him farther than he'd thought possible.

"Anton," she said quietly, "do you mind if I call you Anton?"

He laughed. "I don't even know your name. Sure, you can call me Anton. It's my name."

He twisted and stretched over to the nightstand for the glass of vodka he'd left there. He couldn't quite reach it with her on his other arm. She sat up to let him reach.

Then something hit him. His hand swept the glass off onto the floor, and then suddenly he was on his stomach with the girl straddling flat. She twisted his right arm behind his back.

"Good. We need to talk, Anton."

He tried to grab her with his left arm but she yanked hard on his right, and he gasped with the sudden wrenching pain.

"I have a confession to make," said the girl. "Novotny didn't really send me."

"No matter what you do to me," he gasped through clenched teeth, "there's no way you can get out of this place alive."

"Calm down," she said. "Don't worry, Anton. Nobody's getting hurt. You liked the first part, didn't you? You'll like this part too. We're going to talk about your friend, Mr. Skala."

Kucera groaned. "Ah, Christ. Enough."

"I agree," she said with a smile. "Enough is enough. The man's got all the subtlety of a mob of drunken soccer hooligans. He's blundering into situations he doesn't understand. Stirring things up. Far more trouble than he's worth, all in all. I take it he's something of a thorn in your side too."

"Who the hell are you?" Kucera asked.

"I told you," she said. "Tonight, I'm whoever you want me to be."

Then she flipped him over, caught his free arm, and fell forward so that she was holding both his arms down on the pillows over his head. She smiled and started to move against him.

"The real question is, what are we going to do about Skala?"

CHAPTER 30

Crane wasn't sure what saved his life. A voice in the hallway outside. Some subtle change in the light from the window. A rustle of fabric. Perhaps the faint medicinal smell of hospitals and death.

But he awoke in the dark as a plastic mask fell over his face with a sudden hiss of gas. He jerked his head to the side and felt the hard plastic scrape down his temple. Then he slapped the arm away and instinctively kicked up with one leg, but the bed covers blunted his energy and he accomplished nothing. A fist slammed into his gut, and he gasped and sat up fast. His head slammed into something hard.

Crane rolled away to his right, kicking away the bed covers, and fell off the edge of the bed. He sprang to his feet as a dark shape launched itself across the bed at him. He stepped back and nearly tripped over the nightstand. At least the movement helped. The figure missed him, tried to correct with a wild swing that glanced harmlessly off Crane's shoulder.

Crane stumbled toward the windows, instinctively seeking what little light there was. He registered something unnatural on the attacker's head. Then he was caught up in the long fabric curtains. He clenched one to himself and fell to the floor, yanking the curtain down with him in a rain of metal and plastic clips.

The suddenly uncovered window let in reflections from the streetlights below. The room grew brighter, but only barely. Crane realized the shape on the man's head was a set of night vision goggles, not unlike his own.

Then the man launched a vicious kick into his ribs, and Crane rolled away, struggling to get out of the downed curtain and regain his feet. But the figure followed and kicked him again. This time Crane was able to blunt the impact with a forearm, but it still sent a painful shock through his body. He needed to regain the initiative. Now. He settled onto his back, and the figure closed in to stomp his face. Crane caught the man's boot and twisted hard, throwing him off balance.

The man staggered away, fighting to regain his footing, and Crane used the brief respite to get to his feet. He threw a wild swing that connected and did little damage but did knock the other man off balance once more. Crane dove at his midsection, and they went down together—the other man hitting the bedframe hard on the way down. Then they rolled on the floor, punching, gouging, and grappling. Crane managed to slam the man's head against the bedframe again and this time dislodged the goggles so they sat half on and half off his face, effectively blinding him. He flailed and managed to connect with a kick to Crane's side. But now Crane had the advantage. He deflected a wild punch and fell across the man's chest, weighing him down, and pressed a forearm hard against his throat. He held it there, feeling the man's struggles slowly grow weaker, his ragged breaths fading. Then he was still.

Crane kept the pressure on until he was positive the man was dead. Then he rolled off onto his back, breathing hard. He was dimly aware that someone in the next room was pounding on the wall.

Crane staggered to his feet. He was lightheaded; it was hard to keep his balance. More than just adrenaline and exertion. There was that medicinal smell in the air. Somewhere a hiss of escaping gas. He stumbled to the doorway and switched on the lights. The body lay beside the bed, a shape in blue coveralls, its face covered by the dislodged goggles. Off to one side, where it had rolled almost under the suite's couch, was a dark green metal bottle with a brass valve and a clear plastic face mask. He staggered to it, almost fell beside it, and frantically turned the brass knob until the hissing stopped. Then he forced himself to his feet, turned on the vents and the air conditioning, and staggered to the bathroom. He closed the door, switched on the fan, and sat down hard on the toilet lid and remained there in his boxer shorts until his vision cleared and the metallic taste was gone from the back of his throat.

When he could stand and focus his vision again, he walked back out into the room. The clock on the nightstand said it was almost 3:30 in the morning. The pounding on the walls had stopped. Whoever they'd awakened had apparently been satisfied. Crane could make out the blinking red reflection of a traffic light through the window.

The body was still sprawled on the floor beside the bed. The man had worn blue work coveralls and black gloves. The night vision goggles were built into a rubber mask that covered his head entirely. Crane knelt and peeled them away. The man was perhaps in his forties, with rough skin and salt and pepper hair cut short. He searched his pockets and came out with a set of heroin works in a plastic bag: a length of rubber surgical tubing, a bent and tarnished spoon, a cotton ball, a lighter, and a plastic syringe. In the bottom of the bag were a couple small baggies of black tar heroin.

So the plan had been to knock him out with what Crane assumed was some kind of surgical anesthetic, and then stage a heroin overdose. He sat back and took a long, deep breath. The robbery was one thing, but this was quite another. If whoever he was looking for hadn't been on to him before, they clearly were now.

He finished searching the body and found only a master keycard for the hotel's doors. And he noticed the man wasn't wearing any shoes, just heavy woolen socks.

Crane quickly dressed. He went to the door and looked out through the viewer. The hallway looked empty. He opened the door and found a pair of work boots set neatly against the wall outside. He took them back inside and put them on the body. He put the drug kit back into the man's pocket but kept the keycard. Then he dragged the body to the door and stepped out into the hallway.

He stood there for a long moment, listening. He heard nothing. At some point the hotel would start to wake up. Early risers, newspaper delivery. But for now the coast looked clear. He lifted the body up and hefted it over his shoulder and then took it down the hall to a maintenance closet. The keycard opened the door, and he dumped the body inside, next to the mop buckets.

He looked at the body slumped amid the mops and the cleaning supplies and the barrel of rags. He resisted the urge to feel badly for him. Whoever this was, the man had tried to murder him in a particularly unpleasant way. Crane could sense that he was getting close to the source of all this malevolence, and the closer he got, the more violence he'd stir up. It had been this way in his fieldwork for the government. Now was no time for sympathy. Now was the time to go to ground and let his enemies reveal themselves by searching for him.

He closed the door and went back to his room. The curtain was a mess of ripped fabric and broken plastic rings. There was nothing he could do about that. But otherwise he made sure the room was cleaned up and free of anything damning. He packed what little he would need in a shaving kit bag the thieves had left behind and headed downstairs.

A few minutes later, the valet brought the Audi up to the front entrance, and Crane disappeared into the night.

He avoided the main streets and drove carefully through the side streets and alleys of the old town, streets designed for horses and pushcarts. The Audi stood out here like a tiger in a flock of sheep. He needed to get it off the street before the city started to wake up.

Some exploring eventually turned up a private garage near Zelny Trh square. Once he managed to wake up the owner and hand over enough euros to quell the man's irritation at the ungodly hour, Crane hid the Audi away in a private bay at the back of the building and hit the streets on foot.

He still stood out, of course. The next step was to ditch his expensive clothes and take on a new persona, one that could move around Brno unnoticed. That was tricky since he didn't speak the language. He'd never pass for a local, so he'd become a tourist. Just a considerably less flamboyant one.

He waited until the shops opened in the morning, and then found a second-hand store in a poorer quarter and emerged in an old pair of jeans, a thick army sweater, and hiking boots. The backpack was the perfect touch. It would hold his weapons and gear, and it was festooned with patches from all over Europe, including flags from half a dozen countries, as many cities, and a peace sign. Best of all, it had an honest-to-God Che Guevara portrait sewn onto the back, the young revolutionary's thick-browed eyes glaring out from beneath his beret against a bright red field. Crane was delighted—it was perfect. He had become the very stereotype of an earnest, if not slightly annoying, grad-uate student backpacking around Europe. With his hair ruffled and a day's worth of beard, he was pretty sure he could pass unnoticed now.

An involuntary yawn reminded him that he was exhausted after a mostly sleepless night. The next step would be to find a youth hostel that kept daytime hours. He'd catch some sleep and stay out of sight until he worked out what to do next.

CHAPTER 31

Klement Novak sat at his desk with his office door closed while the security people stomped back and forth outside, checking cameras and questioning his people.

He was not having a good morning.

Everything had seemed so perfect last night at Borgo Agnese. If nothing else, he'd been eating at Borgo Agnese, a place he couldn't usually afford. It was as if the American, John Crane, had swept into Brno bringing the good life with him, and Novak had been caught up in his wake. The demo had gone very well. He was convinced Crane's company was going to buy Dešt-nik, and then he'd be on his way. The sky would be the limit.

Then, somehow, this morning, it had all vanished like a mirage in the desert. Crane had missed his appointment. Novak and his people had waited in the lobby, growing more and more anxious as the minutes slipped by. He'd tried the cell number Crane had given him, and left a couple urgent messages but got nothing. What he got, after almost an hour of waiting, wasn't his angel investor but a dozen security men from Jižni Morova BioKapital. They'd invaded the building—Novak could think of no better word for it—and swept every inch of the place. And then the questions had started.

Who was the American? What was he doing here? What did he say? What was he wearing? During the presentation, which chair did he sit in? What did you talk about at dinner? What did he order?

It had been the same with his people. Anybody who had so much as seen John Crane was questioned to within an inch of their lives. They were being extremely aggressive for company security men.

If that's what they were. They didn't act like any security Novak had seen before. He'd repeatedly demanded to know what this was about and why he and his staff were being subjected to this treatment. He hadn't gotten an answer. He was beginning to wonder if they weren't something else entirely.

He stood and paced around his office for a minute, and then opened the door and stepped out into the central cubicle area. Eyes followed him, his staff wondering what the hell was going on, what he was going to do about it.

The security team was moving from desk to desk, inserting flash drives into all the PCs and doing ... something.

"Did the American come to your cube?" one of them was asking poor Nedda, who was so scared she was almost crying.

"Leave her alone!" Novak called. "She didn't do anything."

The man looked back over his shoulder at him, scoffed, and turned back to Nedda. "Did he touch this computer? Even once?"

Novak stormed down the hall to the conference room where the main detachment had set up. There was a man there who seemed to be in charge. He would complain to him. If that didn't help, he'd call his point of contact at the incubator firm itself. There was no excuse for this. They'd done nothing wrong.

As he turned the corner, two of the men were leaning against the far wall, sharing a cigarette.

"Why's the boss so worked up?" one was saying to the other. "It's one guy."

"Why don't you ask Zajic," said the other one.

"That's the guy that took out Zajic? Shit ..."

Novak stopped short. Both men looked up at him. It wasn't a friendly look. Novak turned around, and they watched him as he walked slowly back around the corner. He returned to his office and sat down behind his desk, stunned.

Zajic. Crane had used that name. Emil Zajic. Crane had thought the man was an employee, but Novak had never heard of him. What had Crane said about him? What was his job supposed to be? He tapped a pencil against the edge of his desk until it came to him. Mergers and acquisitions.

It couldn't be a coincidence. Apparently there really was an Emil Zajic somewhere. And Crane thought he worked for Deštnik.

Novak got up, walked over to his door, and locked it. Then he sat down at his computer and started to go through the company's HR files.

———

Crane sat cross-legged on the bottom level of a wooden bunk bed in a dormitory room surrounded by other wooden bunks. It had taken some looking, but he finally found a hostel on a back alley in one of Brno's older neighborhoods that would let him check in at midday. The other guests were out during the day, and Crane had the room to himself for now. It was time to check in with Josh. He'd want to know what had happened.

Crane checked his phone's clock. It was a little before 8:00 in the morning in California. If Josh was still in bed, Crane would wake him up. He hadn't had any sleep last night. Let Josh share a bit of the hardship.

The phone rang several times before Josh picked up. "Just a moment, John," Josh said in an unusually restrained voice. Then Crane heard voices in the background. Far from waking him up, it sounded like he'd caught Josh in a meeting.

"Sorry, John," Josh said finally. "What's up? How's Brno?"

"It's been better," said Crane. "Somebody tossed my room last night."

"Are you all right? Are you in trouble?"

"I'm fine. I was at dinner with Novak when it happened. I went through the motions with the police. My cover's intact with them, at least. But the opposition's made me."

"That doesn't sound good. How do you know?"

"Because after the police were gone, somebody else broke into my room while I was sleeping and tried to kill me."

Josh was silent for a long moment. "My God," he said at last. "This is getting bad. I'm starting to think you should scrub and get out of there."

"No," said Crane. "I'm getting closer. That's why this happened. We've poked the bear, Josh. You don't run now."

"Okay," Josh said. "I agreed we'd do this your way, so okay. Am I clear on the sequence of events? They robbed your room first. Then they came *back* later and tried to kill you?"

"That's right," said Crane. "I think the robbery was a coincidence. The police certainly didn't seem very surprised. Part of the act was flashing my status symbols around. Someone was staking out the hotel when I got here. I think we're looking at thieves who got more than they bargained for."

"Oh God, yeah, what did they get?"

"The surveillance gear mainly. The weapons and most of the really incriminating stuff was in the car. But they were probably very surprised when they opened those suitcases. In fact," he added, "that might be what triggered the attack. Our opponent obviously has criminal connections. If the thieves sent up a red flag about my gear, that might be what tipped him off."

"So what's your next move?" Josh asked.

"I need some guidance. I think Novak's a pawn," said Crane. "I don't think he has any idea what's going on. So the next question is, who could use his company like that without the CEO having a clue?"

There was a moment of line tone, then, "You said they get their office space from an incubator, right? That would be my guess. They provide seed capital, office space. If they're providing shared back-office support, that means they're probably doing the books for every startup on the campus."

"Internet too?"

"Internet backbone would be part of the turnkey office package. All the companies would be working off their servers."

"So they could set up their people with a Deštnik cover that would pass muster."

Josh laughed. "They could do a lot more than that. Most of these startup guys are tech bros. Bio bros in this case, I guess. They know their stuff, but they don't know squat about business. That's why they turn to these incubators in the first place. So they work around the clock on their research and take the rest of it for granted. They'd have no idea what's really going on."

Crane let out a low whistle as the pieces started to fall into place. This could go well beyond just providing fake jobs for smugglers operating overseas. They could be laundering money through Deštnik and the other startups, using them to ship things into or out of the country. The possibilities were endless.

"I'm sold," said Crane. "The incubator's called Jižni Morova BioKapital. Can your people run some checks?"

"I'll get somebody on it right away."

"I'll call you in a couple days. I'm going to try and plant the sniffer you sent me. So watch for data packets from .cz addresses."

"We'll be watching," said Josh. "Be careful, John."

"Always."

Then Crane hung up and slipped the phone in his pocket as a young couple came in speaking German, nodded to him, and dumped their packs on a pair of bunks.

He was always careful. That was what had gotten him this far. The question, as always, was where was that line between too careful and not careful enough?

CHAPTER 32

Jižni Morova BioKapital occupied a four-story building in a downtown neighborhood that was shifting from residential to commercial. The building had a gray metal façade with the company name in machined letters over its glass doors. It perched on a street full of white houses with steep, red-tiled roofs like an alien invader.

Crane walked around the block to a narrow street lined with small businesses—book shops, a hair salon—and went into a coffee shop to wait. He'd spent most of the last two days casing the building and getting a feel for the surrounding neighborhood. He was as ready as he was going to be.

Crane watched the movement of people and cars outside as the evening rush hour passed and the streets gradually emptied. He left the coffee shop before he became conspicuous there and wandered the streets for another hour.

It was dark when he was ready to move. He stepped into the shadowy murk of an alley and removed his gear from his pack. He still had a set of lockpicks, the flash drive with Josh's mysterious spyware, and Emil Zajic's pistol. He'd spent a couple hours yesterday modifying his beaten up jacket to hold the pistol with its long silencer so it would be readily accessible.

The flash drive went into the watch pocket of his Levi's. Josh had promised that all he had to do was find an active computer connected to the network and plug in the drive. The software would do the rest, digging through the company's files and sending what it found home to Josh's people over the Net.

The building was on a slight grade, and at the lowest corner was a small loading bay that should lead into the basement. Beside it was a small access door, long unused from the looks of it. The company didn't deal in truckloads of cargo. Crane guessed the bay itself was used rarely, and when they did use it, they simply used the rolling garage door itself for access. The hinges and lock were rusted, but Crane had prepared for that. Crane was betting the building's security system didn't cover it.

But there was only one way to be sure. He oiled the hinges and lock from a small bottle he'd picked up earlier that day from a sewing machine repair shop around the corner. Then he took a small flashlight from his pack and held it in his teeth as he picked the lock. It gave way reluctantly, with a small shriek that Crane actually found reassuring under the circumstances. No one had used the door in years.

The door still creaked despite the fresh lubrication. Crane slowly edged it open with a series of tiny metallic groans, just far enough for him to squeeze through. His flashlight revealed only stained concrete, electrical junction boxes, and dust.

He now had two objectives: get a keycard so he could move around the building, and find the server room. The doors and elevators all had black plastic card readers set in the walls at waist level. Crane had watched people coming and going with ID cards clipped to their belts or on lanyards around their necks. They would wave the cards at the boxes, which would beep in confirmation and then let them open the doors. It was a corporate ritual, like genuflecting at church. There were ways around the system, but Crane didn't have the equipment anymore. Even if he did, it would be easier to just get a card.

He pulled up the hood of the sweatshirt he wore under his jacket and made his way to the stairs.

Thankfully, fire codes were universal, Crane thought as the stairwell door opened for him. The doors would let anyone into the stairwell, even without a card, to avoid trapping someone in the building in an emergency. Of course, to get out of the stair-well anywhere other than on the main floor, he'd need a badge. So Crane made his way upstairs, found a nice-looking spot between the second and third floors, and sat down to wait.

He was already familiar with the first floor. Beyond the glass doors was an expansive marble and aluminum lobby with reception and security desks at the back and walls lined with colorful educational displays, as if the place spent half its time hosting groups of schoolchildren. The second floor was a mezzanine, open to the lobby to create a large, airy space. A huge mobile of a DNA molecule hung overhead. Two spirals of multicolored balls and rods ran almost the whole length of the lobby. Below it was a pushcart with racks of pamphlets and magazines, presumably touting the region's research infrastructure and industrial prowess.

The security office was on the main floor, and it was possible the servers were down there too, but Crane doubted it. The IT workers would be housed near the servers, and there was no office space for them on the ground floor. The second floor was unlikely too. The architects wouldn't want to waste the view into that huge open space on windowless storage closets. That floor would be offices and conference rooms. That left three and four, with four being executive country. So Crane was betting on three. But it didn't really matter until someone brought him a keycard.

So Crane waited, staring at the institutional beige walls and doing dips on the handrails until he heard a sudden electronic beep from below. An instant later, there was the click of the magnetic latch on the door to the second floor releasing.

Crane stood facing the door and put both hands on the stair rails.

The door opened and a guard entered. The door closed behind him before he looked up and saw Crane smiling down at him.

"Hi there," said Crane. Then he put his weight on the handrails, raised both legs off the step, and kicked the guard hard in the chest. He pushed off the rails and dropped to the landing as the guard slammed hard against the wall and staggered. Another punch put him down. Crane gently lowered his unconscious body to the floor and took his radio and keycard.

The third floor hallways were quiet and dimly lit. Crane made his way down the corridor, pointing his phone's camera at the signs beside the closed doors. A translator app replaced the Czech words with English on the screen. Most were the names and titles of the people who worked behind them. All of them had panels of frosted glass beside them to let some light through. But eventually Crane found a door that lacked the glass panel but did have a keycard reader nearby. He pointed his phone at it: "Computer Apartment," the translator app decided. Close enough.

Crane swept the card over the reader and let himself in. The lights came on as he entered, revealing racks of servers trailing bundles of Ethernet cable. Bingo.

On a table was a PC with a monitor, keyboard, and mouse. The screen ran a continually updating series of line and bar charts labeled in Czech. Crane assumed it was displaying the network's status, metrics like server loads, volumes of data moving through the connections, and memory utilization.

Crane found an open USB port on the side and plugged in Josh's flash drive.

He was expecting a beep from the machine, so he was startled to hear a voice speaking Czech, and then realized it was from the guard's radio. A quick interrogative, followed by a few seconds of silence, and then another query. It sounded like the man he'd knocked out had been missed. Time was short.

The screen displayed an upload bar crawling toward completion. A different voice crackled on the radio. The voices were growing more concerned. Other voices started checking in on what Crane took to be a roll call. Then the radio suddenly went silent. Someone had found the downed guard, and they'd realized their communications were compromised and switched frequencies.

The upload bar finished filling its box and vanished. The screen went back to displaying the same real-time network metrics it had been showing before. Crane hoped that meant all was well. He pulled the drive and stuck it back into his pocket.

The hall was still empty and quiet as he slipped out. He was closer to the far end of the building from where he'd left the guard, so he went that way. He came upon a set of elevators and had an idea. Maybe he could send them out of his way. He called a car, reached around the open door, and sent it up to the top floor. Then he hurried back the way he'd come and entered the stairwell.

Noise echoed off the concrete here. Crane tried to be quiet, but the door had made some noise, and his footsteps could still be heard. Then someone shouted in Czech, and Crane heard footsteps hurrying up from below. He almost made it to the second-floor landing when a uniformed figure burst around the corner. Crane drew the CZ-80 from his jacket and fired a flurry of shots over the guard's head. Even silenced, the gun echoed like a thunderclap in the confined space. The guard fell back, and Crane dove for the door to two.

But the door refused to open. The damn keycard. He ducked as the guard reappeared around the bend in the stairs and snapped off a shot. Now Crane heard shouting from above and more footsteps descending. They would box him in in seconds.

There was no more time to play softball.

The guard popped around the stairs again, leading with his pistol. Crane shot him in the upper chest, watched him fall back, and heard the gun clatter down the stairs.

Then he stopped thinking about him and swept his stolen keycard across the reader to open the door.

He emerged into a long hallway with offices and conference space on one side, and the yawning open space of the lobby on the other. Two guards stood in the middle of the lobby. As soon as the door opened, one saw him and shouted. Then they both opened fire. There was a metal safety railing and Lucite panels meant to keep dropped objects from falling to the floor below. Crane dove for the floor, and bullets started to splinter the Lucite all around him.

He crawled down the hallway on his knees and elbows, and the guards stopped firing. The Lucite panels were enough to protect him, but they kept their guns trained on him. One was shouting into his radio.

A moment later, the door behind him beeped and flew open. Crane rolled onto his back and fired two shots, center mass, into the figure emerging from the stairwell. Another bullet from below smashed into the panel next to him with a slapping noise, and the clear Lucite went opaque white.

One of the guards had left, Crane realized. They had him pinned down here so one would stay to report Crane's movements and take a shot if he got one. The other would join the rest of the detachment and take him here. He assumed they had people in both stairwells coordinating their attacks on him by radio.

If he was going to escape, he needed to get the initiative on the one below him. He whirled toward the far stairwell and fired a shot into the closed door. As he hoped, the guard below was thrown off, assuming Crane must be firing at his companions. Perhaps someone had moved too soon and ruined the plan. He spun in that direction to see what was happening.

The instant's distraction was all Crane needed. He popped up over the railing and took the man out with a single shot.

Then, just as both stairwell doors beeped, Crane vaulted onto the railing and pushed off hard with both legs. For a moment, he soared through the air, feeling the sickening lurch in his stomach as gravity clawed at him, tried to smash him against the marble floor below.

Instead, Crane slammed hard into the enormous DNA molecule that hung in the middle of the space. He managed to hook an arm around a rod that linked a yellow atom to a green one a few feet away. But the model was made of wire and thin plastic, not meant to bear weight. He heard cables snapping as the whole thing began to pull loose from the ceiling.

Then the guards opened fire from the mezzanine. Bullets whistled past him, punching holes in what remained of the blueprint for all life. Crane was going down fast, anyway. He swung toward the only thing he could see that looked likely to break his fall—the pushcart full of pamphlets—and let go.

He hit the fabric cover hard, and the cart disintegrated under the impact, throwing out a blizzard of informative marketing material. The remains of the mobile followed, crashing down and scattering plastic and wire across the lobby. The guards lost him for a moment in the chaos.

Crane shook off the impact and was getting ready to sprint for the front doors when he saw the bright red and blue glow of police lights approaching down the street. This just kept getting better, he thought.

He looked for another way out and decided his best choice was the door behind the receptionist's counter. He took a deep breath and sprinted for it as a hail of bullets slammed into the marble around him.

He vaulted the counter, scattering flat-screen monitors and telephones. He was directly beneath the mezzanine hallway now, and the guards no longer could see him. He heard shouting from above as he whipped the keycard across the reader and opened the door. Beyond was a straight, dark corridor. Crane sprinted down it, past side doors to the emergency exit. Again he practically threw the keycard at the reader and let his shoulder knock the door open.

Crane emerged in the alley behind the building, breathing hard. He took a moment to recover in the cool night air. But he could hear sirens on the main avenue and knew he wasn't out of this yet.

Across the alley and three doors down was a locked door that Crane was reasonably sure was the back door of a café on the next block. He quickly picked the lock and let himself in. He found himself in a cramped space lined with shelves crammed with cardboard boxes. There was just enough light to see his way through a beaded curtain to the front of the house.

Then Crane noticed a small blinking light at his side. An alarm panel. He shook his head. This was not his night.

Crane dashed to the front door and flipped the lock. He managed to get out to the sidewalk moments before the alarm started loudly whooping in time with the police sirens. They were now two blocks away. But the police would take notice before long and realize which way he'd gone. He needed to get off the street, or they'd eventually run him down.

He hurried around the corner and nearly collided with a

shapely brunette in a revealing micro-dress. He backed up a step and said, "Sorry," in English.

"No problem," she replied in accented English. "So where are you off to in such a hurry? Maybe you are looking for a party?"

He was in no position to reject an opportunity to get off the street, Crane thought. He grinned. "I love a good party."

She smiled through brightly painted lips. "Well, all right. I know a place. Let's go party!"

Crane offered her his arm, and they strolled off down the street together.

CHAPTER 33

The girl's name was Natalya. She took Crane to her small apartment and had the grace to feign disappointment when he said he didn't want to sleep with her. Instead, he paid her for her time, and they talked about life in Brno while Crane searched her kitchen and came up with enough to put together a passable meal for them.

She was Ukrainian but had been working her way west since leaving home two years ago. She'd been in Brno for a little less than six months, but she was well versed in the local criminal scene.

"Start at the top," Crane said as he added a bit of green pepper to the sausage and onions frying in a pan on her small gas stove. "Who's the big man on campus?"

"Kucera," she said. She sat at a small kitchen table of aluminum and Formica. "Anton Kucera. He came from the street gangs. I think he just pushed out the old boss not too long ago. Everyone is scared of him. I saw him once. He scared me too."

"What did he look like?"

"Not much older than me. He doesn't look Slavic. They say his mother was Italian. Blond hair, not tall. Dark eyes. He had a scar over one eye, I remember. He's handsome, I guess, but very intense. I didn't want to be around him."

"So he runs everything now." Crane vigorously beat some eggs in a bowl and then splashed some white wine she had open in the refrigerator into the pan. She sat at the table and watched him cook for her with a curious expression.

"What do you call this?"

"It's a Greek omeleta. Nothing fancy." He dumped the eggs into the pan and then covered it with a plate. "So is one of Kucera's lines of business robbing hotel rooms, by any chance?"

"Oh, yes. The rich tourist hotels. Very much."

Well, that was probably who had ended up with his surveillance gear, then. May it serve him well, Crane thought. It seemed pretty useless to him at the moment when he didn't have any idea who he should surveil with it.

"Here comes the tricky part," he said. He flipped the pan over and then took it away to reveal the omeleta on the plate. "And now the other side." He slid it back into the pan and adjusted the heat slightly.

Before long, Crane was satisfied with it and slid it back onto the plate. Natalya produced more plates and some mismatched silverware, and they ate it with the rest of the wine at her little table while an electric clock hummed on the wall above.

"Nobody ever cooked for me before," she said.

"Really? Nobody?"

"Well, my mother, of course. But apart from that ... no."

"That's too bad." Then his phone chirped in his pocket—Josh's ringtone.

He gave her an apologetic smile. "I need to take this. Go ahead and eat."

He wandered into the apartment's small living room and took the call.

"Yes?"

"Can you talk?" Josh's voice. He glanced over his shoulder. Natalya was still at the table, but the apartment was small. It wasn't as though she couldn't hear him. He decided she was no danger.

"It's okay."

"Well, we got what there was to get from their computers, but we hit a dead end."

Crane really didn't like the idea that he'd done all this and killed at least two men for nothing.

"What do you mean?"

"The guy in charge of BioKapital is one Dalibor Cermak. I'm sending you pictures and a brief on him now. But trust me, this is not the kind of man who sends a squad of dirty cops with assault rifles to shoot up a research facility in the rainforest. Guy's about as interesting as a box of saltine crackers. And I wouldn't want you to think there's an interesting picture on the box or anything. We're talking generic saltines. He's that dull."

"Is he leading a secret double life?"

"No. Or at least, he's doing it really well if he is. There's more. The company's financial structure is all screwed up. Everything's triple blinded through trusts and holding companies. My people got nowhere. And they're very good at what they do."

Crane didn't doubt it. So this Cermak had to be a distraction, a squeaky clean puppet for whoever was really running the company.

"Do you want to meet him?" Josh asked suddenly.

"Cermak? What do you mean?"

"One thing we turned up, there's a state trade congress that he's part of. They're holding a function for some Chinese investors tomorrow night."

"Can you talk somebody into giving me an invitation?"

"We can do better than that. My guys can get into that system, no problem. We'll just add you to the list. Your name?"

"No, I'm persona non grata around here. Make me German. Gerhard von Brandt. With BASF." He thought for a moment. "And a plus one."

He lowered the phone for a moment and called back over his shoulder to Natalya, "You want to go to a real party?"

———

Crane stepped out of a rented limo in front of a building that could only have been built by Russians. Its huge, brutalist facade was hung with long, spotlit banners displaying the Czech and Chinese flags.

"What are you smiling at?" Natalya asked as she took his hand and got out of the limo. Crane nodded toward the flags. "Strange world. All those former and current communists in there talking about making money."

"I suppose," she said with a disinterested shrug.

They looked stunning as they walked up the wide steps to the main entrance. Crane wore the Brioni suit, freshly cleaned and pressed. He'd added a new pair of Stefano Bemer shoes because he thought they fit this new, temporary character and because he wanted Josh to feel he was getting his money's worth. Natalya wore a sleek Fouad Sarkis dress in a soft green, with a halter neckline and a long slit up the left leg. It cost more than the rent on her apartment, and Crane was sure she'd never worn anything remotely that expensive. But he had to admit she knew exactly how to wear it.

All eyes were on her at the front entrance. Just as Crane wanted.

"Von Brandt," he said in accented English to the large, tuxedoed man at the door. "And my companion." The man struggled to keep his eyes off Natalya as his second checked the name against a list on his tablet.

"Good evening, Herr von Brandt," the second said after a moment. "Welcome."

Inside, the main atrium was strewn with flowers and banners with slogans in Chinese and Czech. Guests made small talk while a string quartet played, and waiters distributed wine and hors-d'oeuvres.

There were a few shallow steps down from the entry to the main floor. They stopped at the top and surveyed the crowd, searching for Cermak.

"Got him," Natalya said in triumph. "Ten o'clock, near the wine bar."

She indicated a man with a subtle flick of her fingers, and Crane realized that was indeed Dalibor Cermak standing at the bar, although he had a different haircut than in the picture Josh had sent. Natalya had spotted him first. "You win," said Crane, and he passed her a folded one hundred Euro note.

"I don't even know what we're doing here."

"We're here to figure that man out. See how he handles himself. See who he talks to."

They walked down the steps to the main level and accepted glasses of wine from a waiter.

"That sounds like a very dull party," she said with a bit of laughter in her voice.

"Probably," he said. "If it stops being dull, put some distance between us. Get out of here by the nearest exit and catch a cab."

She looked at him with sudden concern. "He doesn't look dangerous. What are you planning to do?"

Crane tried his wine. It was a local varietal, sweeter than he liked, but he thought Gerhard von Brandt would probably like it, so he smiled and nodded.

"I'm just planning to gather information. But things haven't been going the way I've planned them lately."

A photographer appeared in front of them and told them to

smile as he snapped off a couple quick shots. Then he moved on through the crowd, turning and snapping and moving in quick bursts of speed.

"Who's this for again?" asked Natalya.

"Chinese trade delegation," said Crane. He nodded toward a group of Chinese in boxy gray suits talking with a group of what he took to be Czech government officials. The Czechs' suits had wider lapels, and they seemed to be drinking more. The Chinese looked more uncomfortable than anything else as their hosts made sweeping gestures and spoke a little louder than necessary.

"Like I said," Natalya murmured. "Bad party."

Cermak took a drink from the bartender and stalked away to the center of the room. Crane watched him join a stocky fireplug of a man with graying hair and another who had to be a body-guard based on the musculature and the suit.

Crane moved closer, Natalya following in his wake. She traded a couple words in Russian with someone as they passed. Then a waiter with a tray moved into Crane's path, and he stopped short. When his view cleared again, he saw the gray-haired man staring straight at him. Their eyes locked for a moment, and Crane felt an animal hatred in the other man's gaze. Hatred and fear. He'd gone pale, as if he'd seen a ghost. Cermak was trying to talk to him, but the gray-haired man wasn't even hearing him.

Crane broke the eye contact and glanced around. Every-thing seemed normal. Nobody else was paying attention to either him or the other man. No, there was no question who the older man was looking at or what his reaction meant. Crane had never seen him before, but he knew beyond doubt that the man recognized him, and he was no friend.

The bodyguard had picked it up too, following his boss' gaze and homing in on Crane. Crane saw him instinctively slip into a combat-ready stance.

Then there was a squawk from the PA system and the sound of someone tapping on the mic. Everyone turned toward the dais where someone made a quick announcement in Czech.

The sightline between Crane and the gray-haired man was broken as the crowd shifted. He turned to Natalya. "What did he say?"

"Speeches now," she said in disgust. "This just keeps getting better."

The first speaker introduced another one, and everyone applauded. "Deputy minister of industry and trade," Natalya murmured. "Hurray."

Crane noticed a slim figure moving through the crowd a step or two at a time, apologizing and excusing himself as he came. A moment later, he recognized Klement Novak. Damn it, he thought. Not now.

He turned toward the dais and focused on the speaker. Perhaps Novak wouldn't recognize him. Or at least wouldn't want to make a scene in the middle of the speech.

But Novak brushed against Crane as he passed. "You have to get out of here," he said softly but with urgency. "Right now. You're not safe here."

Then he moved on in a straight line past Crane and vanished into the crowd.

Crane glanced over where the gray-haired man had been, but he was gone. He scanned the room and spotted the bodyguard, without his boss, leaning in to speak with one of the event's security personnel.

There was an emergency exit on the far side of the space, near one of the bars. He nudged Natalya and guided her through the crowd in that direction.

"What did that man mean?" she asked. "What's the matter?"

"It'll be okay," said Crane, his voice as reassuring as he could make it. They made their way to the edge of the crowd, and Crane swept this side of the room. There was the bar, and the fire exit just beyond it. To his left was a hallway. Crane watched two waiters walk down it with their trays at their side. They passed restrooms—identified by icons on frosted glass panels—and then disappeared through twin swinging doors into what had to be the kitchen.

"What's happening?" Natalya repeated a bit more urgently.

"It's okay, but I don't know the score, so we're going to fall back. You first. While I'm getting a drink at the bar, you go to the ladies' room." He nodded toward the hallway. "Except you're really going through the kitchen and out the back. Get a cab and go home."

"Come with me! You're frightening me!"

"You'll be safe on your own. It's me they're interested in."

She hesitated but finally she bit her lip and nodded. "You'll come back to my place?"

"I will. You'll be fine. Go now."

He stepped away from her toward the bar, and that seemed to shake her out of inaction. She walked into the side hallway. Crane watched her walk past the restrooms and disappear into the kitchen.

He ordered a vodka and tonic and watched the security people get nervous, one after the other, as word that something was up spread across the room.

He tried looking for the gray-haired man—he decided he had to call him something better than that and settled on "Ivan." He looked for Ivan but couldn't find him. Either he was just lost in the crowd or he'd left without his bodyguard.

The speech ended suddenly, and the crowd applauded. The next speaker was Chinese. He came to the podium with a translator, and the whole cycle began again.

Crane was watching Ivan's bodyguard when he noticed the photographer pass by and head down the hall toward the kitchen. Crane followed.

He walked through the swinging double doors into a steamy, loud expanse of white tile and stainless steel. The place was peppered with chefs and waiters lounging while they waited for the end of the speeches to signal the next course. Nobody paid any attention to him.

Crane found the photographer in a disused corner, pulling lenses out of a shoulder bag. He looked up as Crane approached.

"You shouldn't be back here," he said.

"No," Crane said, "probably not. But I'm going to offer you a thousand euros for a copy of your pictures, and I didn't want to do it out there in public."

The photographer wasted no time. He pulled a spare card out of his bag and slapped it into the camera's second slot and then copied the first card over to it. A few moments later, he traded the card for a handful of bills.

"I'll be back with more pictures later," the photographer said with a wide grin as he stuffed the money into his pocket.

Crane smiled back. "These will do. Thanks."

The photographer headed out the doors toward the main space, and Crane was about to do the same when the doors swung open and Ivan's bodyguard came through.

He and Crane startled each other. Crane could see him tensing to attack. Crane slapped the guard's fist away and stepped inside the arc of his swing. Then he punched the man hard in the solar plexus and knocked the wind out of him. He followed up with a palm strike that broke his nose, and finally grabbed the lapel of his suit and threw him over his hip. The bodyguard hit the floor hard and stayed down.

Crane turned and realized the entire kitchen was looking at him in stunned silence. He smiled at them.

"Sorry," he said. "He's an awful tipper. You all work too hard for that."

Then he walked past them, between a pair of long prep tables and out the back door.

CHAPTER 34

Branislav Skala stalked through the building's security office like a caged panther. He'd retreated here for his own safety and to give his bodyguard freedom to operate. He didn't like being alone with only a handful of the building's security men for protection. They looked useless, and they weren't his people. But at least the head of the security division knew very well who Branislav Skala was and knew better than to stand in his way.

Skala watched the party on the monitors. The assorted trade functionaries had no idea what was happening. The man from Team Kilo must have come here for him. But at the moment, he was nowhere to be seen. That just made Skala more nervous. He'd sent his bodyguard Pavel to search the parts of the building that weren't on camera, but there'd been no report yet. He'd also called back to his estate for reinforcements. They'd be useful even if Team Kilo's man—this "John Crane" or "Gerhard von Brandt," or whoever he was—had backed off and fled. Whether he could find him in the building or not, at least he could start cutting off his enemy's lines of support.

"Show me the recordings," he told a nervous camera operator. "Show me that man from the moment he entered the building."

The door opened and Skala's hand instinctively went to his jacket, but of course, there was no gun there tonight. He'd wanted to become a gentleman, and gentlemen let others do their killing for them. He was beginning to miss the edge of adrenaline, even the taste of blood in his mouth. This was a strange, desiccated world he was moving into, where every signal was subtle, every move obscure, and its results invisible to the eye but only felt in the gut.

It was his reinforcements. Four of his best men filed in. They looked wary, on edge.

"Boss?" said the leader.

"Do you have that footage yet?" he snapped at the security guard.

"Monitor two, sir," the man stammered. He pointed to a screen, and Skala saw a view of the front door. An annoying, fat manufacturer of plastic goods came through into the party with a blonde on his arm who was way too young for him. Too tall as well, Skala thought.

"According to the log, he checked through the front door about three minutes from here," said the operator. "I'll fast-forward."

Skala let a bit of cold slip into his voice. "Yes, do that."

The image raced forward, and there he was, the same man he'd seen in the pictures from San Juan airport. He walked beside a sleek woman at his side and stood at the top of the stairway, surveying the party.

"Freeze that," he snapped. "Print half a dozen of them."

He turned to his own men. "Find the girl," he said quietly. "She's local. If he's not with her, she'll know where he is."

The office printer spit out screen grabs of Crane and the

woman, and Skala distributed them. "Go now. Call me the moment you know anything."

Two of his men nodded and walked out. A moment later, the door opened again and two of the building's security brought in his man Pavel, holding a bloody handkerchief to his face.

"What the hell happened to you?" Skala snapped. This was bad. It made him look weak in front of the outsiders.

"He broke my nose," Pavel said through the blood and the handkerchief.

"I can see that! Where is he now?"

One of the guards holding Pavel said, "According to the kitchen staff, after he beat up your man, he went out the back. He's gone."

Skala shook his head in disgust. "Get him to the car," he said to his other two men. "The side entrance! Not through the damn party!"

They took Pavel from the security guards and helped him out into the hallway.

"We're done here," Skala said to nobody in particular, and walked out after them.

"And put someone on Klement Novak," he said to the backs of his men as he followed them down the hallway. He'd seen a glimpse of something earlier on the party floor. He'd seen Novak moving through the crowd toward the man Crane. It might be nothing, but Skala had learned never to assume something was unimportant.

"He'll know something," he muttered, and followed his men out into the dark where his car waited to take him to the safety of his estate.

———

Crane had the cab drop him off several blocks from Natalya's apartment and walked the rest of the way. He doubted anyone had had time to follow the cab, but he wasn't positive. He also didn't understand the chatter between the driver and his dispatcher. Cab outfits seemed to have a connection to the seedier side of life everywhere Crane had been. It wasn't beyond question that a call had gone out to the drivers asking after him and his drop-off location had been sent back to whoever was after him.

So Crane walked a twisted, complicated route through darkened side streets, looking for signs of a tail. The night was growing colder. Some of the old alleys were still paved with cobblestones in this part of town, and the streetlights gleamed off the stone. He took another turn and checked over his shoulder. He saw no one, heard no footsteps on the cobblestones besides his own. Finally he decided they hadn't followed him.

A coffee shop was still open across the street from Natalya's building. Its bright lights cast shadows out across the pavement. A lone patron was visible at a table by the window. Crane passed by and turned quickly into the entryway of her building. He pressed the button for her apartment, and the door buzzed and let him in.

He took the stairs to the top floor and knocked at her door. There was no answer. Several seconds went by. Crane knocked again and this time heard something fall over inside. He had a terrible thought. They hadn't found him; they'd found her.

Crane turned the knob, and the door opened. He eased inside, listening, but heard nothing. As he passed out of the tiny entry foyer and into the sparse living room, he caught movement in his peripheral vision and instinctively let himself drop.

A figure in a dark overcoat moved out from behind a battered display cabinet, holding a pistol with both outstretched hands.

The gun went off with a roar in the enclosed space, and the

bullet drilled through the air over Crane's head. He hit the floor and dove for the man's legs as the shooter tried to readjust. Crane hit him hard in the shins and knocked his legs out from under him. He fell hard and fast, instinctively throwing out his arms to catch himself and fumbling the gun. Crane grabbed for it but only succeeded in knocking it across the floor toward the kitchen door. As his eyes followed it, he registered a thick spray of blood across the kitchen wall.

Then Crane was fighting with no thought for anything beyond staying alive. He kicked hard, connected somewhere. His enemy grunted in pain but then drove an elbow hard into Crane's ribcage. Crane tried to grab him, but he slid away and threw himself across the floor toward the gun. Crane grabbed his ankle as he rose to all fours, and pulled him down again.

The killer gave up on the gun. Instead, he rolled away to one side and drew a switchblade. It opened with a solid click, and the man scrambled away and got to his feet as Crane got up, breathing hard.

His opponent didn't rest. He moved forward, making a wide swing to drive Crane back against the wall. Then he followed with a thrust. Crane moved to the side, let his training come to the fore. Sidestep, strike the forearm. Try to trap it. But Crane wasn't in the right position for that.

Fall back and reposition. Crane felt the cabinet against his shoulder and leaped to his left as another thrust came in and smashed the cabinet's glass doors. It spilled a dozen little porcelain figures Natalya must have collected. Crane moved in and felt them being crushed beneath his shoes as he made simultaneous strikes at the man's throat and knife arm. This time he hit the arm on the nerve he'd been aiming for. The arm went briefly numb; Crane could see it in the way the grip on the knife softened. He slapped the knife out of the man's hand, and it fell among the shattered figurines.

The man tried to respond with a punch, but it had no energy. Crane twisted and let the blow glance off the side of his abdomen. Then he smashed the heel of his palm into the man's chest and knocked him back toward the window. The killer staggered back, trying to catch his breath and regain his balance.

Crane calmly took four steps toward him, his eyes cold with rage, and backhanded him hard across the mouth. He caught the man's attempted off-hand punch and used it to pull him down into his upthrust knee. The man gasped and went limp for a moment. Crane pushed him to the floor beside the window and fell onto his back with both knees. He grabbed for the blind and found the cord. The blind flew up with a metallic protest as he pulled the cord hard and looped it around the man's neck.

Then he pulled it tightly and held it. Crane could feel the man's struggles, but his eyes were locked on the kitchen door and the arcs of blood on the cabinets and walls.

When he knew the man was gone, he pushed off him and ran to the kitchen, knowing what he would find.

Natalya lay on the floor near the stove where he'd cooked for her. The man had fastened her arms to the back of one of her aged aluminum chairs with duct tape. Then he'd gone to work on her with the knife. It was bad. It was very bad. Crane knew she was dead, but he checked her pulse anyway and listened for breath. More than anything, he wanted to look away, but he forced himself not to.

He didn't have the right to look away.

Finally he let out a long breath. He went back to the living room and took off his jacket. He was checking the man's pockets when he noticed he was wearing an earpiece. He took it out and listened. Someone was calling out in frantic Czech. Crane dropped the earpiece, edged over to the window, and looked out. The coffee shop window was empty now.

Crane locked the door and then finished going through the

man's pockets. Besides his wallet, Crane found a few pairs of latex gloves, a phone paired to the earpiece, some keys, and another clip for the pistol.

He put on the gloves and used the switchblade to carefully cut Natalya's body free of the chair. He laid her out on the floor and wiped down the stove and areas he'd touched while he was here before. His movements were rote, mechanical. Guilt was there, but he ignored it the same way someone might ignore pain during the first rush of adrenaline. It could crash down on him later. When he was finished here.

Finally, Crane put himself back together, checked the load in the pistol, and stuck it into his belt. He listened at the door and then opened it onto an empty hallway. He took the stairs slowly, a flight at a time, and then stopped after each one to listen and sense the vibrations of the place.

The spotter was still out there. The one who'd sat with his coffee in the shop window and watched the street while his partner was upstairs torturing an innocent girl to death. The one who'd warned him when Crane arrived so he could buzz Crane into the building and then wait to murder him.

Crane made it to the front lobby without interference. He kept one hand on the butt of the pistol as he opened the door and let himself out. The street was empty. Through the window of the coffee shop, he saw only a bored barista reading a magazine behind the counter.

Crane turned left and walked down the street. What a sight he must be, he thought randomly, in his very expensive suit and shoes, with latex gloves and a stolen pistol. Then the thought vanished in the whirl of heightened sensory impressions. Crane felt the cold night air on his cheeks, heard the cries of a cat in the distance. He instinctively evaluated every reflected flash of the streetlights off glass or metal. He could feel each beat of his heart. Crane sensed something primal inside himself, something ruthless and pure.

When the spotter came, Crane was more than ready for him. He was a shape hurtling out of the darkness of a narrow alley, a blade catching the light with its particular shade of gleaming reflection. Crane caught the knife arm by the wrist and pivoted. He redirected the man's surging energy into an arc around himself and hurled him into the corner of the building on the other side of the alley. The spotter hit the stonework hard, lost the knife, and staggered back with a face full of blood. He stumbled a few steps down the alley, bleating like a sheep.

Crane followed and kicked him hard in the crotch. The spotter fell at Crane's feet, and Crane calmly drew his partner's gun and shot him twice in the head.

He dropped the gun beside the body and continued down the alley. At the other end, he turned onto a street of darkened shops and walked away.

CHAPTER 35

Crane stalked the streets, barely aware of where he was going, distracted by equal measures of rage and guilt. Eventually the night's chill got to him. He looked around and realized he was only a few blocks from the garage where he had left the Audi.

He headed that direction and jammed his hands into his jacket pockets to keep them warm. He felt something in one pocket and took out a folded piece of notepaper. He stopped under a streetlight to read the words scrawled in blue ballpoint pen. "We need to talk." A phone number. "Novak."

He remembered Novak's warning at the party. Apparently Novak had managed to slip this into his pocket at the same time without him noticing it. That was surprising by itself. But Novak had known about the threat from "Ivan." The notes suggested he had more to say. It could be a trap. But maybe there was more to Klement Novak than Crane had thought.

He took out his phone and punched in the number. It was obscenely late. By all rights, Novak should be fast asleep. Crane didn't care. He could damn well wake up.

Novak answered almost immediately.

"What do I call you?" were Novak's first words.

"Crane will do."

"And I guess you won't be buying my company. But then, it was never really my company, anyway, was it?"

"Do you have something to tell me or not?"

"You asked about an Emil Zajic," said Novak. "You were right. He worked for Deštnik, but I'd never heard of him. It turns out there's a lot going on at Deštnik that I didn't know about."

Crane was hurrying toward the garage. He let Novak have his weighty silence.

"I don't know who you are," Novak said at last, "why you're involved. But we need to meet. I have what you need."

Crane stopped short. "What do you have?"

"The files, all of them. The real ones. Names, account numbers, payments, delivery schedules. Once I knew it was buried in there, it wasn't hard to find. You can have the whole damn thing."

"Why would you want to help me?"

"Because they took everything from me!" He could hear the pain in Novak's voice. "All I was! All I poured into my work, they took it and they stretched it like a fake skin over their own rotten bones ..." Novak sighed. "Somebody with money around here, you know going in they have to be shady. Everybody knows that. But I thought they just wanted to invest. It's all useless now. And I can't do a thing about it. Who am I? I'm nobody. But you scare them. That's why I want to help you. Because whatever you are, you scare the hell out of them, and that means you can hit them back."

Crane had no idea who they thought he was. Back in Puerto Rico, Zajic had demanded answers to questions that he didn't understand. The cop, Acevedo, had said something about Team Kilo. It meant nothing to him. And now Novak was telling him people who shouldn't even know he existed were frightened of him. Frightened enough to torture a young girl.

To splash her blood shoulder-high up her kitchen walls in great arcs.

They were right to be afraid of him now.

"Where are you?"

"At Deštnik."

"Stay there. I'm on my way."

"All right. I'll meet you out front."

Crane hung up and hurried the last few blocks to the garage.

Thankfully, no one had tampered with the Audi. Crane unlocked the reluctant wooden doors and hauled them open. The R8's nose gleamed ominously in the glow of a streetlight.

He quickly checked the car and then got in and pulled the silenced CZ pistol from beneath the seat. He checked the load and set the pistol on the passenger seat. Then he turned over the engine. The car growled as he pulled out into the empty streets. It was an angry sound that fit his mood perfectly. Slaughter-house images of Natalya's kitchen kept intruding into his memory, and he fought them back. He'd deal with those thoughts later. Now he had work to do.

He let the GPS guide him back to the research campus through empty roads and past darkened houses. Brno still slept. There was a mist in the air that swirled in ghostly tendrils in his headlights and gave all the lights a hazy, yellow glow.

This could still be a trap, he thought as he drove. Novak still didn't strike him as a man who kept secrets. But Crane had just been reminded that he could make mistakes sometimes. Bad ones.

He remembered a small rise that looked down over the campus. It would offer a good view of Deštnik's building. He killed the lights and slowed as he approached. The Audi rolled slowly up to the crest, and he stopped. The research campus spread out before him. Empty parking lots, darkened buildings. Sodium lights that turned all the colors to black.

There was a figure outside Deštnik's building. Crane opened the glove box, took out a pair of high-powered binoculars. He adjusted the focus until he could see Novak stamping his feet against the chill.

Crane swept the parking lot, the spaces between buildings, even the roofs. But he saw nothing. Perhaps Novak was, once again, being up front with him.

He was putting the binoculars away when he saw a corona of headlights enter the parking lot. He yanked the binoculars back out.

The car was a dark Škoda sedan. Novak stepped forward to meet it. Crane saw him suddenly tense, then whirl and sprint back toward the building. The Škoda's driver gunned it forward, leaping the curb and following. The passenger door flew open and another figure dove out and tackled Novak just outside the front doors.

Crane swore, tossed the binoculars into the passenger footwell, and put the car into gear. He turned the lights back on and floored it. The Audi accelerated down the slope as if kicked. He took the turn into the campus at speed and flicked the lights to high.

Ahead, the car's passenger looked back at him, his face gleaming in the high beams. Then he finished stuffing Novak into the trunk. He slammed the lid, dove into the open door, and the Škoda took off.

Crane followed them out onto the main road. They took a hard left, heading back toward Brno. The car was running flat out, but it was no match for the Audi. Crane closed fast and fell in behind them.

The Hurricane Group had given him extensive training in defensive and pursuit driving. Crane was qualified in the PIT technique. All he had to do was overtake them slightly and steer into the Škoda's rear quarter to fishtail it and spin it out. But they were doing more than ninety miles per hour through this semi-rural stretch of road. His instructors had emphasized that the method wasn't recommended for speeds over thirty-five—unless the goal was to kill everyone in the target car.

But they were headed into town. Eventually they'd have to slow down to speeds where it would be safer. In the meantime, they weren't going to lose him.

He hung a couple car lengths behind them and waited for them to make a move.

Soon they did. The passenger leaned as far as he could out the side window. Crane dropped back and swerved as he opened up with a small submachine gun. Then he sped up in the far lane, putting as much of the sedan's body as he could between himself and the gun. It was probably unnecessary, he realized, as the shooter emptied the clip, spraying bullets with no control. He heard one thud into the bodywork somewhere in the rear, but nothing more.

Then the Škoda vanished. Crane checked his mirrors, looked over his shoulder. The car was simply gone, swallowed by the night. He jammed on the brakes and spun the Audi hard around. Tires squealed, and the car lurched to a stop, facing back the way he'd come.

There. A gap in the fences and a small sign in his headlights. There was a narrow side road. With his focus on the gunner, Crane had missed it completely. But they'd killed the lights and made that turn at high speed, with a man hanging out the window. He had to admit that was impressive. They did have one edge on him. They knew the territory.

Crane downshifted and hit the gas. He steered the Audi into the gap between the fences and flew down a short embankment. Then the road leveled out and led straight off between abandoned fields. Crane floored it.

Before long, he made out the shape of the Škoda ahead. He

kept his distance and followed them as the road wound through a light industrial area of metal buildings, chain-link fencing, and razor wire. The sedan was still doing more than seventy over the rough road.

Novak must be terrified bouncing around in the trunk, Crane thought. He hadn't asked Novak to stick his nose where he shouldn't. But if it wasn't for him, the man would be safe in his bed right now. Another innocent bystander Crane had put in danger. He wasn't going to get this one killed too.

The Škoda veered onto another side road, and Crane smoothly followed. He gunned the Audi forward and closed fast on them before dropping back again. Just reminding them he was there and could overtake them at will.

Then the sedan braked hard and drifted into a smaller road that led back into a neighborhood of weather-beaten old houses. Crane braked and followed. The road was barely wide enough for two cars to pass. In places, parked cars and pickup trucks choked it down even further.

The Škoda was already taking a right between two homes. Crane downshifted, and the Audi's engine complained as he braked and flung it around the corner. They'd found a way to negate his advantage. Here he was no faster than they were.

He lost sight of them after a series of tight corners. He stopped, rolled down the window, and listened. The Škoda didn't like to be pushed the way they'd pushed it. Its engine was running loud and rough somewhere to his left. Crane hit the gas, took the next corner well over its design speed, and wiped out a scooter parked near the curb. Then he raced down the straight, checking side streets as he went.

The Škoda suddenly shot across his path a couple blocks ahead, a dark shape bouncing over the road gradient with its lights off. He had them again.

Crane gunned the Audi forward, jarring over potholes. He

took the left to follow them and saw them racing down another country road, this one headed back away from the lights of Brno.

This road was straight and empty, passing through forest that gave way to marshy flood plain along one of the rivers. The Svratka and the Svitava converged at Brno. Crane was lost now. He had no idea which river that was off to his left. But he knew the road was straight and empty. It was time to stop this.

He took the Audi up over one hundred, closing rapidly on the sedan and easing into the far lane. He caught a glimpse of a battered hatchback parked far over on the shoulder as it flashed past. Then a running figure ahead of him, throwing something. Then the narrow black line that fell across the road.

He jammed the brake hard into the floor, but he knew it was too late. The Audi hit the spike strip at more than eighty, and all four tires shredded into a cloud of rubber and steel. The wheel wrenched out of his hands. Crane's training cut in, and he instinctively crossed his hands over his chest and braced for impact.

For a brief moment, the Audi was airborne. Its engine whined so loud, it almost sounded like it might take off and fly. Then the car slammed into the mud flat. The airbags exploded into Crane's face and chest, and he rode it out as the Audi was flung around to one side and rolled.

He was alive when the car stopped moving and the bags deflated. He'd been slammed around, but the airbags and driver's harness had done their job. Nothing was broken. The car was upright, canted over to Crane's right. Mud was oozing through the passenger side door.

He took a moment to clear his head and realized the CZ pistol had ended up in his lap. He grabbed it and tried his door. It opened with a protest of metal, and Crane slid out into the muck.

The car was finished. Crane staggered a few yards away and found a clump of scrub bushes on a dry hummock. He knelt behind them and took an inventory. He hurt, but he could function. He was in the middle of nowhere. He stood out like a sore thumb in his torn suit. He'd need different clothes.

A burst of gunfire interrupted his thoughts. Bullets slammed into the back of the Audi and shattered the rear window. Crane went prone and moved around the clump of bushes. A few moments later, there was another burst; the muzzle flashes were like a flare. He made out a figure running awkwardly over the marshy ground. The figure stopped again a few yards farther on, fired another burst, and started running again.

He didn't seem to think Crane had made it out of the car. Good.

Crane let him come closer and fire another burst. Then he checked the CZ, knelt beside the bushes, and shot him three times. The man fell and didn't move.

Crane made his way to the body. The gun was an HK 417. Whoever he was, he'd gotten his hands on what was most likely a stolen military assault rifle. He checked the pockets and found what he assumed were the keys to the hatchback. He took those and the gun.

Either the crash or the gunfire had punctured the Audi's fuel tank. The smell of gasoline was strong. He found a cigarette lighter on the body and, regretfully, started a fire in a small pool of leaking gas. He was halfway back to the road when the Audi went up in a loud fireball.

Josh wouldn't be happy about that.

When he got back to the road, Crane took a moment to clear the spike strip. Then he walked back to the hatchback and started it up. He could see distant police lights coming closer as he drove away.

CHAPTER 36

The river, as it turned out, was the Svitava. Not the Svratka. Crane had learned that from the old woman who ran the second-hand shop where he'd bought the clothes he was wearing. Natalya was dead. Most likely Novak as well by now. But at least Crane knew which river he'd been driving alongside all night. That was something, he supposed.

He'd reached the little town called Blansko not long after sunrise and stopped, drained and exhausted. He didn't know if the hatchback had been reported stolen, but the safe move was to get it off the street. Crane found a gloomy side street and parked in an alley behind a boarded-up shop. In the back, he found an oil-stained coverall that made him a little less conspicuous. There wasn't much he could do about the Bemer shoes. They were worth more than the car, but they were already scuffed and muddy enough to pass if nobody looked too closely.

He'd found the second-hand shop, bought some more appropriate clothes, and gotten the lay of the land from the owner in broken Russian. He'd gone back to the car long enough to change in the alley and collect the things he needed. The last thing he'd done was remove the plates and hide them under the back seat so some passing cop wouldn't run them. An abandoned car wouldn't look out of place here at all. Once that was done, he'd walked several blocks over to a decent-looking coffee shop, gotten a cup, and sat down at a small table in the back.

Then he couldn't think of another damn thing to do to put off thinking about it. He sat with his coffee and closed his eyes and let the despair wash over him. It was mid-afternoon now, and he was still there in the back of the coffee shop. He didn't know how to get past it. He'd seen people die before. He'd killed them himself and slept like a baby. Killing Emil Zajic and that team of drug runners in Puerto Rico hadn't bothered him at all.

But, of course, this was different. They'd all chosen to play the game. They all knew the stakes, and the world was better off without them. Natalya and Novak never made that choice. They were pawns he'd used for his own ends, and they'd both died for it; they'd died badly.

Crane hadn't just failed. He'd been reckless and irresponsible. He'd gone into a situation without the right skills or support because he thought his training would let him operate alone. He'd been in freefall when Josh found him and threw him a rope. But Crane had ruined that. He'd set that rope aflame, and now it was turning to ash in his hands as he dangled over the abyss. If he'd taken the damn consulting job when they fired him, Novak and Natalya would still be alive.

But then he realized something didn't sit right with him about that idea. He ran it back and forth in his mind, unpacking all its little pieces. It wasn't just that he used two people and got them killed. There was more to it than that. He'd always lied to people, used them to find information, to smoke out a target. It was part of the job.

The job. That gave him a finger on it. In the Hurricane Group, he was a field agent following orders that filtered down from God knew where. From shadowy figures with their own agendas stalking the corridors of power. He was as much a tool as the people he used. But now there was no government above him. There was no command authority to shoulder the responsibility. If this was a Hurricane operation, he'd have been under orders to use Novak and Natalya to achieve his mission goals, and he could lay their deaths squarely at the invisible feet of invisible figures in Washington. It was all on him this time.

Strangely, the realization helped a little. Crane always felt better when he had a defined problem to face. He bore the responsibility. Responsibility was something that came with power. He had the power to decide how to respond to the situation he found himself in. Natalya was dead, and probably Novak too. They'd died in terror and agony. That was past, and he couldn't change it. But from this moment, he would decide what to do about it. Not mysterious figures in Washington, not a detached mission commander. If there was something that could be done to balance out what had happened, no one would tell him he couldn't do it.

And he knew what he had to do to balance it out. He drew Novak and Natalya into this, it was true. But it was the man he'd taken to calling "Ivan" who had them killed. Ivan had put all of this into motion. Crane still didn't know why Ivan wanted to take down Melissa Simon's research project halfway around the world. He didn't care anymore. What mattered was that he was brutal and ruthless and was crushing anybody who crossed his path. The best thing Crane could do for the future was stop Ivan cold. The best thing he could do for the dead was to make him pay.

But how?

Crane grimaced as he took a swallow of cold coffee. That was a sign it was past time to leave. He'd processed it enough, and he'd been stationary for too long. A basic principle they'd drilled into him in Hurricane for situations like this was to make a choice and commit to it. To make things happen, he had to be moving.

He left a handful of coins on the table and walked out to the streets. He pretended to window shop as he wandered the town's small, struggling commercial district. But his mind was turning over his options, discarding them one at a time. Eventually, he would be left with the best move available to him.

He began with where he was now—at a dead end. Josh's research had led to the CEO of BioKapital, Dalibor Cermak. But Cermak meant nothing. He was just a smokescreen. Knowing who Cermak was got him no closer to Ivan. He supposed he could go after Cermak and beat Ivan's identity out of him, but he knew that was a bad move.

Next mystery: who or what was "Team Kilo," and why was Ivan so terrified of them? If he knew that, perhaps he could use it. But he didn't.

A mission briefing would be helpful about now. A bland-looking briefing room with a file on the table. The whole mission planned with all the Hurricane Group's resources and expertise laid out for him. But, of course, there was no briefing to consult. No orders, no backup. He was on his own. In a place where he could barely operate because he couldn't blend in. He didn't even speak the language. He could get by well enough in English or Russian, but there was no way he could infiltrate the Czech underworld because he couldn't pass as anything but an outsider.

He needed help. There was no way around it any longer. He'd exhausted all his options, and all the help Josh could offer. But there was someone he could call. Crane didn't want to call him, but he had run out of other choices.

With that, there was no more hesitation. His training again. If there was only one way forward, no matter how unpleasant, then move immediately. Hesitation would only make things worse.

Crane took out his phone. What time was it in the States right now? It would be early on the West Coast, but he'd be up. Crane punched in a number from memory.

There were several seconds of silence, and then a few electronic clicks and a fuzzy ringtone.

On the third ring, it picked up, and through the static, Crane heard a familiar voice.

"Stoppard."

"Malcolm, it's John Crane. I'm sorry to bother you so early."

"John! Hell, you know I'm up. Almost got breakfast ready. How're things in the Beltway?"

"Couldn't say. I'm in the Czech Republic at the moment."

There was a long silence, and when Stoppard came back, the jovial tone of an old friend catching up was gone. "Well, that explains it. Getting a lot of line noise, John. You want to hang up and call back in?"

Crane sighed. Malcolm Stoppard had been a field agent back in the day, and then an instructor for new Hurricane Group agents. He'd retired when Hurricane was shut down. But he was still connected and too important to be ignored. The reference to line noise was meant to tell him that Stoppard's phone was probably still scanned by NSA and perhaps other even less friendly groups. He was suggesting that Crane call back using a secure phone that could encrypt its signal. Which would have been a fine idea if Crane was still a government agent and had anything like that.

"Don't think that will help, Malcolm," he said at last. "The phones are the phones over here."

There was another pause. Then, "I'm eager to hear why you're over there, John."

"Just a vacation. I'd never been before. It was kind of an impulse thing."

"That's the best kind of vacation," Malcolm said, his voice carefully neutral.

"Yeah. Thing is, I didn't really prepare, and I don't know my way around. I could sure use a local guide. And I remembered you spent some time over here. I was wondering if you know anybody who could help me."

"Where are you again?"

"Little town outside Brno."

There was another long silence. Then, finally, "I know someone in Prague."

"Prague is fine. I can get there in a few hours."

"They won't be cheap," Malcolm warned.

"Money's no object."

"Really? Well, you've piqued my interest. Can you write down an address?"

"Go."

Malcolm gave him a street number. Crane dropped the phone in his pocket long enough to scrawl the number on the back of his receipt from the coffee shop. When he fished the phone back out of his pocket, he heard a dog barking loudly in the background.

"Hey, is that Molly?"

"She says hello," said Malcolm. "We're both happy to hear from you. But you've got us worried now. Is this something you can walk away from?"

"I'm afraid not. I've paid in full already. I'm going to finish the tour."

"All right, John. If your mind's made up, maybe my friend can help you."

"Thank you, Malcolm. I appreciate it."

"It's nothing. But come see me when you're back in the

States. We'll take Molly on a long walk up the beach, and you can tell me all about it."

"I'll do that," he said. "Until then."

"Take care, John."

Crane hung up. He checked the street ahead and behind and then walked briskly around the next corner he came to, and the next. Checking for tails. Standard tradecraft. You lost control, he thought, but you're back in charge now. Build it back up, step by step.

With the decisions made, Crane's mind was clear and focused again. There was a path forward once more, and Crane was ready to walk it.

CHAPTER 37

Crane put the plates back on his stolen hatchback and drove into Prague just before sunset. He pulled up outside the address Malcolm Stoppard had given him and found a place to park. The building turned out to be the Alphonse Mucha Museum. Crane shrugged and went inside. He bought a ticket and a guidebook and began immersing himself in the Czech art nouveau tradition. He was admiring a series of theatrical posters of Sarah Bernhardt when a man shuffled up beside him. He was old, grizzled, dressed like a panhandler, and he smelled horrible.

"Your name is Crane?" he said in a thick Russian accent. "Sorry it took me a while. Malcolm said you were a better dresser."

Crane laughed. "I'm making concessions to circumstance."

"Hah. My name is Yermolayev. Alexei. Good to meet you. You have something for me?"

Crane passed him a thick envelope. It vanished into the many layers of greasy wool and cotton shrouding the man.

"And now even better to meet you, Mr. Crane. I have a blue van around the corner. We can talk there. Five minutes."

Then he turned and shuffled away, the museum guard watching him go with distaste.

Crane didn't let himself think about whether Yermolayev's van would really be there when he left. He was in no position to dictate terms. He had to trust Malcolm's judgement.

Crane made his way slowly to the exit, stopping every so often to admire a painting. Outside, night was falling. Young couples walked the street arm in arm. A bike messenger flew by and disappeared around a corner. People leading ordinary lives. Crane had had a taste of that in Key West. It was all right, as far as it went.

The van was there.

So much for ordinary life.

As Crane approached, the side door opened with an indignant shriek and Yermolayev swore at it in Russian.

"Come in, come in," he said. "Pull up a trunk."

The back of the van was strewn with papers and junk. Empty beer cans drifted around. The paint was almost stripped from the metal, leaving only bare gray with an occasional reminder of the original blue. A weak dome light cast barely enough light to see by.

Crane sat on one of two large Russian army trunks as Yermolayev dragged the protesting door shut again. He sat down across from Crane.

"So your money is good. What do you need?"

"I have some pictures of a man," he said. "I'm hoping you can tell me who he is."

Yermolayev shook his head. "Why do you think I would know this man?"

"I think he's big in the criminal scene in Brno."

"Well, that narrows it down a little. Not much, but a little. What have you got?"

Crane took out the SD card he'd gotten from the party

photographer. Yermolayev nodded and made his way forward, through a curtain that blocked the back of the van off from the front seats. He came back with a battered laptop and booted it up.

"If there's anyone in these pictures you recognize ..." said Crane.

Yermolayev took the card from him and inserted it into the laptop. A few moments later, the pictures came up, and Yermo- layev flipped idly through them.

"Fancy party," he muttered. "Very nice. Nobody, nobody. Now she's a looker—but too young for him. He thinks she makes him look like a big man. But he just looks like a fool. Who else? Waiter with tray of drinks. Boring man, boring man, Chinese boring man. Oh ..." He paused and looked over the top of the screen at Crane. "You have very good taste in enemies, Mr. Crane."

He turned the laptop around and Crane looked into the eyes of Ivan glaring at the photographer as Cermak stood beside him, trying to make some point.

"That's the one. Who is he?" Crane asked.

"That, my friend, is Branislav Skala. He isn't 'big in the crim- inal scene in Brno.' He owns Brno."

"I thought Kucera ran Brno."

Yermolayev laughed, a deep belly laugh that echoed in the small van. "Oh, look who knows all about the Czech underworld all of a sudden! Yes, that's the official story. Skala was the old bull, and finally the young upstart fought him and drove him off. But the truth is a little different. The end of the war wasn't so much surrender as negotiated truce. Kucera gets to be the big boss man, but Skala still pulls his strings."

He pulled out a phone and tapped the screen several times. "Here's Kucera," he said, showing Crane another photo. Kucera was a young man with short blond hair, compact but muscled, wearing a bomber jacket. "In case you run into him in your travels," Yermolayev said. "Another dangerous man."

"Where do I find Skala?"

"He bought some old manor south of Brno. A mansion with a vineyard. I can show you. He's retired there to pretend he's a country gentleman." He spat into the corner of the van. "Fucking peasant."

"Does the name Emil Zajic mean anything to you?" Crane asked.

"One of Skala's," Yermolayev said, nodding. "Used to coordinate drug shipments coming through Russia from Central Asia. Now word is Skala's trying to work with the narco cartels. I assume he's got Zajic someplace over there, maybe in the Caribbean."

"Puerto Rico," said Crane. "Except Zajic's dead now."

Yermolayev stopped and gave Crane a long look. "I hadn't heard that," he said at last. "Skala won't be happy."

"Is he ever happy?"

"No," Yermolayev admitted, "he is not."

"I've got one more name to try," said Crane. "Does 'Team Kilo' mean anything to you?"

Yermolayev considered, shook his head. "You have some context?"

"Not much. A name some of Zajic's pawns heard him use. Apparently Skala's terrified of them. So who scares him?"

Yermolayev let out a whistle. "Nobody I know of. Someone who scares that old bastard I would not want to meet. But they say Skala's got his own private archive. Keeps notes on everybody—who works for who, who stabs who in the back, where all the bodies are buried. Maybe if you took a look at that..."

Crane shrugged. Maybe. The idea didn't seem to get him any closer to his goal, so he discarded it.

"Can you get me a clean car?" he asked. "For the right price, obviously. The one I drove here ..."

Yermolayev grinned, like he couldn't believe his good fortune. "I like you, Mr. Crane," he said. "You're like the golden days of the Cold War come back again. I can find you something. Nothing flashy."

"That's perfect."

"Let me make a call. And while we're waiting, we must crack open some of the good stuff. I've been saving it for a day like this."

Yermolayev started toward the front of the van. Then he clapped his hands and turned back and to gesture toward the trunk Crane was sitting on. "You're going after Skala, yes? You need some hardware? Guns? Ammunition? Explosives? Incendiaries?"

Crane looked down at the trunk for a moment with a raised eyebrow. Then he looked back up at Yermolayev. "Let's make it a day to remember."

———

Branislav Skala was pacing the sterile, museum-like corridors of his mansion when the head of his security force came looking for him.

"What?" Skala snapped as the man entered the room. What was it called again? A day parlor or something. A woman's room, he thought. The idea of his underling finding him here suddenly irritated him.

"Sir. The winery says the man's still said nothing useful. They're sure he knows nothing. He'd have told them by now."

Skala swore silently. Novak was supposed to tell him where to find the Team Kilo operative, Crane. If he really knew nothing, that avenue was closed.

CHAPTER 38

It was just after midnight when Crane pulled off the road and into the trees near Branislav Skala's estate. It was a clear night with enough moonlight to let him make his way through the trees. He took another look at the map Yermolayev had provided. Making his way a quarter mile through the woods, he would come to a low stone wall at the property line. Then the vineyards formed an open bowl descending the hillsides to the mansion. The whole property was much too large for Skala's men to patrol. They'd have a smaller perimeter closer to the house, and he'd have room to move.

Crane got out of the car. He'd changed into black clothes and boots. Carefully laid out in the trunk was the arsenal he'd bought from Yermolayev. He had the silenced CZ pistol and the HK 417 carbine he'd taken from the man who wrecked the Audi. Next to that was a Russian SV-98 sniper rifle with night vision scope and a 10-round box magazine. There was a backpack full of incendiary grenades and explosives, as well as spare magazines for all the guns. It was a hell of a load, but Crane expected he'd need everything he could carry.

He took some time getting everything checked and loaded.

Finally he fastened the HK to his pack and shrugged it on. He closed the trunk, picked up the sniper rifle, and jogged away into the forest.

He found the stone wall readily enough. It was waist high, built by hand from stones some farmer had removed from the fields, probably centuries ago. Crane ducked down behind it and listened for a full minute but heard nothing. Finally he decided no one was here, and he climbed over it and onto Skala's land.

He found himself on a shallow hillside. In front of him was a great expanse of grapes, staked out in long, straight lines stretching down the slope. He could make out buildings in the distance: barns, a winery, various outbuildings. Beyond them all, gleaming white in the moonlight, was the house itself. Three stories of white stone with a black roof. There were wings and connecting passages, formal gardens, and a large lawn. Low walls separated the grounds from the farm.

To his right, the hillside sloped slightly up. Up there would be the highest point on the estate. It would give him the best field of fire into the compound. Crane took five minutes to walk there, his boots crunching softly on turned earth.

When he found a likely spot, he shrugged off his pack and sat down on the dry dirt between two long rows of grapes. He knew Skala's men were down there somewhere. He opened up the SV 98's bipod, lay down, and switched on the night scope. He swept the outbuildings and found two men with rifles standing behind a fence, looking out over the fields. He kept scanning and found another one moving toward the winery. Crane watched him disappear through the building's large double doors. Then he turned his attention back to the pair by the fence.

Range to the two men was a little under four hundred meters. The bullet would cross that distance in less than a second. Crane chose one, sighted in, let out half a breath, and held it.

He squeezed the trigger.

He heard the crack of the gun but didn't even see the first man fall as he worked the bolt to reload. He placed his eye to the scope and saw the second man just starting to react. He fired again, and the second man fell. He reloaded and waited. Another man came running from off to the right. Crane's third shot dropped him.

He looked for another target, but they'd figured out that running around in the open was a bad idea. He saw the muzzle flash as someone edged around the corner of a shed and fired a wild burst off into the fields. Crane put a round into the corner of the shed where the fire had come from. The shooter appeared again, firing in his direction now. This time he remained in sight long enough for Crane to reload and fire. That was four down.

Floodlights came on around the outbuildings. Someone started sweeping the fields with a bright spotlight. They must have realized he was using night vision and were hoping to blind him. Crane's next shot took out the light.

There was more return fire now, and it was focused in his direction. They had his location now. If he stayed here too long, they'd flank him. It was time to move, but he would leave the men who came out here after him something to remember him by.

Crane took several bricks of plastic explosive from his pack. He wired in a detonator and placed them in a row beneath the rifle. Then he clipped an audio pickup to the barrel and put its corresponding receiver in his ear. When he was satisfied with his bomb, he picked up the rest of his gear and jogged away. There was still sporadic fire from the outbuildings. Through the earpiece he heard the occasional round impact near his former position.

Crane carried the HK 417 in both hands and kept up a steady pace. Moving was easier now without the bulk of the sniper rifle and its night vision scope. But he was still carrying a lot of grenades and explosives, and they were heavy. Why not lighten his load a bit more, Crane thought with a grin.

He veered into the long rows of grapes and started working his way through the trellises, moving from row to row as he headed downhill toward the farm buildings. At each row, he removed one of the incendiary packages from his pack, slaved it to the same detonator channel, and left it among the vines. He kept going until he was out of incendiaries. His pack was considerably lighter now, with only a half-dozen old Russian efka fragmentation grenades and a few other small items remaining.

Crane peered through the grapes. He could see lights moving up the slope well off to his right. They were closing in on his former position, but he didn't hear anything through the mic on the rifle yet. After a few more rows, he came to a packed dirt access road for tractors and farm equipment. It ran straight down the hill between the long trellises and into the cluster of garages and outbuildings. He switched the HK 417's safety off and jogged down the road.

As he approached the cluster of sheds, he heard voices ahead and took cover behind the large rear tire of a John Deere tractor. Two armed men walked past, talking in low voices. Crane carefully edged around the tractor to keep hidden from them, and then turned and sprinted toward a long, windowless storage building. A pile of crates had been stacked against the rear wall, and Crane used them to launch himself up and catch the edge of the roof. He pulled himself up and lay flat on the metal roof, listening. Nothing suggested he'd been seen.

He crawled to the other side of the building and looked out over the compound. He counted four men visible. Two were looking out the window of a garage full of tractors, but the other two had resumed walking around outside as if the emergency was over.

It had been about five minutes since he'd fired his last shot. Already the combat discipline of Skala's men was starting to fade. It was something Crane was familiar with from his training. With an active threat to point to, their senses focused and adrenaline kept them on edge. But without a threat to direct it toward, that heightened posture turned into a drain on their energy. Eventually it would exhaust them, and they would gradually let their guard fall. And that was when Crane would hit them again.

He heard a voice through his earpiece, shouting something Crane didn't understand. Someone had made it to the rifle and seen that he'd abandoned it. It was almost time. He heard more voices, visualized others approaching seeing the rifle positioned on the ground.

Crane took the detonator from a pocket and flipped open the cover over its small actuator switch. Someone was saying something in his earpiece. The tone of voice suggested a first hint of confusion. Crane took out his earpiece and dropped it on the roof beside him. Then he pressed the switch.

The explosion was a loud *whump* behind him. There was a brief flash, and Crane knew there would be a cloud of smoke dispersing in the wind, even though he couldn't see it in the darkness.

Shouts erupted all around him. Crane heard doors open. He peered over the edge of the roof and saw a group forming nearby, at a point where they could see between buildings up into the vineyards. They clustered together as they pointed and tried to understand what had happened. Crane took one of the efka grenades from his pack, pulled the pin, and tossed it off the roof. It exploded and spattered the walls with shrapnel and blood.

Someone started firing up at him, so Crane slid back from the edge. He moved quickly to the back side of the building and leaped off into the night. He rolled into a crouch and readied the HK 417 just in time for someone to come running around the corner of the building toward him. Crane cut him down with a burst and then sprinted in the opposite direction.

The shadow of the winery was perhaps two hundred feet away. Crane kept low and ran for it. When he reached the shadow, he scurried around the corner and pressed his back flat against the stone wall.

Crane could hear shouts in Czech from around the compound. They were looking for him, but he didn't think anyone had seen him come back here.

The wall felt cold against his back. It felt somehow very old. It was a long building, oriented perpendicular to most of the others, and Crane figured it was probably empty now. If he could get inside, it would give him cover and take him considerably closer to the main house.

The large double doors at the end of the building were well lit and probably noisy, but Crane could make out a gable farther down, presumably protecting a small side door. He moved that way. There were windows on this side of the building, but Crane saw only blackness inside. He reached the door and forced the lock with his knife. The door swung smoothly open, and Crane slipped inside.

He was in a small storage room full of wooden hand carts and old barrels. At the other end of the room was another door, with a bar of pale yellow light along the floor. Crane moved quietly across the tiles. He heard a voice and then someone crying out in pain.

Listening at the door, he heard someone speaking in Czech and then the unmistakable sound of a hard slap and another short, strangled cry. Someone was getting worked over out there.

The door was cracked open. Crane knelt down below eye level and looked out. The door opened into the winery's enormous central corridor. The doorway was flanked by huge wooden casks stacked in tiers and held in place by frames of roughhewn wood. Crane saw more casks in the same kind of racks on the other side of a wide, central aisle. He assumed the casks lined both walls for the length of the building. The voices were coming from somewhere to his right.

Crane slipped quietly through the door and edged up against the casks, moving slowly toward the main corridor. The rich smell of fermentation and centuries-old wood reached his nose. Peering around the corner, he saw shadows and then figures lit by portable lanterns. There were three of them around a table. There was a fourth man on the table, and Crane made out leather cords around his ankles, securing him to the tabletop.

Someone said something in Czech and backhanded the man on the table. He grunted in pain and said nothing. The man who slapped him moved a bit, and Crane saw the face of the man on the table. He was bruised and bloody but alive.

It was Klement Novak.

CHAPTER 39

Crane jerked back around the corner of the casks. His first thought was a rush of relief. Novak was alive. At least that was one less death on his conscience.

His second thought was that he couldn't leave Novak there. That was obvious, but it still jarred him. Trying to rescue Novak would compromise his mission. Crane's goal was simple: to reach Branislav Skala and kill him. Once that was accomplished, he meant to withdraw, fighting where he was forced to, and return to his car in the woods. There was no place for a wounded civilian in that. He didn't even know if Novak could walk. And he could hardly carry an injured man all the way back out through the vineyards with Skala's men in pursuit. The operational procedures the Hurricane Group had drilled into him said Novak was a liability.

But nothing was as it would have been if he were still with Hurricane, Crane thought. If he was still with Hurricane, he wouldn't even be here. Once he'd returned from Puerto Rico with clues pointing to the Czech Republic, they'd have assigned this part of the mission to someone else, someone who at least spoke the language.

Again, Crane felt himself hanging from that burning rope. If he was going to do this, it would mean disregarding his training —the one thing he was counting on to keep him alive here.

But then he considered the alternative. Suppose he abandoned Novak to his fate, took Skala out, and made it out safely. Suppose he went back to Josh Sulenski, reported his success, and enjoyed a well-earned break on a beach somewhere, knowing he'd left an innocent man to die.

No, that wouldn't do at all. There was no decision to be made when he looked at it that way.

A radio crackled in Czech. Crane peered around the corner again. A handset sat propped on top of a barrel near the table. One of the men picked it up, thumbed the switch, and made a report. Then he put the radio back down and turned back to Novak.

Crane considered how to take the three men out quietly, without getting trapped in the winery and without harming Novak. He couldn't simply open fire with the rifle or he'd draw outside attention. And he had to keep them away from the radio.

Crane edged back toward the door. He checked the gap between the casks and the rear wall. It looked as if he could wedge himself there and climb the rack. The shadows there would help conceal him, and the rafters and the framing that held the casks would let him move around the building.

He set the HK 417 down beside the casks. Then he shrugged off his pack, retrieved the silenced CZ 70 pistol, and left the pack beside the rifle. Between the silencer and the thick stone walls, he hoped he could get away with firing the pistol without alerting the men outside. But if he was wrong, he'd be swarmed and killed. Last ditch option, then.

Crane wedged his fists into the gap between the casks and the wall and hauled himself up. The wood was rough enough to give his boots some traction, and he was able to scramble up to reach a heavy oak beam and use that to pull himself the rest of the way. Finally, he stood on top of the casks, some ten or twelve feet above the floor. It was gloomy here, and the wood smelled of old pitch and dust. Crane tested one of the beams in the frame and decided it would hold his weight. He started edging forward, toward the table where Novak lay. None of the men were looking up. Crane kept moving, slowly, half-step by half-step, until he was almost directly above the table.

One of the men said something, and the others laughed. The speaker had a shaved head and a nasty scar running up his forehead. He drew a knife with a thin, curving blade. A fillet knife for boning fish. He made a point of showing Novak the blade, how it flexed under pressure. He pressed the back of Novak's hand down onto the table to flatten out his fingers.

Crane couldn't see a way to take all three out without firing the pistol, and he was running out of time. The man with the knife pressed its point against the tip of Novak's index finger, and Novak wailed in terror. It was a primal, animal sound, and Crane couldn't listen to it any longer.

He cocked the pistol and put a round through the scar in the bald man's forehead. The soft crack echoed off the vaulted ceilings. Between that and the silencer, the others couldn't easily locate the sound. They were still looking for an enemy at ground level when Crane killed the second man.

The third was behind Novak's table. He dove for the radio, but Crane shot the handset and it exploded into a rain of plastic fragments. The third man dove back, using Novak for cover. He drew a knife and shouted something Crane didn't understand. He assumed it was a threat to kill Novak.

So far no one had come in response to his shots, but he needed to end this now. Crane jumped off the beam and hit the stone floor with a jarring impact. He dropped the pistol and rolled, coming up on the other side of the table from the last man. Crane let his momentum carry him as he roared and charged the table. He went low and hit the table hard with his leading shoulder. The man sprang backward in surprise, but too late. Novak shouted in fear and pain as the table tipped and then toppled over. The other man stumbled away but then went down hard as the table landed across his legs.

Novak's restraints kept him hanging off the side of the table. Crane scrambled over him to reach the other man. Crane was coming from behind him, and the man waved the knife blindly over his shoulder as he fought to free himself. But Crane caught his wrist and wrenched the knife free. The man was screaming something in Czech when Crane thrust the knife into the back of his neck.

They lay there in a tangled heap. Crane, the man he'd just killed, and the tortured Novak hanging by his wrists and ankles from the side of the table. Crane breathed in great gasps. The jump to the floor had hurt.

But that was nothing compared to what Novak had gone through.

Crane found the fillet knife and slashed through the leather cords tying Novak to the table. He caught him and gently lowered him to the floor.

"It's okay," he said. "I've got you."

"You came," Novak gasped. "They kept asking where you were. I couldn't tell them."

"I know," said Crane. "We've got to get out of here before someone else comes. Can you walk?"

"I ... I don't know. They were going to..." He closed his eyes and shuddered.

"I know. It's over now."

Crane helped roll Novak flat on his back and quickly checked him. There were no broken bones at least, but plenty of contusions around his face. One eye was swollen nearly shut, and he suspected Novak's nose might be broken. But there was nothing permanent.

Crane retrieved his pack and rifle. Then he bent down enough to get Novak's arm around his shoulders.

"Come on, we're getting out. Stay quiet and let me know if you think you're going to fall."

He helped Novak stagger between the long rows of casks. So far, so good, he thought. But Novak would never make it back to the car. He needed another way to get him out.

At the far end of the building, a smaller door was set into one of the large double doors. Novak was walking on his own by the time they got there, but not quickly or steadily. Crane cracked the door open and peered out. He saw nothing moving. Off to his right, flashlights swept through the vineyards in ragged lines. That was a break, he thought. When he'd disappeared, they must have assumed they'd driven him back, and now they were trying to flush him out of cover out in the vineyards. But there would still be men back here guarding the house.

He surveyed the nearby buildings. One stood out. It looked less rough and utilitarian than the others, made of the same white stone as the main house. It was oriented along the paved road leading past the house, and four arched sets of double doors faced out onto the road. It had to be the garage for the main house. Perfect.

Crane checked the area again but saw nobody. "Let's go," he said quietly. Then he half trotted out into the open, Novak struggling to keep up. Crane kept the HK 417 in his right hand as they moved, and checked for anyone approaching. But he hoped he didn't have to engage an enemy under these conditions.

They had nearly reached the shadow of the garage when Novak cried out and stumbled. Crane caught him and fell into a crouch.

"I can't ..." Novak's breaths were hoarse and ragged.

They were exposed here. They needed to move.

"I've got you," said Crane. "You're getting out of here alive. I promise." He slung the rifle over his shoulder and half-carried, half-dragged Novak the rest of the way to the pool of shadow.

Crane found a side door and forced the latch with his knife. He helped Novak inside. In the darkness, he could just make out the bulky forms of cars. The nearest was a large, black Mercedes sedan. That would do. Crane opened the back door and helped Novak lie down on the back seat. He rolled onto his back and seemed to breathe easier.

Crane knew he could open the garage doors here, hotwire the Mercedes, and take his chances on making it out to the road. But his mission was still in play. And there was little point in running if Skala was still alive to chase him. Skala held all the cards here. They wouldn't make it far.

"I want you to wait here," he told Novak. "I've got something to do. Then I'm coming back, and we'll get out of here."

"You're leaving me?" Novak sounded confused, almost childlike.

"No," he said. "I'm going to go kill Skala. You'll be safe here until I get back. Stay here and stay quiet. When it's done, we'll drive out."

Novak was quiet for a long moment. "Good," he said at last. "Kill him. That's good."

Crane took a small bottle of water from his pack. "Here, take this. I'll be back as quick as I can."

Novak nodded, and Crane made his way to the far end of the garage. Novak apparently wasn't coherent enough to consider what would happen to him if Crane didn't make it back.

Standing on the hood of the car in the next bay, Crane could see out the windows set high in the garage doors. It was a straight shot across the road to the wall surrounding the house.

And there was a gate not far away. But he knew that gate would be locked, guarded, or both. And there would be more men in the house. He needed a diversion.

Well, he thought, that was why he'd set one up.

He took the transmitter off his belt and switched the channel. Then he took a deep breath and hit the button.

Outside in the vineyards, the incendiaries Crane had set went off in a great arc of flame that slashed across the hillside. The explosions spread thermate burning at four thousand degrees Fahrenheit. Some of the men searching the vineyards were killed instantly. Others fled in panic. The dry vines flashed and ignited, and fire spread up the hillsides in fast-moving parallel lines.

Crane jumped down from the hood of the car, opened the garage door, and sprinted toward the house.

CHAPTER 40

The staff offices off the manor's old kitchen had become the house's de facto command post because there were radios there to coordinate workers across the large estate. Branislav Skala was there with two bodyguards and a small knot of frightened members of the manor staff when the vineyards went up in flame.

Suddenly there was panic and shouting everywhere. Skala heard someone screaming over the radio. The pale orange glow of firelight lit up the night outside. The staffers ran out to the main dining hall where the tall windows gave a sweeping view of the vineyards to the east of the house. Skala followed. Someone ran past him in the hallways, screaming, "Fire! The vines are on fire!"

It was true, he saw, as he swept into the dining hall. In the dark, lines of fire raced up the hillside. The members of his civilian staff were wailing as if it was the end of the world. He didn't think the fire would be able to reach the house itself. There would be some major rebuilding to be done once this was over, but Skala had rebuilt from disaster before.

"Anton!" he bellowed. "Anton, where are you?"

Kucera was hurrying through the doorway from the kitchen. "I'm right here, damn it!"

Skala took in the fiery panorama with a sweep of his arm. "Where are the men we sent out there?"

"Team two and team five are cut off from the house. They'll get back here when they can get around the fire. They've got men down. I ordered teams one and four back here." After a moment, he added, "I can't raise team three."

Skala thought for a moment, adding up the numbers in his head. First the sniper rifle. Then the bomb in the fields, followed by the grenade and the brief firefight outside the storage sheds. Now this. More than half his men were dead or missing. It was time to cut his losses.

"Take command of the men, Anton," he said. "You know what to do. I'll be in my suite. There are things I need to take care of."

He stalked off without waiting for an answer. One of Kucera's soldiers stood near the doorway with a submachine gun in his hands. "Give me that!" Skala snarled, and ripped the gun out of his hands. Then he stormed down the back hallways toward his private suite. This place was lost, he thought. One man had done this. One man by himself. He had been right to fear Team Kilo.

In his suite, Skala closed the heavy, oak main doors and locked them. He went to the bedroom where French doors opened out onto the back lawn. He drew the curtains and turned off the lamp he'd left on beside his bed. The room was dark, the windows covered. It was the best he could do. He just hoped the man from Team Kilo didn't know the layout of the house.

He went back to the front room and closed the bedroom door so no light would make it through. Then he opened up his laptop and powered it on. He slid his fingertip across the reader and brought up his list of contacts. The men he'd done all this for would understand. He'd done what they needed done, and he'd drawn Team Kilo's wrath down on himself in the process, redirecting it away from them. He'd done it all to help them. One of them would send a helicopter to get him out of here. When it was settled, then he could rebuild. He'd come back before. From worse.

Skala took his cell from the charging cradle on the desk beside him and started to dial.

———

Crane crouched behind a lacquered wood cabinet in a second-floor hallway. He leaned out and fired a long burst down the corridor. Two gunshots came in reply. Both bullets slammed into the cabinet, sending splinters of wood flying. Louis XV, Crane thought, though furniture styles were hardly his specialty. It didn't really matter now. The thing had been shot to hell. But the cabinet had been a hideous mess of curlicues and gold leaf. If anything, Crane thought, he was doing Skala a favor.

Then he heard running footsteps moving away. Whomever he'd been shooting at must be out. But he'd been located, and that meant he should move before more enemies appeared.

They knew he was in the house, but the place was huge, and he gathered most of the thugs with guns didn't spend a lot of time here. They probably didn't know the place any better than he did. And the sound of gunshots echoed off the marble floors and stone walls until nobody could tell where shots were coming from.

Since fighting his way through a library and a music room out of a period drama, Crane had been stalking the hallways, learning his way around, looking for Skala. But so far there'd been no sign of him. He couldn't keep this up all night. He needed to find the man.

Crane ran down the hallway, past several closed doors. He'd checked a couple when he first entered the corridor. They were empty, unused bedrooms. He didn't feel like checking the rest of them. The hallway ended at a stairwell, narrow and plain compared to most of the house he'd seen. He realized he'd wandered into the old servants' routes through the house. He took the stairs down, moving quietly, hearing the occasional creak.

There was a small alcove at the foot of the stairs with a plain wooden door leading out. He was turning around the last landing when the door was smashed open and two figures in black sprang through, guns raised. Crane cut them down as a burst tore into the wall beside him and sprayed him with plaster dust.

He ran down the last few steps and through the doorway, leading with the rifle.

"Don't shoot!"

In the hallway, a man in a white shirt and black vest and pants threw up his hands and cringed at the sight of Crane's gun. He was unarmed. A civilian. Part of the household staff, Crane assumed. He'd spoken English.

Crane leveled the gun at him and closed the distance between them in a few quick strides. "You speak English?"

"Yes! Yes! Don't shoot!"

"Then tell me where I can find Branislav Skala!"

———

"I'm sorry," the recording said once more, "the number you are calling is not accepting incoming calls at this time. Please try your call again later. Thank you."

Skala roared like an angry bull and hurled the phone across the room. It smashed the glass covering a Manes painting of naked women frolicking in the woods, and then clattered to the floor among the fragments.

"Fuckers!" Skala screamed. "Fucking bastard fuckers! I did this for you!"

None of them were taking his calls. Not one would help him. After he'd gone out of his way to protect their interests. After he'd taken such terrible risks and paid such a price.

He looked at the laptop sitting open on the baroque desk across the room. The screen glowed pale blue in the dim light. That laptop contained secrets. Not just about their enemies but about them too. The fucking coward turncoats. They'd learn what it meant to betray Branislav Skala. He crossed the room to an antique cabinet beneath a crossed pair of heavy broadswords on the wall. Inside the cabinet was a safe. He quickly opened it and took out a money belt with emergency funds in both Euros and gold coins along with credit cards and the key to a safety deposit box in a bank in Prague. Just in case.

Skala took off his shirt and strapped the belt on against his skin. He was buckling the last strap when there was a burst of gunfire outside in the hall, a beat of silence, and then another. Skala's breath caught in his throat, and he froze for a moment. Outside, someone screamed.

He was here.

More gunfire, bullets thudding into the heavy oak doors. Skala's eyes swept across the room. What did he need? What could he carry? He slammed down the laptop's screen and gathered it up, clutched it against his side.

Then the doors exploded inward in a cloud of smoke and a shattering noise. Skala screamed. On pure instinct, he grabbed the machine pistol and sprayed bullets through the doorway. He screamed in rage against the gun's deafening roar and kept squeezing the trigger until the gun ran dry.

A silence fell over the room. Skala stood there for a moment, the gun in his outstretched arm. He saw only smoke and darkness in the hall outside. He dropped the empty gun. Nothing seemed real anymore. As if in a dream, he turned, walked around the desk, and took the only weapon he could see—one of the heavy swords on the wall. With the sword in one hand and his laptop in the other, Skala walked through the bedroom door and then out the French doors to the back lawn.

It was time to leave.

CHAPTER 41

Smoke swirled around Crane's boots as he climbed over the wreckage of the oak doors and into Skala's suite. The room was ruined. The explosion had thrown the doors into the room and knocked over furniture. Fragments of glass and spent shell casings lay scattered around the floor. Beside a desk lay an empty Scorpion EVO III submachine gun.

Crane knew Skala had been in this room when he blew the doors. He'd emptied a clip from that Scorpion through the shattered doors at him. He hadn't gotten far.

Crane made his way around the desk and across to the closed door on the far side of the room. He kicked the door open and fired a burst through the doorway. The room beyond turned out to be the bedroom. His bullets ripped up Skala's expensive bedclothes and sent a white cloud of down into the air. Otherwise, the room was empty. Skala had left through the open French doors to the right. Crane loaded a fresh magazine into the rifle and followed.

The night air smelled of smoke, and the hillsides still glowed with firelight as the vineyards burned. Crane stood in the doorway and swept the backyard with the muzzle of the HK. The rear garden was an orderly arrangement of square beds outlined by low hedges, cut perfectly square themselves as if they were made of leafy green bricks. The hedges, perhaps two feet tall, enclosed beds thick with flowers and ground cover, many with trimmed conical evergreens at the center. Straight ahead of him was a circle of carefully trimmed shrubs surrounding an ornate fountain with carved birds and cherubs. Flagstone pathways wound among the plants.

Nothing moved.

Crane stepped out from the house, listening, trying to make out shapes in the shadowy darkness. He heard distant shouting, men fighting the fire, trying to save the vineyards. The moon shone through a pall of smoke. The fighting, the fire, everything seemed distant now, as if the chaos he'd created hadn't touched this orderly garden, this little piece of the estate where peace still held.

Crane walked slowly forward, looking for movement, listening for any sound. He had to go one way or the other around the fountain. He chose left for reasons that weren't entirely clear to him at first. Then he realized what was bothering him there.

The light wasn't quite the same from that side. Behind a hedge on the far side of the fountain, something was giving off a pale glow—something with a powered screen. He circled around the fountain and headed that way, the HK leveled and ready, his eyes focused on whatever was putting out that light behind the flowerbed.

He sensed the movement from his right as a disturbance in the air more than anything he saw or heard. He spun in time to see a shape hurtling at him from the shadows of the fountain. A figure. Something in its hands, swinging hard.

On pure instinct, he raised the rifle to protect himself. He felt a jarring impact that sent a shock up his arms and ripped the rifle out of his grasp. Crane staggered back as the HK tumbled away into the night. His attacker pressed forward, silent, wild-eyed. It was Skala, Crane realized, armed with ... a sword?

Skala swung the sword again, wielding it like a baseball bat. Crane dove and rolled, and the heavy blade swept through the space he'd been in a moment before. Skala charged after him. The only sound was his grunt of exertion as he swung again and narrowly missed Crane's head.

Crane scrambled around the corner of the hedge and saw the source of the glow that had distracted him. It was a laptop sitting upright and open on the ground. It was displaying a login screen asking for a password. He heard Skala's footsteps right behind him on the gravel at the edge of the path. Heard his hoarse breath, knew the heavy blade was swinging toward him.

Crane grabbed the laptop and rolled onto his back, holding it up in front of him as a shield. The blade smashed into the hard plastic case and sliced through the hinges with a grating noise. The keyboard portion hit the ground, and Crane was left holding the suddenly dark screen. He hurled it into Skala's face and then rolled to one side and used the distraction to spring to his feet.

Skala was turning toward him again, so Crane ran in the direction the rifle had flown. Skala regained his bearings and ran after him with the sword held high.

There. An incongruous shape inside one of the flowerbeds, projecting up from the hedge on the far side from him. It was the HK 417. Crane adjusted his course and headed for it.

Skala saw it too. "No!" he screamed, and hurled the sword at Crane's back. It glanced harmlessly off Crane's shoulder. Then Crane dove over the hedge and reached for the gun.

"No!" Skala screamed again, and leaped over the hedge after him. Crane got his fingertips on the gun's muzzle and pulled it toward him, but Skala landed on his back, clawing at him like a madman. Crane pulled the rifle closer as Skala pounded him with his fists. He brought the rifle closer, inch by inch, until he could get a firm grasp on it. Then he swung it back over his shoulder blindly, felt it hit Skala hard.

He threw Skala off and rolled onto his back, the rifle in both hands now. As Crane sat up, Skala hurled himself at him again, grappling with him for control of the rifle. Skala was breathing heavily, keening with a strange, high voice. It was as if all reason had left him, and Skala was reduced to pure animal rage. He was an old man, but his strength and endurance were remarkable. He bore down on Crane with all his weight, trying to force him into the orange lilies to press the rifle down against his throat.

Crane saw movement over Skala's shoulder. One of Skala's men coming to rescue his boss and finish Crane off. He needed to gain control of the gun, now.

He put all his strength into one upward thrust and threw Skala off. But Skala kept his death grip on the rifle. The newcomer raised a pistol, and Crane saw the muzzle flash, heard the loud crack of the gun. Skala cried out as the bullet hit him in the side.

Skala spun away from Crane, and the man with the pistol fired again. Then a third shot, and a fourth. Skala fell limp against the ground, and Crane wrenched the rifle from his hands. He raised it to point at the man who shot Skala and found himself staring down the muzzle of his pistol.

They remained there, both frozen in place for a long moment while Branislav Skala lay dying amid the flowers at Crane's side. Finally Skala groaned, let out a long, rattling breath, and was still.

Crane kept his eyes locked on the man with the pistol. He recognized him, he realized, from Yermolayev's phone.

"You're Anton Kucera," Crane said at last. "You speak English?"

"Little bit," said Kucera. "You know me? I don't know you. But I know you are not who he thought. Not the man from Team Kilo."

"How do you know that?"

"Because it turns out I'm the man from Team Kilo." Kucera let out a short laugh that seemed empty of all amusement. "It is funny," he said. "He wanted to be like them. But he was a fool. When rich men want someone for their dirty work, they want a real thug. From the streets. Not a ... dressed-up clown who wants to come in by the front door and be one of them. They sent someone to ..."—he smiled for a moment—"to make me an offer. It didn't take much. I hated that old bastard."

"So you'll tell the local gangs that I killed him," said Crane.

Kucera nodded toward the flaming vineyards. "Not hard to believe."

Crane had to admit it made sense. Skala was out of the way. Kucera was rid of him and so were the people whose business he'd been interfering in, whoever they were. And Crane himself had provided the perfect screen to hide what they'd done.

"So who are you?" Kucera asked.

"Just someone who works for somebody he picked a fight with."

Kucera nodded. "Plenty of those."

They remained there for another moment, staring into the muzzles of each other's guns. Maybe Crane could get off a burst before Kucera pulled the trigger. Maybe he couldn't. Either way, he didn't stand to gain anything from finding out. He imagined the same calculations going on in Kucera's mind.

Finally Kucera nodded at him. "You have a good night," he said. Still holding the gun on Crane, he took a single step backward. Then another. Then he simply melted away into the night.

Crane waited perhaps thirty seconds. The garden was still, empty. He stood up, stepped over the hedge, and walked back the way he'd come. On the ground near the main pathway, he found the smashed wreckage of Skala's laptop. Or half of it, anyway. He picked it up and tucked it under his free arm.

Then he walked back toward the gate that led to the garage.

CHAPTER 42

Three days later, a helicopter took Crane back to Josh's yacht, the *Normandy*. It was anchored near the Cordillera now, off the northeastern tip of Puerto Rico. As the helicopter circled the *Normandy* and came in for a landing on the top deck helipad, Crane saw a boat a few hundred yards away with dive flags up. He could just make out figures in the water near the reefs.

Josh was waiting as Crane stepped onto the deck. As the helicopter lifted off and headed back toward Fajardo, he explained that Melissa Simon was taking advantage of the snorkeling. She could hardly have failed to notice the helicopter, though. Josh expected her back soon.

In the meantime, they went over what had happened and decided what to tell her.

"There's not much to protect her from," said Crane. "She saw me kill a man."

"Okay, we'll tell her everything," said Josh. "If you're comfortable with that."

Crane just nodded. He'd killed far more than the one man Melissa had seen. And he'd gotten an innocent girl murdered. At least Klement Novak had survived. He was in a hospital in

Prague, where Josh had seen to it that he was getting the best possible care.

Off to the port side, Crane saw the *Normandy*'s excursion boat returning. The doors in the side of the yacht slid open, and the boat coasted inside. Josh led Crane back to the rear deck where they'd eaten lunch and discussed Josh's problem.

"By the way," Josh said while they waited, "we cracked the encryption on that hard drive you sent back. Let's talk about that later."

Meaning not in front of Melissa, Crane noted. He nodded as the glass doors slid open and Melissa stepped out, her hair soaking wet, wearing a white bikini top and a pair of gray dive shorts. Crane had to admit the woman knew how to make an entrance.

Over a round of drinks, Crane and Josh told her what had happened in Brno. The broad strokes, at least. Melissa listened with increasing surprise.

"I don't understand," she said at last. "I've never even heard of this guy. Why would some Czech gangster want to shut down my project?"

"Apparently because of the actinomycetes," said Josh.

"What?"

"Your team weren't the first people to go digging in the mud in that rainforest," Josh explained. "There was a German biotech firm that sent people into the general area a few years ago, looking for undiscovered microorganism species. They found some. Apparently they've been working on pharmaceutical applications ever since."

"But nobody published! What good—" Crane saw realization cross her features. "Of course. They were keeping it secret until they had something to patent."

"And then you came along and started putting all that data

out on the Internet," said Josh. "Dumping it into the public domain."

Anger flashed in her eyes. "So they hired some gangster to shut me down? We can crush them in court!"

"It's not that simple," said Crane. "They'll say they had no knowledge of what Skala was doing. I think it's even true. I think he took it on himself to shut you down because he thought it would help him curry favor with them."

"Son of a bitch," she muttered behind the rim of her glass. Then, louder, "So this Skala, his corrupt cops and his drug runners, who pays for what they did?"

"I think they've paid," Crane said quietly.

Melissa's anger folded up and collapsed. All of them were dead now except Acevedo, who he imagined would be spending a very long time in prison.

"You're right," Melissa said softly. "Of course you're right."

"Look at the bright side," said Josh. "It's over now. You can bring your team back in and get back to work. There'll be funding for new equipment, computers, gene sequencers."

"Are we talking about a blank check here?" she said with a sudden grin just at the corners of her mouth. "I can come up with a hell of a shopping list."

Josh laughed. "Within reason."

She turned to Crane with a smile. "Come out and see me when we get everything up and running. I'll show you around again."

He thought she meant it this time. He nodded and smiled back. "I'll do that."

———

Josh and Crane stood at the stern and watched the boat taking Melissa back ashore.

"About the hard drive," said Josh.

"I take it you found something interesting."

"Skala's personal notes. He was trying to map what the ultra-rich are up to behind the scenes."

"People like you."

"Not exactly," Josh said with a laugh. "Let's say people in my tax bracket. Members of the Bilderberg Group, the Council on Foreign Relations. Corporate elites. He was trying to understand what they do behind the scenes. It's full of code names and connections and rivalries and secret alliances."

"Kucera said he wanted in," said Crane.

"Makes sense," Josh said. "I went hiking once, place called Klaksvik in the Faroe Islands. There was this steep hill. I mean really steep. I looked up and saw what I thought was the top, and up I went. But when I got there, I realized it was a false summit. There was more hill that you couldn't see from the bottom. So I kept on going up, and there's more hill beyond that. And then again. Every time I thought I'd made it to the top, there turned out to be more hill to climb. Skala made it to the top of his world, and then he found out there was more. He wasn't at the top at all."

"I don't think he's someone we wanted at the top of the ladder," said Crane.

"That's just it," Josh said, turning from the rail to face Crane. "Neither are the people he talks about in those notes. He thought governments ran the world, but he found out they don't. The people on that hard drive run it, and that's not good for anybody. They play their little reindeer games because there's nobody to make them play fair, and people get caught in the middle. Lives are ruined. People live in poverty and fear. It's not how the world is supposed to work, John."

Crane had the feeling this wasn't a new idea to Josh. It was a presentation. Something rehearsed. He realized Josh wanted something from him and was afraid he wasn't going to get it.

"What are you getting at?" he asked.

"Cards on the table," Josh said. "There are plenty of people I could have hired to look into Melissa's problem. But I had my reasons for choosing you. I wanted to see what you could do. But I also wanted you to see the world Skala saw."

"Are you saying you already knew why someone attacked the project?"

"No, no. I wouldn't have kept that from you. Believe me. But I knew it had to be something like what you found. Who goes to all that trouble to take out some post-grads collecting mud samples?"

"So this secret world of Skala's ..."

"It's real," said Josh. "When you get to where I am, you can see it. You get a seat at the table, and you can join in the game if you want. But I'm not like them. Most people in that world are born into it, or they claw their way in by any means necessary. I just tripped and fell into it, I guess. I was just an ordinary guy."

Crane smiled and raised an eyebrow. He was pretty sure there was nothing ordinary about Josh Sulenski.

"Okay, point taken," said Josh. "Let me rephrase. I'm a guy who wasn't born with a silver spoon and my own hedge fund. I was just a math nerd who liked solving puzzles. And then one day I solved the stock market, and everything changed. I'm a normal person who lucked out and got handed a seat at the table. And it bothers me what they do to normal people there."

Josh fell silent for a moment, looking out over the boat's fantail at a flight of gulls heading in toward the shallows to fish.

"What's that got to do with me?" Crane gently prodded.

"I had to do something," said Josh. "Suddenly I had all this money and power. I couldn't just spend it all on airplanes and Italian supercars and private islands. I had to find a way to use it that would let me look at myself in the mirror. Bill Gates is wiping out malaria. Elon Musk has his own space program. His own *space program*! Can you believe that? What could I do?"

Crane sighed. "Your own secret agent. I don't want to be your toy spy, Josh."

"You were the Hurricane Group's spy."

"Because I wanted to serve my country," said Crane.

"No, you wanted to do good in the world. You joined the Hurricane Group because you thought it would let you do that."

Crane thought for a moment. "Yeah, okay. I wanted to make the world a better place."

"And how did that work out? Governments aren't the ones in power anymore. This is a new gilded age. We're back to just giving all the money and power to whoever's clever, or ruthless, or just lucky enough to grab it. Then we let them decide what to do with it, and hope they decide to do something good. And sure, some of those people are working hard to do the right thing. But a lot of them are monsters."

Crane had to admit, he'd felt less comfortable in the field for Hurricane than he'd thought he would. He didn't know where the orders were coming from. He didn't know what the real agenda was.

"Governments are weak," Josh was saying. "They're paralyzed. The powers fighting over the world now are beyond them. There's a whole new Cold War going on, and that's where we need a good spy."

A crewman brought a tray with two glasses of champagne. Apparently Josh was confident in his persuasiveness.

"We both want to do good in the world. You've got the skills, I've got the resources. Seriously, who needs a covert government agency? I've got more money, and I make my own rules. Don't think of it as losing your license to kill."

"That's not really a thing," Crane interrupted.

"Think of it as gaining your very own black budget. Come on, John, what do you say? Want to help me save the world? It'll be fun."

Josh took a glass of champagne from the tray. Crane hesitated. He had no doubt this was a key moment in his life. It wasn't the life he'd planned for himself, but that life had evaporated. There was a huge difference between working for the United States and working for an idealistic Internet billionaire —one who'd apparently watched too many Bond films.

But it wasn't all bad, he realized. Josh was about as ingenuous as a billionaire could be. And Crane would work directly with him. No long chain of command to conceal the agenda, no shadowy figures stalking the corridors of power. With Josh, he realized he would always know what he was doing and why. The question was whether he could trust Josh, and he realized he did. Josh might not always make the right choices, but he'd never sell Crane out.

The more he thought about it, the more the offer sounded like what he'd wanted from the Hurricane Group all along.

And he could always quit and find a job if it came to that.

He took the other glass from the tray and tapped the rim against Josh's glass with a clear, crystal sound that rang like a bell. Josh beamed.

"Where did you want to start?" Crane asked.

EPILOGUE: I HATE TO DIE

Italy, the Adriatic Coast

A green Jaguar F-Type sped south down the SS 16, the old coast highway, carving its way through the road's long, sweeping curves. To the right was farmland and scattered houses, the fields a rolling backdrop of deep green and tan. To the left, the sea gleamed in the mid-afternoon sun, stretching out to the horizon where it merged with a deep blue, cloudless sky.

In the driver's seat, John Crane smiled. This was a change he could live with.

Until recently, Crane had been a field asset for the Hurricane Group, a U.S. covert operations team. That was over now. The Hurricane Group's budget had suddenly been pulled and their operations folded up. Crane didn't know why. Like all the agents, Crane had been offered a mid-level consulting job at a beltway bandit firm with ties to the intelligence community. It was comfortable money in exchange for letting them put him away safely in a box.

Crane had turned it down. That had been a risky decision at the time, but as he downshifted and floored the accelerator to whip around a battered Fiat, Crane thought the gamble had paid off. He'd been approached a few months later by a 25-year-old Internet billionaire named Josh Sulenski. Crane had handled a security issue for Josh, one that had proven to have larger implications. Josh and Crane were still tracking down leads and considering how to respond.

In the meantime, Josh kept coming up with small tasks for Crane to do, and he supposed it was a real job at this point. Josh had a rare combination of extreme wealth and earnest naiveté. He could come up with some very odd ideas, and he had the means to implement them. But to his surprise, Crane had found that he enjoyed working for Josh.

If nothing else, the Hurricane Group had routinely sent him into blasted, chaotic warzones to risk his life against heavily armed terrorists. Josh had sent him here to meet a vacationing French scientist—presumably an unarmed one—who would pass him a data card. Given the choice, Crane thought, he'd take this.

Crane slowed as he approached the outskirts of Pesaro. He drove past rows of vacation rental houses, then the elegant gardens of the Villa Caprile. He crawled through the town's crowded commercial district, the streets overflowing with pedestrians and teenagers on bicycles. Soon, however, he passed out of Pesaro again and climbed the large hill to the south of town, the Monte Ardizio.

At the top of the hill, he decelerated into the small parking lot of the Hotel Brunelleschi, the Jaguar's tires crunching on gravel. It was a small hotel, a couple sun-bleached white stories dotted with black cast iron balcony railings and spots where the plaster had crumbled away. The Brunelleschi still recalled past glories, but it was clearly more down at the heels these days. The tourists had come to prefer the tall luxury hotels in Pesaro with their modern conveniences and better beach access. The Brunelleschi had a great view, but no beach access at all. On the other side of the building was only a steep slope that plunged several hundred feet to the railroad tracks, and then the beach beyond.

Still, Crane decided, he liked the place. It wasn't crowded, which was to his benefit. It would be quiet, and the cliffside bar would be an excellent place to enjoy a drink and gaze out over the sea. He turned off the engine and got out of the car.

John Crane stood a bit taller than average, his body disciplined and taut. The wind off the sea whipped through his short, dark hair and he stood there a moment, reveling in it. He wore gray Thom Browne chinos and a navy Sunspel polo shirt. He'd had the pants custom tailored to accommodate the Sig Sauer P938 he wore holstered inside his waistband so it vanished beneath his clothes. Crane hung his sunglasses from the placket of his shirt and walked to the main entrance, his motions economical and confident.

He passed through an empty lobby, gave the desk clerk a smile, and nodded toward the glass doors leading out to the patio bar. The clerk wished him a pleasant afternoon.

Outside, Crane could see how tightly the hotel was squeezed between the highway and the edge of the cliff. The bar sat at the end of a path that descended the cliffs some 100 feet. There, the slope leveled out just enough to accommodate a narrow white structure with a red tile roof.

At the bottom of the steps, Crane opened the door and stepped through into a darker space. A small bar was immediately to his right. It wasn't set up; at this hour, they were probably serving from the restaurant bar. To his left, tables stood against a low outer wall giving an open panoramic view of the sea below. Behind them, across the center aisle, a line of booths ran down the rear wall.

There was one person here, sitting in the back-corner booth Crane had been hoping to claim for himself. A young man, he realized as his eyes readjusted to the darkness. Indian ancestry, about Crane's age ... and then his stomach seemed to drop out from under him.

It was Chris Parikh.

For a moment, Crane stood stunned. Parikh's face registered the same astonishment. Crane let out a breath and slowly walked over to the booth.

John Crane had only gone on two field missions for the Hurricane Group before the government pulled the plug, and Chris Parikh had been a key part of both of them. He'd been a trusted partner—maybe even a friend, if Hurricane agents had friends. Crane had assumed Parikh had taken the job with the consulting firm in Virginia. Obviously, he hadn't.

Of course, Crane would have known that if he'd taken the job himself. He couldn't fault that decision. But what the hell was Parikh doing here? It couldn't be coincidence. Would he have to kill him before this was over?

They nodded to each other as Crane eased into the booth. Slowly, subtly, he slipped the Sig Sauer from his waistband and pointed it at Parikh beneath the table. The moment dragged.

"Been a while, John," said Parikh at last.

"A year, almost. You're looking good."

"You too."

Another uncomfortable silence.

"Christ, we can do better than this," said Crane. "We spent five days locked up in a safe house in Peshawar with nothing to pass the time but a DVD of *The Princess Bride*. Surely that kind of shared experience forges a bond between men."

"You'd think so," said Parikh. "So why are we sitting here with guns pointed at each other under the table?"

"Because each of us is pretty much the last person the other expected to find here?"

The door opened and a waitress appeared to take their order. Parikh ordered a Campari and soda and Crane followed suit.

"So, I guess you didn't take the consulting job," Crane said as she left. "Where are you working these days?"

"Not at liberty to say, I'm afraid. You passed on it, and yet here you are." Parikh shook his head. "And I'm really trying, John, but I can't think of a single good reason for you being here. Lot of bad ones. But nothing that ends with us sharing a drink and talking about the old days."

"Well hell, Chris, I'm not going to just sit here and let you shoot me."

Parikh winced. "Damn it, Crane, tell me you're not working for the White Eagles. Be convincing."

Crane had no idea what Parikh was talking about. He tried to remember anything from his Hurricane days about something called the White Eagles, but nothing came to him. "Uh, okay," he said at last. He held up two fingers in a mock Boy Scout salute. "I'm not working for the White Eagles. Was that convincing enough? I don't actually know who that is."

Parikh studied him; Crane could see him wanting to believe him.

"Your turn," said Crane. "Tell me you're not here to take out a skinny French guy in a Yankees cap."

"I don't know what you're talking about."

Parikh's confusion seemed genuine, and Crane decided he believed him. "Maybe we should both put some cards on the table. We can always shoot each other later if we decide it's called for. So who are the White Eagles?"

Parikh thought for a moment. Finally, he let out a sigh. "They're Serbian gangsters. They claim they're the same paramilitary that fought in the war back in the 90s. But they're just some thugs trading on the name. They do the usual gang stuff, and they hire out to anybody who'll pay them. They run drugs and weapons, traffic people, do the occasional hit. We're interested. Then we picked up some chatter that suggests they're doing a job here. We don't know what exactly. But whatever it is, I'm here to make sure it goes badly. Maybe bring one of them home for questioning."

A job here, at the Brunelleschi. The occasional hit. Crane felt that little thrill he always felt when the pieces finally fell into place. "I get it," he said. "You're here for the hounds. I'm here for the fox."

He let Parikh see the movement as he slipped the Sig Sauer back into his waistband. A moment later, Parikh did the same.

"You really thought I joined a Serbian militia?" Crane said, letting a bit of irritation slip into his voice.

"Word is they're working with a spotter," said Parikh. "A local guide with papers for the cops if they get pulled over, someone to do the advance work and let them stay hidden until they're ready."

"Oh," said Crane, "well then allow me to rephrase. You really thought I was freelancing for a Serbian militia?"

Parikh gasped in exasperation. "Well why are you here? You're supposed to be in a bloody cubicle in Northern Virginia doing enterprise operations ... something."

"So are you ... wait a minute. You're still working field ops for the government! What the hell, Chris? Did they fire me and just pretend they were shutting down the whole department so I'd think I didn't know anything about current operations?"

Parikh started to speak, but fell silent as the waitress returned with their drinks. "Two Campari and soda," she said as she set down the glasses. "Do you need anything else?"

"No, thank you," said Crane. "You don't need to come back down. We can pay the check at the main bar, right?"

"Of course, sir." Then she left and they were alone again.

They sampled their drinks, then Crane said, "So?"

Parikh sighed. "You don't know my parents," he said with a sardonic smile. "They're already pissed off that I'm not married. Unemployment wasn't an option, so I took the consulting job. Then a couple months later, somebody else showed up and recruited me back out into fieldwork again. It's pretty much the same job, really."

"So they shut down Hurricane and then turned right around and started up another group just like it?"

"You know the government," Parikh said. "Right hand, meet left hand. I think Hurricane just lost a bureaucratic turf war. Something behind the scenes that we never saw."

Crane shook his head. "And they picked you up, but not me."

"You know I didn't have any say in that."

That was true enough. But it didn't mean Crane found it any less irritating. Maybe if he'd taken the damn consulting job they'd have taken him back too. But then he would have missed so much.

"Your turn," said Parikh. "If you're not working for the government, who the hell are you working for?"

"You won't believe me," Crane said.

"Try me."

"Okay. I'm doing covert missions for a naïve Internet billionaire with utopian ideals and some serious James Bond fantasies."

"You're kidding!"

Crane grinned. "Told you."

"You're serious." Parikh drained his glass and set it down hard on the table. "Jesus, do you have any idea how much trouble you can get in? Are in? They don't just let private citizens do this stuff!"

Crane shrugged. "You'd be surprised how much legitimacy being a multi-billionaire gets you."

"Who's the French guy?"

"Dr. Julian Mesnard," said Crane. "He works for a Swiss biotech concern. He developed a technology that doesn't fit into his company's market strategy. He wants to make sure they don't bury it."

"What kind of technology?"

"I don't know the details. That's what he's bringing me. But it pulls carbon dioxide out of the air. A lot of it apparently. And creates a very effective soil fertilizer as a by-product. Assuming it scales to industrial volumes, my employer thinks it could play a big part in fixing the climate."

"Who would want to kill him for it?"

"Somebody with the connections to hire your Serb gangsters for the dirty work. His employers most likely. The agri-chemical industry. A few others I can think of."

Parikh considered. "Here's what I don't get," he said at last. "I get the rich guy indulging himself. I get the conspiracy theories and the whole 'never trust the man' thing. But I don't get you getting mixed up with it. You've got solid skills, and your head was always screwed on straight. How'd you get involved with this? You could have taken the damn consulting job if you needed the money."

"What can I say? I like him. And whether your bosses like it or not, it's a world of non-state actors now. The good news is, they're not all bad guys."

Crane conspicuously checked his watch.

"Showtime?"

"Soon now."

Parikh eased out of the booth. "All right, I'll do my thing. You and your Frenchman can be my bait. I'll be in the hotel. When they head down here, I'll bring up the rear. Be careful coming out that door until we're finished."

"Keep the waitress off the field," said Crane. "People show up, she'll come down to take their orders. She'll walk into it."

Parikh nodded. "Got it under control." Then he offered his hand and Crane shook it. "I always did like you, Crane. I'll keep your name out of this if I can."

"Appreciate it." Crane retrieved a card from his wallet. "This number will get to me if you want to talk sometime."

Parikh produced his own card and they traded them.

Parikh walked away, then stopped at the door. "If you're going to do this, for God's sake stay clear of the U.S. Government, okay?" He slipped into his best Inigo Montoya accent. "You seem a decent fellow. I hate to kill you."

Crane grinned. "You seem a decent fellow," he answered. "I hate to die."

Parikh smiled back; then he was gone.

Crane looked out at the sun on the Adriatic. A boat slewed across the water behind a great arc of white sail. The warm breeze swept gently through the bar. He was just starting to regret sending the waitress away when the door opened. A slightly built, middle-aged man came in and blinked in the sudden darkness. He wore slacks and a t-shirt, with a New York Yankees cap over black hair that was graying at the temples.

Crane rose. "Dr. Mesnard. I'm John Crane."

Mesnard let Crane settle him into the booth but kept checking the door over his shoulder.

"Something's wrong," he said. "They're following me. They know!"

"Calm down, Doctor." Crane eased back into his seat. "First things first. You have something for me?"

"I need protection! If I just give it to you, I don't have any leverage."

"That's not true, Doctor. You're much more important than an SD card. And the men following you are going to get a lot more than they're expecting."

Mesnard blanched. "You know about them? Oh god. I hoped I was just being foolish."

Crane shook his head. "No, you're being followed. But my job is to protect you. And there's someone else here whose job is to stop those men."

He held out his hand and waited until Mesnard took a small datacard from his pocket and handed it over.

"Thank you. Now this is important. Do you have any reason to think the people after you are working for anyone besides your employer? Does anyone else know what you've created?"

"I don't think so. What am I going to do? I can't go home! My—"

Behind him the door opened. Crane reached out and pressed gently on Mesnard's shoulder to slide him farther back against the rear wall.

The newcomer was Crane's age, lean with a shock of surfer blonde hair. He wore baggy, pocketed cargo shorts, boat shoes, an unbuttoned Hawaiian shirt over a t-shirt for some band Crane didn't recognize. Plenty of places he might hide a gun. By the time Crane had assessed him, the man's eyes had adjusted to the inside light. He looked back at them and waved.

"Afternoon," he said in a loud, American-accented voice. "You two guys Americans? Me too."

He walked straight toward the booth. Crane slipped the Sig Sauer from its holster and passed it to his left hand; he wanted his right free, and even off-handed he wouldn't miss at this range.

"You've got a great spot back in this corner, don't you?" the man said. "Fantastic view. Hey, you a Yankees fan? All right, go Yanks!"

He didn't seem concerned that they weren't answering him. Then Crane realized he wasn't talking to them at all. He was passing intel to the men outside. The mic would be concealed somewhere in his shirt.

The spotter had almost reached them, and Crane was already starting to power himself up from his seat when he heard shouts from outside, then the crack of gunfire.

The spotter whipped out a pistol but Crane caught the man's wrist with his right hand and smashed it hard against the edge of the table. The gun flew free. It bounced across the table, and for one terrible instant, Crane thought Mesnard would grab for it and try to defend himself. Then it slid off the table's far edge and fell into Crane's seat.

The man tried to yank his wrist free from Crane's grip. With his other hand, he pulled a knife from his waistband. But before he could bring it to bear, Crane jammed the Sig Sauer in his left hand into the spotter's navel and fired two shots up into his torso.

The spotter looked at Crane in shock. He stumbled backwards and Crane went with him, adding his own strength to the dying man's momentum. As they reached the wall, Crane grabbed his belt and powered him up and over the edge.

He toppled over the wall, hit the ground with a thud, and slid thirty feet down the slope until his body came to rest against a buckthorn bush.

Just as Crane passed the gun back to his right hand, the door crashed open and a shape flew through it. Crane whirled to fire, but realized there was no need. A heavyset man in track pants and a blood-soaked t-shirt hit the nearest table hard, then slid to the floor and didn't move.

Outside, the shooting had stopped.

Crane turned back to the booth. Mesnard cringed in the corner, pale and wide-eyed. Crane holstered his pistol, took Mesnard's arm and guided him out of the booth.

"Oh god," Mesnard muttered. "Oh god. What do we do?"

"We're leaving," Crane said calmly. "Stick close to me. Walk fast, and look scared. Can you do that?"

Mesnard nodded. "Oh, yes."

Crane led him out of the bar keeping himself between Mesnard and the dead Serb. Outside, another body lay sprawled near the steps. A few yards uphill, Parikh's knee was jammed into the back of a third man, face down in the dirt, his hands secured by a plastic zip tie. Parikh jabbed an ampoule into the man's neck and his struggles faded.

As they passed, Crane and Parikh traded a glance and a quick nod. Then Crane moved on, hurrying the trembling Mesnard up the stairs.

A small knot of guests and staff had gathered in the lobby. Crane threw the door open and rushed Mesnard through. He put some panic into his voice. "Call the police! They're shooting each other!"

Then they were gone before anyone had time to think too much. Crane swept Mesnard out the front door and bundled him into the Jaguar.

"Is there anything in your car that you need?" he asked.

"Just clothes and a toothbrush," said Mesnard. He made a sound that was probably meant to be a bitter laugh. "Nothing that matters now. They know what I did. I'm a dead man."

"No," said Crane. "You're unemployed. But you're not going to die."

Crane swung the car onto the highway and drove fast to the south. Behind them, police lights approached the hotel from Pesaro. Crane gave the car its head and put some distance between himself and the scene.

"Why not? They can kill me whenever they want."

"It's too late for that," Crane said. "Cat's out of the bag. All killing you gains them now is the satisfaction of revenge. And

I'm going to make sure they understand that pleasure would be very short-lived."

He accelerated around a Renault. "As for your career problem, you should talk to my employer. He's fascinated by your work. I know he'd love to talk to you. Pay's good." Crane patted the leather-wrapped steering wheel. "Nice perks."

Five hours later, at Ancona Falconara Airport, Crane watched Mesnard board an Alitalia shuttle to Rome. From there he was booked on four different flights, but he wouldn't be on any of them. Instead he would be on a chartered jet to London.

As the turboprop took off, Crane walked back out to the parking lot. His own flight left from Perugia just before midnight. Crane pointed the Jaguar west on the SS 76. If he put his foot down, he'd have time for a late dinner.

The console chimed to signal an incoming call. Crane didn't recognize the number, but he checked Chris Parikh's card and smiled. He tapped the answer button.

"Saw you got your guy," he said.

"Being questioned as we speak," said Parikh. "You get your man out?"

"On his way to a new life."

"Glad it worked out for you. Just be careful out there. You don't have the government backing you up anymore."

"Fair enough," he said. "But don't mistake official orders for legitimacy. You know the things governments get up to."

"I don't make the policy. I just finish the mission."

"Well, if you ever need to get out, talk to me." Crane grinned. "Have you ever considered piracy? You'd make a wonderful Dread Pirate Roberts."

Parikh laughed. "Screw you, Crane. Stay safe." The call clicked off.

This had been a good day, Crane thought. Parikh was right. He didn't have the full force and resources of the United States

Government behind him anymore. But he was pleased to discover that he really didn't mind.

Then he dropped the pedal, the Jaguar's V-8 responded with a throaty roar, and Crane sped into the night.

The End

John Crane returns in Wrecker.

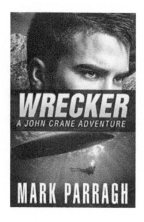

Available now at:
Amazon

Want even more?

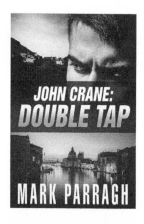

John Crane: Double Tap collects two novella-length adventures that expand John Crane's world and flesh out what happens between the first three novels.

And you can get it **free, right now**, when you join Mark Parragh's VIP email list. You'll get updates on new releases, sneak previews, and free bonus material available nowhere else, starting right away with your free copy of *John Crane: Double Tap*.

Join us at MarkParragh.com

Contact Mark Parragh

Mark Parragh's web site is at markparragh.com. There you can find a complete list of his books and much more. You can also find him on Facebook at facebook.com/MarkParragh, or email him at inbox@markparragh.com.

———

If you enjoyed this book…

…please help someone else enjoy it too. Reviews are hugely important in helping readers find the books they love. Reviews help me keep writing and they make sure the books you enjoy keep coming. Just a few moments to leave a review of this book pays off in so many ways. I'd really appreciate your help.

Thank you!

— Mark Parragh

Made in United States
Orlando, FL
10 December 2022

26003027R00200